David Coles and Jack Everett have been co-authors for many years. Fantasy & Science Fiction have been and still are their favourite genres; a number of short stories and two novels are referenced 'out there' on the net. There have been articles and fiction, including a written soap for pool & snooker magazines and, more recently, historical novels which are a bit like writing fantasy except that someone else wrote the back-story.

The day jobs—to support the writing habit—are a sports bar in Jack's case and computer software in David's. Both live in God's own county: Yorkshire, England.

Visit their websites:

www.davidbcoles.co.uk
www.jackleverett.me.uk

The right of David Coles & Jack Everett to be identified as the Authors of this Work has been asserted by them in accordance with the Copyright, Designs and Patents Act 1998

Copyright © David Coles & Jack Everett 2007

All characters in this publication are fictitious and resemblance to real persons, living or dead, is purely coincidental.

All rights reserved. No part of this publication may be reproduced, stored in a retrieval system, or transmitted, in any form or by any means without the prior written permission of the publisher, nor be otherwise circulated in any form of binding or cover other than that in which it is published and without a similar condition being imposed on the subsequent purchaser. Any person who does so may be liable to criminal prosecution and civil claims for damages.

ISBN: 1-905988-18-4 978-1-905988-18-1

Cover by Sue Cordon

Published by Libros International

www.librosinternational.com

THE ABBOT & THE ACOLYTE

in

DEATH AND TAXES

A Medieval Mystery

by

DAVID COLES & JACK EVERETT

Libros International

Acknowledgements

The authors would like to acknowledge the support and forbearance of their wives while this book was being written; their help and advice made it a better book than it would otherwise have been.
We owe thanks to *Libros International*: to the readers who made thoughtful and valuable suggestions resulting in a much improved book. To our editor Pete Moore, who combed the manuscript for anachronisms, hanging pronouns and unfortunate phrases—those that remain do so in spite of his efforts to convince us. Finally, to everyone at *Libros International* who have worked towards publishing *Death and Taxes*, thank you.

This book is dedicated to our wives—
Wendy and Janet.

The villages of St. Guilhem le Desert and St. Jean de Fos are situated in the Languedoc region of southern France, not far from Montpellier and date back to before the 12th Century when the first William of Orange built an abbey: St. Guilhem le Desert which, colloquially translated, means 'St. William in the Back of Beyond'. By 1281, when Simon de Brie was elected Pope, the two villages had long been on the pilgrims' route to Compostela in Spain.

PROLOGUE

A candle burned late in the shrine where a monk tended a sick goat. The monk had a reputation for caring for animals but this particular animal, a wilful beast, was one that he treated more often than most.

The goat's appetite extended to all sorts of snacks but it was those not intended for eating that brought it back so frequently suffering from throat obstructions. But for the monk's skill, the creature would have met death many months ago.

Feeling along the neck, the monk found the hard shape of the blockage and gradually worked it free. Now it was just necessary to strike behind the object to make the animal cough it up.

The candle flame flickered as the postern was opened and closed. Abbo, the monk, was too busy to notice the entrance, to hear the slur of sandal on tile, to see the new shadow in the candlelight join that of man and beast.

Brother Abbo made a fist and struck the goat just as the nasty, long bronze pin pierced the back of his neck.

The goat and the monk convulsed.

The man fell forward, toes drumming against the floor for the few moments it took him to die. The goat vomited up its last meal – a small wooden crucifix that clattered to the floor at the feet of the assailant.

The murderer tried in vain to pull the weapon free but the vertebrae had closed like a vice and it seemed solidly embedded in the sacristan's neck. There was nothing to be done but to twist and bend the metal until the outer part broke away. There was little blood though, a mere trickle that the monk's black cowl absorbed easily and invisibly. With some effort, the killer dragged the dead body to the lectern and arranged it to appear as though Abbo were kneeling in prayer.

The goat was tied up and, about to pinch out the candle, the intruder had a thought. There was a little room in the corner, hardly more than a cupboard. The candle flared in the draught from the opening door. Inside the chamber, the air smelled musky; it compelled a twitch of the nose, a licking of lips, the faintest of smiles.

Brother Abbo's murderer found a censer and lit the cinders of incense still at the bottom and filled the space with aromatic smoke. Back in the shrine too, the place soon filled with fumes and covered the smell of the goat's vomit.

Then the murderer left.

CHAPTER ONE

The two figures following the ruts left by a lumbering ox-wagon were opposites in nearly every aspect imaginable: years, girth and an alarming complexion of reds and purples on the one hand; on the other, a slim young boy with a face stolen from a pale and shadowed fresco.

The one who seemed never to be far from the thought of his next meal; the other, lean and slender who would have found difficulty in recalling the last good meal he had had.

Trudging through the rain, the larger looked ever and down at the smaller, wondering if he had done the right thing. He had changed the boy's life; there was no denying the fact. *Yet, please God, it had been for the better; it must have been for the better*, he thought.

'You are certain you want to do this?' Abbot Rutilius asked, as the priory disappeared into the rain behind them.

'Oh yes.' The boy's face was stretched into a permanent grin so wide his cheeks hurt. 'Oh yes...' The boy could think of nothing else to say, he nodded.

The abbot was both a worldly and a naïve soul. He travelled a great deal; he came into contact with men and women of all stations and enjoyed company, and could be tempted into paying for drinks and food purely for the enjoyment of conversation. There were lacks though; Rutilius was a naturally gregarious man and was poignantly aware of the pleasures of women, the appeal of family, even the regular comradeship of men of his own calling. All of these were denied him.

The deficiencies were filled by his great delight in food, a satisfaction that helped to insulate him from those other forbidden gratifications.

Now though, the boy would provide him with friendship, discourse, a semblance of family. Now, the abbot had changed not only William's life but his own too.

It had been the previous evening...

Two loud and resounding thumps brought Abbot Rutilius to his feet, afraid some part of the crumbling building had fallen.

'The door,' said the acolyte, and the abbot fled for the door far faster than seemed possible for someone of his plumpness, 'No, no, someone *at* the door, the main door.'

'Ah.' Abbot Rutilius looked out into the hallway where several monks stood frozen in surprise, a foot lifted from the floor, a hand reaching towards a latch. Visitors were few; at this hour vanishingly so.

Then, the bell chain was pulled, the bell jangling somewhere among the rafters; a cloud of dust and less savoury debris drifted downwards. Time and monks moved on once more.

The boy finished lighting the candles and squeezed past the abbot. He went to the door, unlocked it and swung it open. Beyond, a man stood, tall if he had been less stooped, wet, shivering, his fist raised to knock again. Illuminated by the hall lanterns, the rain was a backdrop of golden rods bursting about his feet in hissing explosions; individual rivulets ran from his hat, his nose, his beard, his fingers.

‘We need lodgings. In the name of God, let us in away from this rain,’ he pleaded.

‘Um,’ said the boy.

‘There’s no room,’ said a second voice. Rutilius turned and saw the head of St. Trivier, Prior Stephen, standing in the archway.

‘God’s mercy, man, I’ve a young mother and her child out here. They’re freezing.’

‘There’s a house up the road. A mile, perhaps. They’ll give you shelter.’ Stephen stood silently, a determined expression on his face.

‘I’ll move out of here,’ said Rutilius, gesturing towards the visitor’s accommodation. ‘I’ll sleep in a cell, in the stable.’

The man at the door glanced at him, then back to Stephen.

‘There’s no room,’ he said again, determination becoming stubbornness. ‘Close the door,’ he said, and turned to vanish into the interior.

The boy, William, looked at Rutilius and slowly swung the door closed.

Rutilius crossed the hallway and pulled it open again, he stepped out into the rain; the visitor was already taking up the reins on the little wagon. The abbot raised his hand, called to him, but the downpour drowned his voice, the other shook the reins, as the woman at his side turned and looked back.

The abbot was speechless, his cheeks purple, his nose burning a fierce magenta. He closed the door once more and looked down at the boy.

The monastery of St. Trivier, a small and depressing place where the weed of temptation withered and died almost as fast as the monks in residence, was not a welcoming place. The Order placed great importance on silence, solemnity and frugality. It was no place for an acolyte to start a monastic life.

Looking at the boy, Rutilius could see he had once been a naturally lively and intelligent lad. His face was drawn now, dark shadows loomed beneath his eyes and every movement was hesitant. The gloomy confines of the cold dark halls and cells and the vast dank silence of the place were slowly breaking his heart. The abbot gestured towards the door to his room and William preceded him into the hastily cleared store place.

'Sit down, boy.' And when William had found a chest and seated himself: 'What are you doing in this place? Hmm?'

William was the only son of a minor noble who had led an undistinguished life in the Lange d'Oc. However he was a nephew to Jeanne, Comtesse de Toulouse and had made the mistake of fidelity to the lost cause of the Cathars.

The abbot winced as the heretical group was mentioned and shook his head. 'Surely… No, no. I remain silent, young man.' He immediately asked another question, 'How was he revealed?'

William shrugged. 'He was in Carcason, there was an argument with the Bishop.'

'Unwise, most unwise. I take it you have none of this foolishness in your head?'

'I don't believe so, my lord.'

'So what happened, the Inquisition?'

William nodded, now quite dejected. 'He was sent to the galleys, my mother chants prayers at a convent, I was taken to St. Trivier.'

An awkward silence ensued; neither knew quite what to say. A few minutes passed and William got up to trim the wick on a smoking candle.

The abbot used the opportunity to resume the conversation. 'Did your father employ a tutor?'

William raised his thin shoulders. 'He did, my lord, I can read Latin.' Rutilius nodded. 'I can cipher.'

'Good. That's good. Anything else?'

'I was considered skilled with the sword. Vincent used to say…'

'Vincent?'

'My father's master-at-arms.'

'Ah well. I was not thinking of those sorts of skills. You say you can read, can you write also?'

'Of course.'

'So much in such a young fellow.'

'I'm not so young. I'm fifteen in a month or two.'

The abbot raised his eyebrows, 'Fifteen? In a month or two?'

'I don't know what the date is. One day here is just like another.'

'You're right of course. It's the third day of April.'

'Next month, then,' said William, 'on the twenty-seventh day.'

'Would you like to get away from here?' Rutilius surprised himself, he'd only intended to think about the idea before talking to the prior and here he was saying it out loud.

The pale face became animated, William's mouth hung open in amazement, he half-rose from his seat. 'Of course, but there's the prior…' he said eventually, and Rutilius watched him close-up again, squeeze out the excitement, slump back on to the box.

'You do not have to worry about the prior. I need an assistant,' Rutilius said hurriedly, knowing that he did not really need an assistant, 'to help me write up records, to add up numbers. To read things when my eyes are tired.'

'This is real?' The boy asked, disbelief warring with craving behind his eyes.

'Indeed it is. You see,' the abbot leaned back and wished there was a fire on the hearth, 'I am not like your Prior Stephen, bound to a single community. I travel from one to the next.' He grinned conspiratorially. 'I inspect the accountings, I say what should go to Papa Martin, what should stay in the strongbox.'

There were always ambitions to expand and improve St. Peter's at Rome; it was one of the few constants from one pope to the next. At the end of the thirteenth century as at all other times, such plans needed money; money to buy gold and silver, fine tapestry, silks, carpets, to pay the architects, the stonemasons, the carpenters, artists. Money on a huge scale.

There was only one source of money – the Church itself: those who worshipped God, who listened to the priests exhort them to give alms, who paid for prayers to be said after they were dead, who made donations at shrines. A tide of money, a flood of wealth, which must be channelled across the world until the streams grew into rivers and those rivers of gold and silver poured into the Vatican's bottomless coffers.

All to the glory of God: from those who have not, even that which they have shall be taken.

Such wealth, such riches had to be policed and so the Vatican learned from its bankers and sent out clerics to audit the affairs of its institutions.

But what abbot or bishop would allow anyone, short of another abbot or bishop, to peruse the bills, the records of purchase, the rents and allowances of tenants, of farmers or woodsmen? Though never would the abbot admit that his rank was one of convenience, it was a fact, a necessary fact, that such auditors held the office of abbot.

'Consequently,' he explained to the boy, 'a man properly skilled in accounting is given the rank of abbot, he is granted an authority to examine anything he wishes.'

'Do you go very far, my lord?'

'Wherever the Holy Father pleases.' The abbot chuckled, but the walls of the empty hall seemed to soak up the mirth and leave nothing but a hollow rattle. St. Trivier discouraged cheerfulness within its walls.

'And I would never have to come back here, my lord?'

The abbot shook his head solemnly. 'With God's good grace, I also hope never to do so again, my son, and for you, even less reason. And there is no need to call me lord, yours or anyone else's.'

'Then, what should I call you, my lord?'

'Hmm.' The abbot thought a moment or two. You would become a sort of apprentice, so, Master, hmm?'

He nodded. 'Yes, Master.'

'And you may call me William,' said the acolyte.

'William. Well now.' The abbot was about to chuckle again but desisted. 'So you believe you would like to help me?'

The acolyte's eyes were bright with excitement, he could hardly speak but there was no mistaking his assent.

'You will find me a hard taskmaster,' he warned, wagging his finger. 'I insist upon excellence in all things.

I must have confidentiality and you must learn quickly. I have a slight tendency to forget, so you must remember for me. You understand this?'

The acolyte nodded enthusiastically. 'My lor... Master.'

While the acolyte prayed more fervently than usual that night on the cold stone floor of his cell, Rutilius sought out Prior Stephen in his cramped study.

'A word with you.' he said.

'My lord Abbot?'

Without invitation, Rutilius sat down on a rickety chair and waited for the other to follow suit.

'The acolyte, William.'

'Ah, a troublesome boy,' the prior replied.

'In what way?'

'Too loud, too quick, too young.'

'And there you put your finger on it.' Rutilius held up his own finger. 'Too young. And too much envy.'

'Envy, my lord? What is there to feed a boy's envy?'

'Absolutely nothing, Prior. The envy belongs to your congregation, to you. All of you resent his youth and beauty instead of celebrating it. He will run away before another winter.'

'An end to be hoped for.' Prior Stephen was perfectly serious. 'The boy was wished upon us by the Bishop without regard for the sort of place this is. He disturbs us all in our devotions.'

'Then you'll have no objection to his coming with me? As my assistant?'

The prior raised grey eyebrows. 'With you? When you have finished here?'

'Which will be tomorrow.'

Here, Stephen almost appeared to smile. 'No objection at all. A great relief, in fact.' The prior's haste to agree verged upon the indecent.

'Yes. I would think so.' Rutilius stood to signal he was finished, but could not resist a final admonition. 'At least he will see no more of your appalling treatment of travellers.'

'Travellers?' For a moment the prior was lost. 'Ah,' he recalled the earlier incident and dismissed it with a flick of his fingers, 'the vagabond who wanted lodging.'

'The traveller, with a young wife and babe.'

'Everyone who comes to St. Trivier disturbs us and our devotions. If we have a callow youth thrust into our care by the Bishop I am powerless to prevent it. If I have lazy vagrants begging for a bed and a bowl of soup, I can and I will.'

'That is your prerogative, at least for the present. It will be reported.' The abbot turned towards the door, 'And not just to Montpellier.'

The day that followed was not the best start to a new life.

The road was unwelcoming, taking them through a region of barren soils and deserted hovels. Even weeds and scrub struggled to find sustenance among the stones and rocky outcrops; birdlife and game shunned the uninviting land. There were no inns, no holdings in the neighbourhood.

Nor was the abbot's health at its best; he had expected to obtain a remedy at St. Trivier only to find that all the keeper of the infirmary could provide was prayer. The incessant rain and the rushing of water in the roadside ditches did not help matters and consequently, Rutilius was in a sour mood, having to stop every half-hour or so to find a convenient spot to relieve himself – sometimes successfully, sometimes not. The boy, holding the donkey's halter, would hear him, sometimes triumphant, sometimes not.

Towards the end of the day, though the weather made it difficult to judge how near dusk was, they came upon a tumbledown church; it had once served a village that was now only a huddle of wattle husks and heaps of rotting timber. They pushed the broken door aside and entered the church. They made a fire of broken furniture and settled down to rest.

As the fire burned down to a comfortable glow of coals, the abbot took certain items from his person: a small gold crucifix, a ring, the larger ivory cross from around his neck and somewhat shamefacedly, he placed them in his purse. As one of the Pope's auditors, the abbot had seen knavery in all sorts of people, from cardinals to servants. He had taken the precautions carefully so William's feelings would not be hurt, but it was best not to place temptation in anyone's path. He laid his head on the purse and slept.

Though hungry, the abbot and the acolyte slept well and awoke next morning to a world transformed. Dew refracted the sunlight like dazzling jewels. The brightness turned the old heaps of stone to rock gardens and the bushes to a brighter green. Dragonflies hovered, bees hummed and birds had come to find the insects lured out by the sudden warmth. Light sparkled off puddles and the warmth opened the petals of gem-like flowers. The young acolyte's grin stretched even further across his face.

As they travelled on, the scrub grew into bushes, and the bushes into trees. Patchy grass expanded to cover the darker soil and in the woodlands, there were glimpses of deer, the calling of doves. To their left ran a small stream over rocks and gravel, chuckling through piles of boulders and tangled driftwood along the side of the road. Coming from a place he had never seen and, like himself, going to a place he did not know, the purposeful sound of water was exciting...

'I like the sound of streams,' he told the abbot.

'Boy,' he replied, in some distress, 'like the water, you chatter too much. I am bathed in pain and cannot listen to you. In God's name, leave me to my misery.'

William had learned at St. Trivier the consequences of sitting for years on cold stone seats. The abbot's distress needed no explanation. The boy's grin faded a little though not for long, the world had grown so beautiful overnight that even the abbot's morose mood hardly intruded on his joy. He was happy to keep his own counsel.

The morning followed yesterday's pattern with the abbot visiting the woodlands and, more often than not, returning with an expression of suffering on his features.

They continued on, avoiding the deeper puddles and the stickier patches of mud where possible and shortly, the time for the abbot to seek privacy came again. He slid painfully from the back of the donkey. 'I shall be back presently.' he said, perhaps striving to be more affable. 'Hold Katerine until I return.'

'As you will, Master.'

William waited with the donkey while the abbot took himself to the side of the road, lifted his robe above his knees with one hand and grasping his staff with the other, steadied himself carefully through the long grass into the trees.

There were muttered phrases, and an occasional *Oh God in Heaven*, a long silence and then almost ecstatically, *Oh God be praised* at the full volume of the abbot's voice. A minute or two later, he returned, tightening the thick cord about his impressive roundness, a spring in his step as though he had shed ten years from his age.

His agreeable mood was short-lived however, for when he regained the road, it was to find William with his arms wrapped around one of Katerine's back legs, while a ruffian pulled the animal along the road by its halter.

'Ho now, what's this?!' the abbot demanded, chasing after the thief and brandishing his pole. 'This boy and this ass are protected by the Church.'

With a single bound, the would-be thief sprang towards William and hauled the boy to his feet. He held the boy in front of him with an arm around his neck, a rusty knife pressed against his throat. William's face was pale but his lips were tightly pressed in rage as much as fear.

Rutilius stopped, his breath catching in his throat. To have rescued the lad from the unspeakable priory, only to have his throat cut by this ragged stranger.

'A good day to you, Bishop,' he said. 'Take care, or your catamite shall surely meet his Maker this day.'

Although he was too far away to touch him, the man exhaled a gale of reeking breath powerful enough to fell an ox. 'I'm no bishop,' Rutilius said, his lips curled back in distaste. 'Let the lad go and we'll say no more.'

'Oh, I'll let the lad go, once I have that ring off your finger and that silver crucifix from around your honour's fat neck.'

Rutilius bridled. 'These are the badges of my office, not baubles you trade for with the life of my servant.'

'Badges or no, I shall have them,' he jerked the knife

below William's chin. 'Quickly now or he's a dead servant. The ring.'

The abbot looked at the ring, turned it round and round, shook his head. 'Nothing is worth a life,' he sighed and began to pull at the ring. It would not slide over his knuckle, tug as he might, it would not move. He held it out. 'It's stuck, look.'

The thief reached with his free hand and twisted the ring, pulled at it. 'Very well, I'll take your finger as well.'

'Then you'll have to let the boy go, won't you?'

The ruffian removed his arm from around William's neck and kicked his backside, 'Out of the way, boy.' The acolyte tripped and tumbled full-length in the mud.

The abbot extended his middle finger. 'Do your worst, devil, and look forward to an eternity in Hell.'

The thief attempted to cut Rutilius's finger but the blade was so blunt, it barely grazed the skin.

'Damnation!'

'Just so,' the abbot replied, 'Exactly. Now you see how God protects all his children.' The colours in Rutilius's face were darkening rapidly. He held his staff in a threatening manner. 'Now be off, or you'll be excommunicated the next time I'm at the bishop's palace in Montpellier.'

'Excommunicated? God has cared not a jot for me all my life, why should I care now? I snap my fingers…' Which was exactly what he did, tipping back his head and laughing.

From a crouch, William leaped and wrenched the knife from the thief. He turned, slashed with the weapon and only the very dullness of the edge saved the vagabond's life. A red wheal appeared across his throat with a drop of blood across the Adam's apple where the skin had parted, death avoided by his very slovenliness.

'God's blood,' shouted the miscreant, dancing back out of reach. He put a hand to his neck and gazed at the blood that came away. 'You nearly killed me, with my own knife.'

'A knife? You call this thing a knife?' William shouted back and tossed away the offending weapon. He pulled something from inside his habit. 'Now, here's a knife.' He advanced, brandishing a long shining steel blade. The thief backed up, stooped to pick up a stone to hurl at William, the boy ducked easily and it sailed over his head.

Behind him, there was a dull thud and a cry, and the sound of a falling body. William glanced back, the abbot had been struck solidly in the chest. He was down on both knees, one hand grasping his staff, the other pressed against his rib cage.

'Master!' William ran across to the struggling abbot and helped him back to his feet. 'Are you all right?'

'Ah. Just a moment.' He pushed himself back to his feet. 'By God's good grace, I believe so.' He looked around. 'The scoundrel.'

'I know, Master, I know.'

'No, no you don't,' said the abbot. 'Katerine, Katerine is gone.'

Katerine, the donkey, complete with bags and baggage was four-score yards down the road with the thief bouncing up and down in the saddle, as he whacked her mercilessly into a gallop. The abbot and the acolyte stood and watched them disappear.

'Katerine,' the abbot cried, and his shoulders slumped disconsolately. Apart from the satchel he wore across his back, Rutilius's spare clothes, their food, a little wine and various comforts for the journey were all tied securely to Katerine's saddle. Rutilius shook his head and sighed.

William was a little less doleful, he had no possessions beyond those he carried and had had no prospect of riding the beast in any case.

'Onward, then,' said Rutilius, turning stoically to face the way ahead. 'No doubt the Lord is punishing me for my anger.' They started and a few steps later, the abbot spoke again. 'Or you, perhaps, for trying to kill the fellow.'

William refrained from answering; his philosophy was not yet as refined as the abbot's. Instead, he held up a tattered pouch that, unnoticed by the thief, he had cut from the man's belt with his own rather sharper knife. They looked inside, it contained an odd collection: a leather cosh filled with sand, four battered bronze coins, a slingshot wound up into a bundle, and something much more welcome. 'How do you feel about a slice or two of liver sausage before we go on? Oh, and I do believe there's an apple here, Master.' He smelled it. 'Wrinkled, but still whole and sweet.'

They sat on a log somewhat sheltered by a tree and consumed the thief's dinner.

When they had finished eating, the abbot sat for a long time without speaking, William carved notches into the log. At length, the older man sat upright and turned a little.

'Boy.'

'Master?' William returned.

'Before we walk on, boy, there's something you should know.'

'Master?'

'I did not come to this employment willingly.'

William was at a loss for words; instead, he shrugged.

'I have come to enjoy it, for the most part, but for my sins, I was commanded to it by my lord, the Archbishop at Avignon.'

'I don't see...' William was somewhat perplexed.

'It was a kind of penance, you see.'

'Ah. Then we are two of a kind.'

The abbot laughed, a peel of unashamed laughter. It was the first evidence of humour William had seen but, as the older man gasped for breath amid the chuckles, the boy was just as puzzled as before.

'Well, in a way, I suppose. Yes, let us say we are two of a kind, boy.'

'But what had you done wrong, Master? What was the sin?'

Rutilius sobered. 'I believe the sin was holding to an opinion different to that of the Archbishop's.' Rutilius wriggled into a more comfortable position on the tree trunk. 'Perhaps you will understand this or perhaps not,' he continued. 'Almighty God has blessed me with an understanding of numbers.'

The abbot stood up and stretched.

'But...'

'Listen. There is a new way of giving names to the numbers, a new way to cipher. I learned it before I came to Avignon and I think it shows me, in some small part, how God has built this world for us and it is ... beautiful, beautiful.'

Rutilius fell silent, his eyes focussed on some far image until, just as William was about to say something, he continued. 'But the symbols and the usage are the invention of a heathen people, from the East; therefore it is deemed the work of the Devil.'

William had never heard of numbering as beautiful before, a mountain, a new-forged sword, a girl, maybe. But numbers!

'The mages who worshipped the Christ Child came from the East.' he said, simply for something to say. 'They must have been heathen.'

Rutilius drew in a great breath and looked at the boy. 'Just so,' he said at length and sat down again, smiling. Here was new insight.

'Now. This knife of yours, young man.'

'To cut my bread and meat, Master. Besides, my father gave it to me on my twelfth birthday; it's the only thing I have by which to remember him.' William patted the left side of his habit, behind which the weapon was hidden. 'That was a good trick with the ring, Master,' he said. 'How did you do that?'

'The ring?' Rutilius raised his eyebrows and then remembered. 'Ah, no trick,' he held out his hand with the middle finger extended. 'Well and truly stuck.'

'Begging your pardon, Master. I saw you take it off last night and put it in your purse with the other things.' The boy took hold of the ring and twisted. It turned, it slid easily up past the knuckle, and off the finger, 'There!'

'Well,' he said, perplexed. And again, 'Well.'

And so the afternoon passed: plodding onward, stopping now and then for the abbot. 'I do believe,' he said at one point, 'that the exercise is improving my bladder, I am tired but I'm certain that I feel better.'

The abbot was surprisingly cheerful considering he had to use his feet instead of a donkey's. The rain, now a downpour, cut their vision to a dozen yards or so, a circular space that moved as they walked, he shrugged off the wet and discomfort and tramped along until a noise could be heard above the hiss of the rain.

'What's that?' asked the abbot, pausing and cupping an ear with his hand. 'Something coming.'

'Something with wheels.' William grinned and they both turned to face the welcome clatter of a mule cart approaching from behind. A small rig appeared through the curtains of rain.

'Ho there,' the abbot raised his staff, 'my good man...'

The *good man* slowed a little. He parted the wet sacking protecting him from the rain and looked the two bedraggled travellers over with an expression partway between detestation and delight. The appraisal was brief; he gave an odd cry and cracked the whip over the pony's flank. The mule pulled harder, the cartwheels turned faster, spraying them both with muddy water. It was out of sight before the abbot's eyebrows finished rising.

'That was the man...' started William.

'...that called for shelter at the priory last night,' Rutilius finished.

'He might have been laughing.'

'Well he might,' the abbot said in a resigned tone, 'well he might.'

CHAPTER TWO

'Have you been to a city, boy?' the abbot asked, as they set off again.

William shook his head doubtfully. 'No, Master. The villages near my father's castle, that is all. Ah, except I once went with father to… um… to Venice; it took us nearly a week to get there. He had been before but it was my twelfth birthday and he took me that time.'

'Venice? Long ago?'

William nodded. 'Three years perhaps, I don't remember why. I remember the waves washing up on to the colonnade.' He pointed upwards. 'My father was upstairs with a factor or someone, talking about cargoes. I was watching them being unloaded.' He laughed. 'Got my feet wet.'

'Well, so you know about cities, then. So prepare yourself, boy. We shall be visiting towns and cities occasionally, and I do not want you to be seen gawking at everything like a country boy with straw in his hair, and dirty fingernails.'

'No, Master. The place we are going to, St. Guilhem le Desert, you said? Is this a town or a city?'

'A town, a small town, in fact scarcely more than a large village, I believe.'

'But this will be where we begin our investigations, Master? Into fraud and goings-on at the abbey?'

'The abbey is the Abbey of Gellone, and there will be no *fraud* and no *goings-on*. I shall be very pleased if you do not use language of that nature. I must seek to reassure those who are to be examined, words like that only inflame. Watch me and take note; you will see how I am courteous, never demand, always request, I always seek the gentle way.'

William looked suitably downcast. 'Naturally, Master.'

'When I came to St. Trivier, there were special orders from Avignon waiting for me. My plans were changed. I have to assume responsibility for this abbey, while the incumbent abbot is away on a pilgrimage. We must get on, time is short now that we do not have the donkey, and all roads in these parts seem to go uphill.'

In this way, they came to the Gellone valley, as the daylight ebbed. The upper part of the road could be seen ahead of them still bathed in bright sunlight, while the valley immediately before them was now deep in shadow and darker by contrast.

'The monastery is up there,' he told the boy, waving vaguely in that direction, 'but we shall rest here tonight, St. Jean de Fos. There is a sanctuary here, a shrine, which the abbey looks after; dedicated to St. Jean, naturally.'

A bridge took the road across a wild and rushing river. It had been built sturdy enough to withstand the occasional floods that swept down the gorge, and there they paused for a moment to watch the white waves rushing out of the gloom towards them.

They crossed the bridge and turned up the side road leading around the village to climb up towards Abbey Gellone and the village of St. Guilhem le Desert. Just beyond the village, the abbot slowed.

'There is the shrine but,' he squinted into the gloom, 'that looks like a bier in the doorway, a deathbed of some sort. What do you think, boy?'

William too looked and his eyes being younger and sharper, he confirmed the abbot's guess.

'Then, go and find out what's happened. I shall rest here.' Rutilius sat down heavily on a log at the roadside. 'Come back and let me know.'

The abbot took a deep breath and his head tilted slowly forward until his chin rested against his chest. Not that he slept, even though travelling so far on his own feet was a rare event.

'Master?' William put a hand on the other's shoulder.

'Ah,' said the abbot, drowsily. 'Yes, resting my eyes, you know. What have you found out?'

'There is a dead man laid out on a table, Master. He was the sacristan but now he's dead.'

'Yes? Well?'

'Master?'

'What did he *die* of, boy? What disease killed him?'

'Old age, Master. He died of old age. His time had come, is what they said.'

Rutilius heaved himself to his feet and paced around a little in a rather flat-footed way. 'Well, I can deal with that. Old age is acceptable but contagion frightens me, I've no wish to have some plague or other jump on me in the darkness. Old age will take us all, of course, but not just yet.'

The abbot worked the stiffness out of his legs and they carried on to the shrine, which was illuminated by several candles arranged around the deceased. A small, somewhat stooped fellow stood close to the bier, a proprietary bearing in his stance.

'God bless you, sir, and you, young man.' The words slowed as details of the abbot's dress filtered through to his consciousness. 'Ah, I had not realised Brother Abbo's reputation reached so high, m'lord.'

'Nor does it, sir. Pray acquaint me with the particulars.'

'This is Brother Abbo, m'lord, sacristan of this shrine. He died the night before last; we found him within, yesterday, when we brought the Saint back here.'

Rutilius spoke in a businesslike tone. 'You will take note of all this, boy, so it may be recorded later.'

'Absolutely, Master. Every... um... particular.'

He turned back to the fellow. 'The Saint, you said?'

'It was our saint's day; the statue of St. Jean is carried behind that of the Virgin in the procession. It stays in the church overnight.'

'I understand. Abbo was working on a saint's day?'

The other shrugged. 'He preferred animals, m'lord.'

The abbot nodded. 'I see. And you are?'

'Marcel, m'lord, a lay-helper here. Brother Abbo was, uh, respected by the folk of St. Jean. We, that is, I thought people would like to pay their respects.'

'Very good, Marcel. I see you have a donations box there.'

'Just so, m'lord. We are grateful for anything his friends care to leave.' Marcel smiled, a trifle relieved that the abbot approved. 'Are you going on to the abbey, m'lord?'

'Tomorrow, I think,' said Rutilius. 'I have temporary charge of the abbey, but tonight I shall waste none of your time. If there is an inn here we shall spend the night in St. Jean de Fos.'

'An inn,' Marcel scratched his chin. 'Of course, it is only a step or two from the Devil's Bridge. Perhaps you came by that way already.'

'The bridge. Yes.' The abbot turned back to look at the shrouded corpse of Brother Abbo. 'Have all things been arranged? For Brother Abbo, I mean.'

Marcel made a gesture suggestive of uncertainty. 'Gilbert, a friend of the shrine, arranged for the body to be washed and together we have, as you see, placed him here for his friends to pay their respects. Other than that...' He waved his prayer book.

'And you do not know what to do?'

'No, my lord. We are lay persons merely; we volunteer the time we spend here, for the good of our souls, without remuneration.'

'Sir, was he given extreme unction?'

'That I was able to see to. A priest lives at the village; you will have noticed the church there. I sent for the priest.'

'Then you have done what is most important. Ah, hmm. The Abbey has been informed of the death?'

'No, my lord. I have been here alone since he was washed. Gilbert was away as usual and the other one, he with the candlesnuffer, is my nephew who came to help me.' Marcel pointed to a younger man.

The abbot nodded. 'Tomorrow we will send someone to the abbey with a letter; tonight all that needs to be done is being done. Did I hear your name?'

'Marcel, Master.' William said quickly.

The other raised his eyebrows. 'Yes, m'lord, Marcel de Fos.'

'You have worked here a long time, Marcel?'

'Seven years. Almost. Since my son took over the shop.'

'You are burning many candles.'

'There are many people who want to see Brother Abbo. Many of those bring alms, he was very well respected by the farming folk around here and they show that respect in a tangible manner. Still, the hour grows late and Pierre is putting out all but a few.'

'Ah.'

Marcel had the slightly hunched back of a man who had worked at a bench or a low table. His hair and eyebrows were grey, his eyes a washed-out blue, though nevertheless sharp and penetrating. His beard had not been shaved for a day or more but the abbot, who believed such practice to be slovenly, was prepared to overlook it for the moment. 'Pierre is my nephew. I try to keep him out of mischief.'

The abbot nodded. Marcel de Fos obviously knew the value of money and how to make it work, an intelligent man. 'I see that the shrine is in very good hands, Marcel. Now, for heaven's sake, *where* is the privy?'

Abbot Rutilius absented himself for some time and on returning his manner was more relaxed. He continued with his instructions. 'Now, we must arrange for the monastery to know about the old monk. He was the sacristan, you said?'

'Indeed, is it not sufficient that *you* know, my lord?'

'I am on my way there but I do not plan to arrive until later tomorrow.' The abbot pointed to the snuffer-out of candles, Marcel's nephew.

'Perhaps he can go.'

'Pierre is my nephew, my lord but...' Marcel looked slightly horrified, 'I would not trust him with such responsibility. You understand?' Marcel tapped the side of his head.

The abbot did. He nodded. 'Hmm. So, er, you mentioned a friend, Gilbert?'

'If he is here, perhaps. He is not…'

'Reliable?' Marcel sketched a shrug. 'Well, we shall see

about that tomorrow.'

'Now, to the inn. I and my assistant have come a long way in the past two days... Hmm,' the abbot pursed his lips. 'Now I think on it, where *is* my assistant?'

'He was talking to Pierre a while ago just outside the Lady Chapel. Perhaps he is inside, praying to the Virgin.'

The Lady Chapel was off to the right, where the cave extended into the darkness. They crossed the central part of the shrine to the chapel, which was closed off by a hand-carved trellis, a smaller sanctuary within the greater. Inside were two people: the acolyte and a young woman, both kneeling, hands together. The woman's eyes were fixed upon the Virgin, the boy's eyes fixed upon the girl.

Beneath the white lace shawl, her hair was a gleaming cascade of black. Her eyes were the colour of aged amber, her mouth was small, lips dark, soft as red velvet. William was transfixed; his breathing shallow for her perfume filled the air, as though lavender strewed the floor from wall to wall.

The abbot reached out to touch his arm and the boy jumped, pressing a hand against his chest where his heart still leaped.

'What you are thinking of is best put behind you, forgotten.'

The girl turned to look at the men. There were tear marks on her cheeks; nevertheless, her voice was irritable. 'Can't you leave me alone?' she asked, an edge to her words. 'Must men always intrude upon a woman's solitude?'

'Our apologies, young lady.' The abbot took hold of William's shoulder and pulled him away.

The boy blushed. 'Sh…she is very beautiful,' he said

when they had moved away from the Lady Chapel. 'Very beautiful but I was only looking at her.' He paused, trying to think of a plausible excuse. 'I was wondering what it might be like to be possessed by an unclean spirit.'

'What do you mean?'

'Pierre said she prays here every day, sometimes once, sometimes more.'

'So?'

'The brother has had cause to exorcise her, not once but twice. Twice, at least, he said.'

'Did he?' The abbot rubbed his chin, rasping at the stubble and remembering his unspoken criticism of Marcel's unshaven appearance. He looked at the dead monk's coffin. 'Brother Abbo?'

The boy shrugged. 'That's what he said.'

'But a monk is hardly qualified. The driving out of demons should be performed by a priest. And I believe, preferably a well-trained priest.'

Brother Abbo's demise had caused more delay than the abbot had expected, and the night was well-advanced when they left the shrine to St. Jean. Stars jewelled the black dome of the sky in a myriad pale colours and a three-quarter moon swam through long skeins of cloud that somehow magnified its light rather than diminished it.

The empty road was alternately shadowed by trees and starkly illuminated by the moon's white light. Further on, within the village's circle, a few dim lamps and candles burned behind shrouded windows and cast a small radiance out on to the street.

William's eyes darted this way and that. It had been almost a year since he'd been sent to St.Trivier and to be once again in a place where ordinary folk dwelt, St. Jean reminded him so strongly of the village below his father's keep; it was almost like coming home.

'The church, Master.' he said once.

'Church? Yes?'

'Just like the village of Castres, where I used to live.' Tears came unbidden and he blessed the concealing darkness. 'And the river. Sorry,' he added as Rutilius looked at him.

The sound of rushing waters was all around them, loud in the silence of night. Below in the gorge, the river ran steadily, pouring between its rocky banks and from all around came the sound of streams coursing through deep-cut channels, pouring over shallow falls, gushing below moss-grown boulders. The abbot did his best to ignore the noise.

This time they walked into the village, which was arranged around the church and at length, reached the inn, a long rambling building with a half-dozen windows along the road side. There were two doors, the result of two cottages being made into one, the bush hung above the second door, and the abbot and the boy entered there.

Inside was a long room set with warped tables and benches along each side, the floor was strewn with green rushes. The noise was considerable; there were, perhaps, two-score men and women sitting there in groups of two or three, a few with five or six and more, all drinking and talking. Most of the patrons were local people; workmen, shopkeepers, foresters, smiths and others, some with their wives. There were also two or three guards from the nearby castle sitting in morose silence obviously waiting on the pleasure of a knight and a soldier of rank, their heads bent in intense debate. These two occupied a darker alcove, a sword and baldric removed for comfort, and leaning against the wall within easy reach.

Followed by the boy, the abbot made his way to the end of the room where barrels were set on trestles along a stout shelf. In front of the barrels an equally long table was presided over by a truculent-looking man who dispensed jugs of ale to a pair of boys who scurried from table to table, attending to the drinkers.

The landlord was a hirsute individual with full beard and a mop of black hair. The sardonic mouth was almost hidden by whiskers, but the nose above stood out like a crag on a cliff side, and the eyes were bright and beady beneath the overhanging brow and eyebrows. These same eyebrows rose, as he noticed his new customers and belatedly realising the one was a well-to-do cleric, he donned his best smile. His eyes fastened for a moment on the ring on the abbot's finger and then on the sparkle of precious metal on the crucifix about his neck. 'My lord, welcome to the best inn,' he sketched a bow, 'the only inn for a day's journey in any direction.'

'Bless you, my son. May God bless you and your estimable house. Is there none in St. Guilhem le Desert?'

'Ah, apart from the one up there, which is a long walk up a steep road.'

'Well, I require a room for myself, with a soft bed and clean sheets, preferably with a lock to the door and shutters to the window. For my assistant, I'm sure he would welcome a space with your potboys for the night.'

'Well now, my lord. What you wish can be provided – so long as we can agree a price. The Church often expects me to be as generous as *I* would wish the Church to be in the matter of tithes and taxes.'

Was this witticism or criticism, the abbot wondered, and hoped for the former, though neither way would make the slightest difference. 'I foresee no problems in this regard.' He unlaced the top of his pouch and drew out a few coins. He placed three silver deniers on the table. 'For bed and two meals tonight.'

The landlord looked at the three dully-gleaming coins and launched into a lecture on the cost of providing quality accommodation in such a remote region. 'Distance, my lord. The cost of transportation of provisions and ale is always high.'

'You surprise me,' said the abbot. 'I would have thought the Abbey of Gellone would supply very good quality ale, perhaps even vegetables too, at very reasonable prices.'

'Reasonable prices, sir, are of minor significance only. If I might say so without intending any offence, the mere mention of *reasonable* prices suggests someone who does not understand the lot of an innkeeper.' He stretched out his arms. 'We struggle to provide the necessities of life to travellers, to bid them welcome. We offer ale and a ready ear to all of our customers, we give advice and sympathy.' The landlord shook his head. 'The day is long and hard, my lord, and all this for a sorry profit. Our one reward is the satisfaction of a job well done.'

The abbot appeared to listen politely to all this. 'I'm obliged to you for explaining these money matters, doubtless they are beyond me. However, I have offered a sum more than sufficient to buy the room and food I have requested, even in the city of Montpellier. You have said it can be provided.'

The abbot simply ignored the further protestations and spoke over them. 'I do not wish to disturb – let us say –

the knight at yonder table who will be only too pleased to listen to Abbot Rutilius of the Vatican. So tell me, what can you provide in the way of a meal?'

Startled that his comradely tones had fallen on such deaf ears, the landlord fell silent for a moment, then, sulkily, 'Crayfish and beans. Bread.'

'Be good enough to bring two meals, a jug of your best ale and two cups. We shall be sitting…' the abbot turned again and looked around the room, he spied a vacant table in a corner, '…over there,' and he pointed. 'I shall expect my bed to be ready when we have finished eating. Is all this clear?'

'It is, my lord,' said the landlord with a note of resignation in his voice. 'It shall be as you wish.'

'Naturally.'

He and William took their seats and, presently, a jug of ale was brought to them and thumped down on the scarred and stained tabletop, along with a pair of leather cups. Shortly after, two deep earthenware bowls were brought. In each bowl, a boiled crayfish stared up at them from beneath a generous portion of beans and a chunk of bread.

After several mouthfuls of beans and the partial dismembering of their crayfish, the abbot waved his bread in the air to attract the other's attention. 'Is the food to your liking?'

'Indeed, Master. The best I have eaten since my father was ... well, you know.'

'Just so. I felt you should have a good meal after the distance we have come today and the unpleasant experience of the cutpurse. Do not expect such rich food as a matter of course, now. I, myself, will normally eat a sparse meal in the evening.'

'Of course, Master… Master?'

'Well?'

'The landlord did not seem pleased with what you paid him.'

'No, you are right in this, there are some in whom avarice is deeply rooted. Still, he had a fair price, content or no.'

The abbot took a denier from his pouch and, holding the edges between the thumb of one hand and finger of the other, he spun it on the tabletop. 'A denier represents the cost of living for a day for an ordinary man. Three deniers equals three days.'

The coin spun and flashed in the lantern light. 'The person who caught this fish walked along the river bank turning over stones, they spent perhaps two hours and took, what, half a dozen?'

The denier wobbled a little, veered.

'To plant and harvest these beans and to bake this bread, may have taken half a day though, like the crayfish, we eat only a portion of the whole.'

The denier toppled over and spent itself.

'My bed does not take a day to prepare, even to emptying the chamberpot and laying clean linen – both of which may be overlooked, and I shall have to complain.'

The abbot took up the coin and dropped it back into his purse.

'The landlord, then, has made a good profit of more than a denier, more than a day's labour. All is in balance. Would you say that all is in balance?'

'I'm sure that all is in balance, Master.'

When they had completed their meal, the abbot purchased a second jug of ale and took this and a cup to the chamber indicated by the landlord where, in fact, he had no reason to complain that evening. The acolyte sat by the kitchen fire until other customers had finished, and the potboys had cleaned up to the landlord's satisfaction and were ready to sleep.

In his chamber, the abbot was visited by lice somewhat larger and stronger and more persistent than he was used to. William slept by a fire that burned warmer and longer than he was used to. The abbot was woken several times, as other guests blundered past his locked door, or tried mistakenly to enter his bedchamber. The acolyte slept soundly for six hours, longer than he had ever been allowed to at the Monastery of St. Trivier, and his dreams were filled with the face of the girl he had seen in the Lady Chapel.

Morning came. Birds commenced their morning chorus, cocks crowed, dogs barked, cattle bells rang as a herd was taken to milking, and the landlord roused his company.

When he was certain no more sleep was to be had, the abbot rose and yawned, scratched, availed himself of the chamberpot, washed his person in cold water and dressed.

William washed at the pump along with the other boys who, thereafter, relieved themselves outside the back door, each competing joyously for the farthest reach.

Which enjoyed their lodging more? Which of them received the most satisfaction for the abbot's deniers? Where did the balance lie?

CHAPTER THREE

Breakfast: a cup of water and a loaf of bread and an early morning that promised sunshine and warmth.

The abbot and the boy had been to the village bakery where, despite the regular patrons who had waited for the oven to be opened, the abbot's robe and ring gave them first choice of the batch. The bread was hot enough to burn fingers, and was still warm when they arrived back at the bridge across the river where the abbot had planned to breakfast: just here, set back in a crevice amongst ferns and moss was a stony basin filled by a bubbling spring of ice-cold water.

On the bridge, the boy looked down at the waters swirling below. A hole had been scoured into the bank near the bridge foundation, and almost untroubled by the greater spate, the current circled slowly. Although the parapet was high above, the dark forms of fish swimming among the trailing green weeds and across the golden brown sand were clear. William dropped a few crumbs on to the water and the fish snapped hungrily at them, no doubt saying grace and thanking some finny god for *their* breakfasts.

There was, of course, still unfinished business to attend to at the shrine to St. Jean. As the sun rose high enough to shed some warmth, they left the village where bedcovers were already being aired over windowsills and men were setting off to labour in the fields or in the woodlands. The road turned steeply upward to where the doors of the sanctuary stood open. Here, they met with Marcel, at this time of day, the sole breathing occupant of the shrine.

The abbot inquired after his health and then about sending word to the abbey. 'Gilbert, was that the name you mentioned yesterday?'

'Yes, Gilbert, though I expect he'll grumble at the job, pleasant though it would be to ride up to the abbey.'

'Ride? Is he old and infirm, then? Does he need four legs rather than two?'

'Gilbert has a crippled foot; he limps and can only walk slowly. I think it is this that gives him his gloomy outlook.'

'Hmm. I see.'

The abbot told Marcel to hire a donkey. 'In fact, hire two, for I shall require one later on today.'

'You, my lord? I expected you to have a mount already, a horse, something of excellent breeding. Surely you have not walked all the way here?'

'We lost ours yesterday,' William said, in an abstracted voice, looking through the open doors into the shadowed interior, perhaps in the hope of seeing the young woman who had been praying there yesterday evening.

'My donkey was *stolen* yesterday,' the abbot corrected, not wishing to convey the idea of carelessness, nor of excessive affluence, 'by an armed ruffian who would have stolen everything including our lives had he had the chance. Between us, we saw him off, though we lost Katerine in the process.'

'A terrible encounter,' Marcel said with a shake of his unkempt head and, perhaps, a fraction more respect in his voice.

'Terrible indeed. Now, I shall write directly to the

monastery. To whom must I address it?'

'That depends upon what you will write,' he said in his slow voice.

'So it does. I shall instruct to whomever I write to send a... to send someone here immediately to supervise the management of the sanctuary. Now, you must not imagine this to be a slur upon your own work. It is necessary to have someone from holy orders here to look after ecclesiastical matters.'

They went inside where it was hard to see in the sudden dimness. 'I am an old man, my lord.' Marcel picked up the chalice he had been cleaning before the abbot arrived. He regarded his reflection in the gleaming surface. Already, he had smeared careless fingermarks on the silver and he slowly began to clean and polish it once more. 'Ecclesiastical matters are certainly beyond my scope.' He contrived an elaborate shrug. 'I have no wish to assume duties beyond my capability'

Had Marcel taken offence or was he merely stating fact? The abbot was uncertain and, ignoring ambiguity as he usually did, continued with his own thoughts. 'Once I, myself, have arrived at the monastery, I shall select a suitable person as a permanent replacement for Brother Abbo. Do you have suggestions as to the qualities of such a person?'

'Me?' Marcel was startled at being asked for advice as though his opinion mattered. 'Qualities?' he asked. 'Well, let me see now.' He held up a bony index finger. 'Animals.'

'How do you mean, *animals*?' the abbot asked.

'There are often quite a number to look after. We keep them in a small field just up the road. The shrine itself is a small one but sometimes there is need for three laypersons here even though the third is only my nephew who helps out and is unreliable. At the moment though, we have only Bernard's goat. Brother Abbo was treating it before his death.'

'Animals? How is it that there are so many to look after? Are we a farm, or do we deal in livestock?'

'Brother Abbo was fond of animals. He was good with them, a healer.'

The abbot frowned. 'A healer? For dogs, perhaps? Oxen?' The abbot was not acquainted with many varieties of animal. 'Oh, and goats of course.'

'Dogs. Cows and sheep, hens, goats, mules, horses, pigs, chickens, turkeys, geese. All sorts.'

'I don't know that we could continue to provide medical services for farm animals. Surely there are those among the laity with the necessary skills.'

Marcel pursed his lips and continued buffing the silver cup to a faultless shine, as he considered his answer. 'The farmers will make a donation to the shrine when help is asked for,' he said carefully, 'and often another one if the healing works. Often again, they are very generous.'

'Aha. I see.' The abbot was silent while he considered the financial aspects. Then, at last, he nodded and smiled. Marcel was a font of knowledge, a splendid fellow. 'Yes, Marcel, you are quite right, I must find someone with such a talent. Now, to whom shall I address this?'

'That would be Prior Josephus, whom I expect is presently in charge. I suppose that is what he is there for – when the abbot is away for any reason.'

'Abbot Roget is away quite often?'

Marcel shook his head. 'No, no, I would not say so. Last year he went on a pilgrimage to Montserrat, he returned after six months. The year before it was to

Compostela, that was for eight months. So, not often.' He stood up. 'I will see to the hire of the donkeys, while you write your letter. Brother Abbo has a small writing case in the study there.' He pointed to a door, which the abbot discovered opened into a small room built against the rocky cavern wall. 'Perhaps I can take the boy with me to help.'

'As you will,' the abbot replied, and pushed the door wide open.

'Damnation – begging your pardon, my lord.'

'Something wrong?'

Marcel was feeling through his pockets. 'A bag of nuts. That, da... that goat of Bernard's has probably filched them. The beast will eat anything.'

'A talented animal,' the abbot observed, and entered the study which was strong with the smell of incense while an underlying musty odour suggested damp paper and fabric. A narrow window was cut through the rock, which admitted an equally narrow beam of sunlight swirling with dust motes; it gave some small illumination.

The furnishings included figures of the Virgin and Christ, and a writing desk piled high with papers, offerings from supplicants, and odds and ends of all kinds. There was also a worn couch pressed up against the wall, a pillow with a pair of calf-length stockings partly tucked under it rested at one end and an old habit had been dropped in a heap at the other.

The abbot searched through the mounds for something to use and eventually found some blank scraps of paper. There were a few twigs of willow charcoal that might just do to write with, but he persevered and was eventually rewarded with three pens cut from dried reeds, and a bottle of ink. With these, he wrote – as well as he could, since much of the ink's colour had settled out – a letter explaining the circumstances, and asking for someone to take temporary charge of the shrine. A wooden tray at the back of the desk held an oil lamp, a golden-coloured knob of wax, and a seal. The abbot folded the paper, addressed it to Prior Josephus at the Monastery of Gellone and, striking a light for the lamp, warmed the wax until it spilled on the join where he impressed it with his signet ring.

When he had finished, the abbot returned to the shrine. Gilbert, as Rutilius supposed him to be, had arrived, and was limping around with a duster in his hand, whistling tunelessly between his teeth. He nodded to the abbot without disturbing the tedious whistle, and continued with his work.

The abbot followed and spoke, as Gilbert stopped to flick his duster at a candelabra set on a stone plinth.

'I am the Abbot Rutilius,' he said, introducing himself. 'You will be Gilbert?'

Gilbert nodded, admitting to the fact.

'I am in charge of the abbey while the Abbot Roget is away.'

'May God bless you, my lord, may your sojourn be a peaceful one.'

'I'm sure that… Is something wrong?'

Gilbert's expression had suddenly become furtive. His eyes looked everywhere but at the abbot's face. 'Nothing at all, my lord. Absolutely nothing.'

Rutilius was about to inform the man of the task ahead but his strange facial contortions quite bewildered the abbot, and he backed away with as affable a nod as he could manage to look at statues and icons, as far from

Gilbert as he could contrive.

Was he a madman? Rutilius wondered, and if so, was he a dangerous or a harmless madman? Gilbert must be close to fifty, though a well-preserved fifty and fit, handsome, he supposed, in a heavy, frowning sort of way, despite his limp. The abbot decided he did not like Gilbert and felt immediately guilty that he should dislike someone with such an affliction. The guilt, of course, compounded the dislike and he put a great deal of effort into rationalising the repugnance he felt.

Marcel and William had not yet returned and, since the abbot could not bear to approach Gilbert, he strode purposefully to the doors as soon as the welcome noise of hooves sounded outside.

Outside, there was a man and a boy, but not the man and the boy he had been expecting. Despite the beard and the luxuriant moustache worn by the man, the family likeness between the two made it obvious that these were father and son. A farmer and a farmer's son come some distance, to judge by the huge yawn stretching the youngster's jaw. With them were a donkey and a horse.

'God's blessings upon you,' said the abbot. 'Have you come to visit the sanctuary?'

'God's blessing be upon you too, my lord. To tell the truth, I'm come to see Brother Abbo – about this horse here.'

'I see. I'm sorry to say that Brother Abbo cannot see you.'

'Oh? Not here at this hour? I can wait.'

'Brother Abbo is dead. He now sleeps until Our Lord returns to call us all to be judged. He died yesterday.'

'Oh.' The farmer's face showed consternation, he scratched his head. 'This is most inconvenient. Felise needs a tonic, and I was counting on Brother Abbo.'

'Perhaps you would care to pay your respects to Brother Abbo?'

'Well, I shall have to go to the farrier's now and he'll charge me double what Brother Abbo would have expected.' While he ruminated, the farmer chewed the end of his flowing moustache, a habit that had bleached the left-hand end to a pale-straw colour, while the rest was a rich brown. 'Perhaps just for a moment then.' Reluctantly, he gave the rope that bridled the horse to his son and entered the sanctuary.

The abbot suddenly realised that he, himself, had not yet even glanced at the dead man and it was only fitting he should bless the earthly body for which Abbo would have no further use until the last Judgement. He followed the farmer in and stood beside him at the side of the bier.

The first thing the abbot noticed was that Brother Abbo had been rather a tall man; he spilled over the bier at either end.

'Looks well,' observed the farmer. 'Prime of life.'

And he did look well too, now that it was mentioned: fair hair in tight curls just visible beneath the cowl of his robe, fair eyebrows and eyelashes, thick lips and a stubbled chin that might benefit from a shave, long-fingered hands, long toes. The deceased monk wore a serene countenance with hardly a line on the forehead. An untroubled end to a placid life.

'Not that I liked him, nobody did, so I can't show regret.'

'He was not liked?'

'Cantankerous.'

The abbot made the sign of the cross above the corpse and recited a prayer. He went back outside into the sunlight, which was bright enough to blind him for a few heartbeats. He almost collided with the horse, which swung its head nervously and backed off a little.

'Sorry,' he said, trying to show interest. 'Is this Felise?' The farmer's son nodded. 'What is wrong with her?'

'She won't bear a foal,' the boy said. 'Been served twice and…nothing.'

'And she has ... before?'

'Oh yes. I reckon she's too old but Pa says one more time; the priest would have something to jolly her up a bit.'

'Monk,' corrected the abbot, absently. 'Poor old thing.' The abbot tentatively held out his hand to pat the creature's muzzle. In the past, he had ridden horses occasionally and he seemed to remember that this was the thing to do. The jewel on his signet ring flashed in the sunlight and so close to her eye, it alarmed the beast, which reared and stepped back, placing a back hoof on the farmer's foot just as that worthy stepped out into the dazzling sunlight.

The farmer roared with pain and that frightened the horse still more. She pulled the rope from the boy's hand and galloped off down the road toward St. Jean in a clatter of hooves and legs that seemed in constant danger of becoming tangled. Father and son departed at some speed, chasing after the animal, with the donkey bringing up the rear at a more sedate pace.

'Oh dear, oh dear,' the abbot said to himself.

A little while later, Marcel and the boy arrived. Marcel led a donkey while the boy tugged at the reins of a mule.

'Was that Robert and his son I saw chasing after Felise?' Marcel asked.

'Chasing?' asked the abbot, as though the word needed

some explanation. 'After Felise? Um, there was a man and his son who came by to pay their respects to Brother Abbo. They were taking their horse to the farrier's, I believe.'

'The farrier. Hmm, he would have passed the farrier already. Ah well. We have a donkey and a mule, as you will have noticed. All that was available.'

'I'm certain that that will be fine,' he said, relieved that the mule was at least a mule and not a horse. He plunged his hand into the capacious purse at his belt and felt around until he had the letter. 'Now, here is the letter, and Gilbert may leave.'

'And you, my lord? And the boy?'

'Later. One of the duties I must see to is a valuation of the monastery's assets. Here, we must check the donations box, and the gold and silver hanging before the statues of the Virgin and St. Jean; we might as well do it while we are here. The boy will note down the details.'

'Very good, m'lord. Now where is Gilbert? He was here a moment ago. But then, so he was last week and that didn't stop him disappearing on and off until this morning,' Marcel grumbled off into the further reaches of the shrine, and the abbot and William went about their own business.

As the abbot listed the items and made a shrewd valuation of each one, the boy wrote down the description and the assessment.

'An arm?' he asked, as he handed the silver model of an arm to the abbot.

'And why not, hmm?' He judged the weight and told William what value to note down. 'I expect someone broke their arm and prayed that it would mend well or, perhaps, they are expressing their thanks that it did mend properly.'

There were small strips of pure silver, or gold, or lead, coins, gilded icons. Innumerable small oil lamps hung before the statues, one of them …

'And now a cow,' the acolyte laughed. 'Tell me what that is for, Master.'

The abbot shrugged. 'Well, perhaps a cow that neither priest nor farrier could treat. Only God could make it well.'

When they had finished, he took the papers and made an accounting of the total value. 'You can check this on an abacus later but I doubt that I am wrong.' He smiled confidently, as he looked at the sum that he had calculated.

When the work was complete, the abbot took the boy aside. 'Here is some money. You have used coin in – excuse my memory - wherever it was you lived?'

'Of course, Master.' William was a little hurt by the other's condescension.

'Of course you have, naturally. I am a fool for asking. Go into the village and get us some food – nothing fancy, mind. You remember the baker's, I dare say they can tell you where to get cheese and some beer or…' Rutilius looked at the sky. 'What a fine day, one of the Lord's best. Get us some mead if it is to be had, else get us ale.'

'Marcel?' William asked.

He barely hesitated before nodding, 'Enough for Marcel too.'

Marcel had kept his ears tuned. Wordlessly, he handed the boy a tall jug.

William was away half an hour and, when he came back, his master was sitting on a chair in the shade outside the shrine. Not wishing to let the sleeping abbot know that he knew he was asleep, the boy sang a verse from a song he liked; a moderately holy song but moderately lustily sung.

'Did you think to wake me, boy? Hmm? Heard you singing all the way up from the village.'

'Really, Master? I hope that I had all the words right, Master.'

'Mostly boy, mostly.' He heaved himself to his feet and reached for the cloth in which William had brought back the food. 'I had better teach you some quieter songs though and just a little more sacred. Now, what do we have ... Oh, well done, young man, well done! Marcel, a table if you have one.'

Marcel rummaged around in the dark corners of the cave and brought out a battered table on to the roadside. He found chairs for the abbot and himself, and a box of old lamps and candlesticks that would serve the boy as a seat. When all was arranged satisfactorily, the abbot said grace and they fell to.

'Hmm.' The abbot poured two large goblets of mead and a liberal dash or two into a third. He brought the first goblet to his nose and breathed in, his eyes closed. He nodded. 'Simple, a …' He sneezed and sniffed again, more cautiously, 'a rounded and nutty aroma.' He wheezed. 'Fit to accompany just such a repast as this.'

He brought out some small loaves, set them on the table. 'This was well done, lad. Bread from that same bakery, hmm? And what's this?' He sniffed.

'Venison,' Marcel said. 'I know where that came from and I shall say no more of that – except to recommend it. No doubt your rank purchased this, my lord. Meat is expensive in a place like this.'

'I remember you saying that you had a shop, and wondered. A butcher's, surely?'

'A jeweller's. You may find a butcher in Montpellier, perhaps. I have never been there, but in a place like this? A butcher? No.'

'Ah!' The abbot dealt with mistakes by ignoring them, and he sailed on, 'Three slices of roasted venison and cheese and ...'

He opened a small package. 'Oh...' he lifted the small pot of dark brown paste to his nose. 'Oh yes. Goose liver. An excellent selection, boy, but take heed now.'

'Master?'

'Do not think that we shall be eating rich food like this every day. Do you hear?'

'I hear, Master.'

'I am a frugal man. Usually, I enjoy only dry bread or a biscuit or two, and some water at midday.'

'I understand, Master.'

They munched in silence for several minutes, except when the abbot mumbled wordless appreciation. Then, his immediate appetite blunted, he looked across at Marcel.

'Marcel.'

'M'lord Abbot?' Marcel took another large mouthful of mead and savoured the taste before swallowing.

'Is the mule tractable?'

'Ha! That remains to be seen, m'lord.'

When their midday meal was finished, the abbot had the opportunity to practise with the mule. It seemed a docile creature, Marcel led it to a mounting block and the abbot clambered carefully into the saddle. He shook the reins; the animal took no notice. He jiggled his heels against the flanks; the animal took no notice. William pushed against the rear quarters, and then Marcel tugged at the harness; the animal took no notice – not even when all three together encouraged the beast.

They desisted, and then all of them cheered as the mule walked delicately away from the block, across the road, and lowered its head to reach a small hummock of grass. The cheering stopped.

'Can you suggest anything else?' William asked Marcel while the abbot struggled to bring his leg over the saddle and slide to the ground.

'Some oats and sweet grass, perhaps. Hold it in front of the beast's nose and lead him that way. I can think of nothing else.'

The abbot returned, dragging the unwilling creature behind him by main force. He shook his head. 'This is not going to work. Was there neither horse nor donkey to be had?'

'Nothing, my lord. Nothing at all. This one is mainly used for pulling a cart, m'lord. I doubt she's ever been ridden before.'

'A cart? That sounds safer.'

'Do you have the skills, m'lord, to drive a mule?'

Rutilius pursed his lips. 'I doubt it.'

Marcel shook his head.

The abbot made a gesture intended to signify patience. 'There is nothing else to do but wait for Gilbert.' And with a certain satisfaction, he went back to his seat. 'The mule may be returned to its owner.'

'Very well, m'lord.'

'And while you are away, if you should come by another measure of that excellent brew...'

'If you would have a coin, or so...'

The boy sat on the river bank watching dragonflies, and

spinning daydreams of the future. As for Marcel and the abbot, they passed the afternoon in a convivial fashion, until the sound of hooves heralded the approach of Gilbert returning from the abbey of Gellone.

'Ho, Gilbert!' Marcel rose and looked closely at what was left in the jug. Focusing carefully, he nodded. 'We have saved you a glassful, perhaps two. How went your errand?'

Gilbert pursed his lips and scowled at the jug then fixed Marcel with his glare, and finally the abbot, who still had a cloth tucked into the neck of his undershirt, a cloth with the golden stains of mead on it.

'It went well enough. I was given a trencher in the kitchen and a jug of small beer. Thank you for asking.' Gilbert's tone was not appreciative.

'And my letter, did you bring an answer?'

'What was there to answer, my lord? They are sending someone.' He slid off the donkey and turned to look at the boy, who was now sitting with his feet in the cool water. 'Someone young and inexperienced, I expect.' He took the almost empty jug. 'Have you said anything about the, er, you know?'

'About the..? Lord in Heaven, no!' Marcel was emphatic.

Gilbert gave his head a dispirited shake and patted the donkey on its bony rear. 'Come, Mariette, both of us deserve a drink.' He led the animal across the road to a streamlet, which fell into the river a few yards further on.

'I hope Gilbert is not going to grumble about unfairness,' Marcel said in low tones. 'He has a great collection of wrongs done to him, and his grumbles can last out the day.'

'Oh, I hardly think so,' the abbot murmured back. 'On

a day like this, what can he find to grumble about?'

Gilbert came back and put Mariette's reins into Marcel's hand. 'You have her now. I'm away to my home. It's going to rain again soon.'

'How can you tell that?' asked the abbot.

'You see how clear everything is? You can smell it on the wind too, rain.'

'Really? The talents of you countrymen always astounds me.' The abbot beamed forcefully, to show that he bore no ill will despite the drawn-down-brows glares, and the nose-wrinkling and mouth-twisting he received every time Gilbert looked his way.

'And from the abbey,' Gilbert went on, ignoring the overture, 'you can see beyond the mountains. Big black clouds, bellies full of water.'

The abbot nodded and, with William's help, secured his bag to the back of the donkey's saddle. While he and the boy were thus occupied, Marcel and Gilbert spoke in low voices.

'So, you have not told him?' Gilbert's voice was morose.

'Certainly not! He praised my work, he asked my advice; how could I tell him such a thing? Besides, how can I be sure? Hmm? It is only hearsay. I had it from you, and you from the two women in the village. And what is all this scowling at the abbot? He may believe you to be the murderer.'

Gilbert stood back in amazement. 'Me? Why should he believe that? I was not here. You are as likely as me, a good deal more likely.'

'Nonsense.' Marcel looked sideways at the abbot and the acolyte to make sure they were still out of earshot. 'He likes me. He would never believe such a thing.

Anyway, it's your responsibility.'

'*My* responsibility? Oh no. He says go to the abbey. I go, and when I return there is no food for me.'

Marcel held out his hands. 'We kept some drink and...'

'Dregs and crumbs are all I am offered.' Gilbert turned his back. 'Oh no, my friend. If the abbot is to learn that it was murder, it is you who must explain it to him.'

CHAPTER FOUR

Mariette was a more docile beast than the nameless mule, more like the abbot's stolen Katerine in fact, and she responded too, to the abbot's hand with the same compliance. He was delighted and, with Marcel and Gilbert engaged in whispered recriminations, he was suddenly anxious to be off. They said goodbye and started towards the village of St. Guilhem le Desert.

The road ran alongside the river for a good way, sometimes close, which made the abbot wince at its noise, sometimes separated by a stand of trees. As they neared their destination and turned away from the water, the road became steeper. Scores of small springs from the recent rain burst from the ground every few yards scouring deep channels into the uncertain surface. While the donkey negotiated such obstacles with fortitude and the abbot on her back never gave them a thought, William found the ascent hard work, his calves and ankles soon aching from the struggle.

An hour passed and the road zigzagged now through new-leafed trees tall enough to hide the sun and turn the warm day cool. As the way turned and doubled back upon itself, there was often enough space for a small house to perch; often too, with a small garden of vegetables. Sometimes there would be a wave or a nod from those who lived there. As they climbed, though, their attention was on the road and they failed to notice the dark clouds of Gilbert's forecast until the first drops of rain hit the ground with ominous *plops*.

'Should we shelter, Master?'

The abbot gazed up at the angry sky. 'I don't think so, boy. This does not look like a shower to me, and if I am right, sheltering will only make us later at the gates and therefore wetter.' As if to lend credence to his words, the sky opened and drenched them to the skin in moments.

They carried on; there was nothing else to do. William's legs throbbed from the strain of walking uphill through the sticky mud and even Mariette was disconcerted by the quagmire into which the road had deteriorated.

It was very dark by the time they reached the village and little could be seen in the narrow streets, except the glimmer of oil lamps and rush lights seen through cracks in shutters and their pale reflection in the black, rain-pocked puddles. Walls seemed to press ever nearer, seemed to be in the act of toppling on to them whenever they glimpsed the rushing clouds overhead. Cold water cascaded off roofs, poured out of the downspouts that waited for the unwary around corners, flowed ankle-deep along the steep streets and roared in cataracts from out of back alleys and narrow lanes.

Sudden lightning flashed ever and again; Mariette shied each time and trembled at the terrible rumble of the thunder. They were almost through the village when a bolt struck a nearby tree with an ear-stunning crack. Mariette simply froze, and all of William's urging was in vain.

At length, the abbot got down from the saddle and joined the boy in his efforts to drag the frightened animal onward. Slowly, they coaxed her into motion and wisely, perhaps, he did not remount.

They left the village behind and, once the shelter of the houses was gone, the wind lashed them with cold, driven rain until they were bent double against its fury. Behind them, it howled across the rooftops and set gates and doors banging and finally, they heard the stricken tree creak and snap, and crash to the ground, as it gave in to the elements.

Although still some way off, the Abbey of Gellone bulked above them, the lights of its windows reflecting in the wind-driven water surging along the ruts worn into the road.

When they climbed the last of the hill and reached the monastery wall, the gates were firmly closed and barred. They banged on the iron bars and shook them, they shouted until they were hoarse and the donkey stood rigid again with fear. At last, the abbot noticed the bell in a small niche and exhausted, pointed out the chain to William. The boy tugged weakly on the rope and the bell sounded feebly above the racket of the storm.

Nevertheless, it was enough; anxious ears had been listening.

Mere moments later, the main doors of the abbey opened and light glared out through the falling rain, spilling down across the steps leading to the gate. Against the dazzle, figures appeared and hurried down the steps, the bar was lifted and the wind swung the gates back with a crash. Mariette shied at the sudden light and noise and pranced like a wild pony, pulling the reins from William's cold-stiffened fingers. Had it not been for the tall figure of one of the brothers seizing the trailing cords, she would have been off into the darkness.

'My lord Abbot. Thank God you are come, we have been so worried – and the poor donkey.' He trailed his fingers down between the animal's ears, stroking her forehead in the same movement. 'There, my lovely one.' The rolling eyes turned to look at her comforter and she quietened, standing meekly, shivering in the rain.

'I am Brother Anno, my lord, and though we are too small an abbey to have a greeter for our guests, Brother Sylvan, who has been with us for more than half a year now, will serve as well as any. Brother Sylvan, take our guests inside will you while I take the donkey round to the stable.'

He stroked the animal's head again. 'What is her name?'

'Mariette,' William said, trying to disentangle the abbot's bag from the cords that tied it to the saddle.

'Leave the bag, my friend, I'll bring it in shortly. There, Mariette – oh, the same that Gilbert rode. You *have* had a busy day, little one.'

They followed Anno into the abbey.

'God's blessings upon you,' the abbot said, pulling the wet hood from his head, 'and glory to Him who eases all pain and travail. A dry place, and a warm one.'

'There's a bathroom through here where you can dry yourself, my Lord Abbot, and then ...'

'Is there a privy convenient?' asked the abbot, shortly.

'Why, yes m'lord. Through here.'

'Wait for me, boy. I'll be back directly.'

Directly, in this case, meant a generous quarter-hour.

'Takes his time, your abbot,' Brother Sylvan observed, a stocky, dark man with the eyes of a fanatic.

The acolyte had seen frescoes of men with eyes like that usually pierced by arrows in uncomfortable places and wearing haloes and often, very little else. He also noticed the attention that the girls at the castle gave such pictures.

He nodded in reply. 'He has, you know, certain problems.'

'Ha, yes, I know. Comes from sitting on cold stone seats too long.'

'As a matter of fact,' the abbot spoke from behind them, 'that is not the matter at all. Rather… rather it is pissing that gives me great travail.'

'My lord, I will bring you some dry clothing and towels.' Brother Sylvan left, somewhat hurriedly.

'Sorry, Master, I, er…'

The abbot sat down to unlace his sandals. 'Boy,' he puffed, as he bent over, 'we'll say no more of the matter. Now, you might find an opportunity to suggest that I could be persuaded to use Abbot Roget's rooms. The privy in there is cold enough to freeze the ... Well, you may guess what it is cold enough to freeze. To me, the guest accommodation seems a little shabby.'

'We can ask for a fire to be made up.'

'Well,' the abbot sat up and kicked off his wet sandals, 'I suppose it is a possibility.'

'And you might not like Abbot Roget's rooms. Suppose we were to ask to see the abbot's rooms later – since you need the privacy for your work.'

'Good, good.' The abbot held up a forefinger and nodded. 'And if Roget's rooms were suitable, I could, um ...'

'You could say that you do not want take up the guestroom in case other travellers arrive.'

'Excellent, boy. That is what we should do.'

And with that, Brother Sylvan returned, anxious to make amends. He carried several clean habits over one arm and a pile of rough linen cloths over the other.

'There.' He laid them on the bench seat. 'My lord, you are, um, well proportioned and I was uncertain as to sizes, so I brought several from which you might choose. The boy is more easily suited, being about much the same height as me, though thinner.'

'True. The boy has yet to have his tonsure but, other than that, you are rather alike.' William was less certain; it had been a long time since he had seen his own reflection.

'Very good,' the abbot continued. 'We will change, and then perhaps, there will be a chance of something to eat?'

'Right after vespers, which is imminent, my lord. We shall look forward to hearing you preach during the meal, my lord.'

'Oh, um, well now.'

They took off their wet and muddy clothing and washed themselves in cold water and, while the abbot tried the various gowns against himself, William garbed himself and drew Brother Sylvan to one side.

'The Brother who took care of Mariette our donkey said that he would bring in the abbot's bag. It contains important documents; he would be very angry if anything were lost.'

The acolyte had had no opportunity, and less inclination to tell the abbot where he had left the bag.

'Have no worries on that score... What is your name?'

'William.'

'Don't worry, Brother William.' Brother Sylvan had made certain assumptions as to William being his equal. 'Brother Anno is a very reliable person. I'm certain he will bring your master's things shortly.'

When both were garbed in their clean, black habits,

Brother Sylvan guided them through the empty corridors. Most of the Brotherhood would already be assembled for the service of vespers, so he hurried them as much as he dared.

'Through here, my lord – mind your head, my lord, the door lintel is low – three steps here, my lord.' And he succeeded in bringing them to the church before the prior himself had arrived.

Because of the abbot's station, Brother Sylvan brought them to seats near the front, a distinction that neither abbot nor acolyte desired. The abbot, perforce, had to be seen and to be heard responding to the service and William had to pretend to a familiarity that he did not yet possess since chanted responses at St. Trivier were regarded as frivolous. However, they appeared to perform well enough and, at the end, Prior Josephus bustled forward pressing his hands together, smiling.

The prior had acquired a permanent bend to the right, the one shoulder higher than the other, his palms pressed together in a habitual gesture of hope, or supplication. The man was a fidget, he scratched his chin, pulled at his nose; he would insert a little finger into an ear and agitate it vigorously. His habit was shiny from long use, threadbare at elbows and cuffs. 'My dear Abbot, so pleased to see you, so pleased.' His voice too, was worn out. He ushered the abbot from the church and along the corridor. 'You had us worried for a time. We expected you to be hard on the heels of Gilbert, and when the storm came ...'

'So sorry to have inconvenienced you,' the abbot replied in his best unctuous tones although, since the prior was behind him, there was little need to match expression to words. 'After our work at the shrine was done, we found there to be a shortage of donkeys in the village and we, well, we had to wait for the faithful Gilbert to return.'

A few more corners were turned and several short flights of steps, both up and down, and they came into a small square room behind a door of extra solidity, and with three locks.

'Our chapterhouse,' the prior said, still smiling and dry-washing his hands, 'on the way to the refectory, convenient for a few quick words in confidence.'

'Exactly right, Prior Josephus. You know the position at the sanctuary, of course?'

'I do now, of course, I do. Poor fellow. Do you know from what he died? What were the circumstances?"

'Old ...' began William, and stopped the moment that the abbot's hand gripped his shoulder.

'I am assured that it was natural causes.' said the abbot. 'But I have no skill in such things. As to circumstance, I know of nothing unusual there either. I was told merely that he died. I'm sure that you must have someone with medical talents. I suggest he looks at the corpse as soon as it is brought here, before the body is prepared for interment. Just in case of contagion, though I'm sure I'm being foolish.'

'Very wise, very wise. I shall have to announce the death, of course, but tomorrow is soon enough for that. So far, Brother Simon, whom I sent to help at the shrine, is the only one to know, the only one here at the abbey.'

'Oh?' the abbot said. 'Why is that?'

'Brother Abbo has a relative here and he should be told first. I wished to speak to you first, of course, but Brother Anno must be next.'

'Absolutely. Exactly.'

'I will bring Brother Anno with me to see you after the meal, if I may?'

The abbot shrugged, 'Naturally.'

In his opinion, the meal that followed was adequate. The abbot would go no further than this. Gellone was one of those congregations that eschewed meat, except in cases of illness. It was not a doctrine with which the abbot agreed but was one with which he had often to live. The thin vegetable soup, the preponderance of potatoes – admittedly, with a skilful use of herbs – and the limp, overcooked greens were sufficient to keep body and soul together, but they added no joy to a man's life.

Although, in fact, there was one thing that did make the whole thing bearable: the bread. It was crusty, it had an herby, oniony flavour, and, like the ale, which also engaged the palate pleasurably, it was served without stint. Nevertheless, the abbot saw that if the local tavern served a reasonable meal, there would be a number of occasions when he might dine out, circumstance permitting.

The insistence that he preach to the assembled brothers was something else that did not have his approval. Public speaking was not one of the abbot's strengths either, though he did his best by attempting to impress upon the congregation that man – or monk – did not live by bread alone, no matter how delicious it might be. He feared that the point of his argument was lost on most, if not all, of those present.

During their walk back to the guest suite, where the bleakness of bathroom and privy had influenced the abbot's opinion so drastically, he spoke to the prior about the incumbent abbot's rooms. 'Work space, you see.' He explained, 'Plenty of table room and doors that lock – confidentiality.'

'Ah, um,' the prior replied, 'somewhat cold in there, at the moment. We'll have a look in the morning, get someone to show you round.' Josephus thought some more, possibly seeing the wisdom of his temporary abbot's plans, he nodded vigorously. 'Certainly, we can do something for you and of course, you will be of the same mind as Abbot Roget in many ways.' More nodding. 'Simple, modest, a common man, humble. Yes, yes. Of course. I will conduct you there myself.'

The abbot frowned and bit his lip, himself – a common man, a humble man to boot? Cold? Fortunately, as a courtesy, the prior still walked behind the abbot in the narrow corridor and did not see the other's misgivings. Had he been too hasty? The abbot wondered. It was not like him to be precipitate.

They arrived eventually at the door of the guestroom, with its fine carved frame. Prior Josephus leaned in front of the abbot and raised the latch, then ushered his guest inside.

There was a swift movement from the side of the fireplace, where welcoming flames roared up the chimney; William had arrived before them. He scrambled quickly to his feet and backed slowly away. 'Just um, making sure that, um, the place was warm enough and dry, Master. You mentioned your aches and pains this morning.'

'I did? Well that's very thoughtful ... I did, didn't I?' The abbot recognised an opportunity to hedge his bets in the matter of workplaces. 'Mm… Aches all down my left side. That's well done, boy, and a welcome sight after that steep hill in the rain, eh?' The abbot limped a pace or two.

'Well, now that we're here,' said the prior, 'you will remember I suggested that we meet with our unfortunate brother about this sad affair at the shrine? He will be here directly.'

As if his words were a cue, there was a knock at the door and a monk came in, ducking beneath the lintel. He carried the abbot's bag.

'Aha, I wondered where that had got to.'

'The brother did say he would see to it, Master, keep it safe and sound.' William's tone was anxious. He did not want there to be any thought of his shirking his duty.

But his master hardly heard him. He was staring up at the monk, who was certainly an unusual figure. He was tall, far taller than the abbot, who was by no means a short man. He was also black, as black as the night sky, blacker than his Benedictine habit. Tightly curled black hair surrounded his tonsure, and glistened with raindrops. His thick lips seemed constantly curved in a smile, his dark-brown eyes just on the verge of laughter.

'Have we not met before?' the abbot asked.

'This evening, at the gate, my lord.'

'No, no, I remember that. I mean before that, before we arrived here.'

'I do not think so, my lord Abbot. I'm sure I would have remembered if we had, and that you would remember one such as me, too.'

The abbot shook his head. 'Your face seems very familiar, though not the complexion.'

The black monk passed the abbot's bag over. 'Perhaps you have met my brother. We are twins.'

'Still, I would remember a man as black as you.'

Anno chuckled, a deep fruity sound. 'Identical in every way except in colour. Abbo is as pink and white as you, well, less pink perhaps. I, as you see, am not. Our father was Nubian, our mother came from Britain.'

'Brother Abbo?' asked the abbot, in a shocked voice.

'Brother Abbo,' he said, laughing again, 'and I am Brother Anno. Brothers.' And then he realised that none of the others were laughing and he stopped. The atmosphere was serious, very, very serious. 'There is something wrong, isn't there?' His eyes grew large; the whites showed all the way around, he turned to Prior Josephus.

'Sit down, my son.' Brother Anno sank slowly and fearfully on to a nearby low chair, as the prior continued. 'I am very sorry, Brother Anno, to bring you such sad news. Your brother died yesterday; the news has only just reached us. He has left this world and waits peacefully to live again when Our Lord comes to build His heavenly kingdom here.'

'Dead?' Tears sprang from great round eyes and dribbled steadily down the monk's cheeks and made two darker patches on his habit. 'How?'

'We don't know,' the abbot said quietly. 'I am told that his death was natural, that he did not suffer.' This last was somewhat of an invention but, all considered, the abbot did not expect to be penalised for it at his own day of Judgement.

The abbot had neither brother nor sister, he could barely remember his parents, William was as close as he would get to a having a son. He could only guess at the measure of such a loss. 'We grieve for Brother Abbo, we grieve for your loss, my son.'

'He was so well, though. Abbo never falls ill, neither of us does… did.'

There was a silence for many minutes until Prior Josephus stood and crossed to the black monk.

'Come, Brother Anno, you will want to pray and to ask God to help you bear this sorrow.' Josephus held out a hand and Anno reached up and held it.

The boy stood too, rested his hand on the other's shoulder for a moment until Anno stood up and he could no longer reach so high.

'Thank you.' Anno looked at the abbot and the boy, and tried to smile through the tears that still streamed down his face. 'A poor welcome for you, my lord Abbot.'

The abbot shook his head. 'May you find peace, my son.'

When they had gone, and the abbot and the boy were alone, he looked across at William, who had moved closer to the fire and stood there hunched in misery. He had known him only a few days and already he could hardly recall what life had been like without the youngster's company. A thought came to him.

'Boy, you told me that Brother Abbo had died of old age. He wasn't old; he was younger than I, some years younger.'

The boy looked up at the abbot, whose naturally flushed face glowed positively scarlet in the firelight. 'I never saw him, Master, how could I know how old he was?'

'No, but that is what you told me.'

'Did I? I don't remember.'

'Perhaps that is what Marcel told you, that he died of old age? Can you remember his exact words now?'

William frowned in concentration. 'What he said was...

His time... That his time had come.'

'"His time had come." And you assumed that that was what he meant – he had died of old age?'

The boy nodded. 'I suppose so. Have I told an untruth?'

'No, no. You made an assumption, a natural assumption.'

'It was the other man who told me, the one who came up here on the donkey.'

'Gilbert?'

The boy shrugged.

They sat in silence for a while and, as they warmed up, so their mood lightened.

The boy looked around the room, now mostly illuminated by the flickering firelight. Furnishings were comfortable, indeed, compared to what the young acolyte was used to at St. Trivier, they were sumptuous. Two large couches with square no-nonsense frames and straw-filled cushions faced the fire. Beyond was a plain wooden table and, against the rear wall, a pair of chests separated by a curtained doorway and a set of shelves. A window, now shuttered and hidden by a heavy arras, occupied most of the outer wall, and placed before it was a writing desk and a tall stool.

The abbot followed the youngster's gaze with his own eyes. 'This seems quite comfortable, you know. I believe I was right to choose against the Abbot's quarters; this will be far more suitable.'

The boy grinned at the abbot's change of mind, and carefully kept the smirk out of the abbot's sight.

'Is there a bed anywhere?'

'Through there, I believe, Master.' He pointed to the doorway between the two chests. 'And there's a fire in there too, Master.'

'I'm beginning to like this place, young man. They do have an idea of civilised living, despite the food they expect us to eat, hmm? Man should not have to live on prayer alone, nor on bread and vegetables. Mark what I say, it doesn't hold the spirit and body together.'

It was not very much later that the abbot rose and went to examine the bedroom and the bed that stood before a smouldering fire. Soon the only sounds within were the crackle of flames and the abbot's snores, which William found difficult to separate from the storm's thunder. The boy snuggled himself down among the cushions on one of the couches.

CHAPTER FIVE

Something woke William from a dream where he was climbing a road that grew steeper with every step. Behind came a monster, snuffling and snorting ever closer. The boy stirred among the cushions and opened his eyes. He looked around him, realising that he had just escaped from a dream, but wondering for a moment or two where in the waking world he was. Then he recalled the past few days and realised the snuffles and snorts of his dream were the abbot's snores. He wriggled back into the cushions in delight.

He had missed the service of lauds, shortly after midnight, mainly because the abbot had forgotten that he was buried somewhere in the furnishings and had gone alone. So, with the exception of prayers a few hours since, he had slept soundly since the late evening before, and felt wider awake than usual for this time of the morning. Perhaps he should get up and explore.

The room was almost dark. The fire was little more than a mound of glowing ash, and all that seeped in around the window shutters was a ghostly grey light. The remains of a log toppled over in the grate, exploding a shower of sparks. A rosy glow shone briefly on the white plaster, a wisp of smoke curled up into the chimney.

Soft cushions and warmth. Even now, so early in the day, the room was warmer than he had been used to for a long time. He grinned into the darkness and burrowed down once more, drowsy and with his resolution forgotten.

A little later, another long drawn-out snore rose like the rasp of a saw cutting wood, followed by a series of snorts and wheezes. While the abbot was still asleep, wakefulness was thrust upon the boy. There was no going back this time. William climbed out of his nest and set about repairing the fire. A handful of kindling on the hot ashes, cautious puffs until tiny blue flames licked around the twigs. Then a few finger-thick sticks and, when finally these were alight, some of the smaller logs.

He tarried there a little while longer on the edge of the hearth, basking in the growing heat and wondering what to do next. At St. Trivier, matins was said at this hour in a cold, austere church, where breath plumed like wood smoke on the chill air, and feet numbed with cold. He could hear faint sounds now: footsteps; sandals slapping against stone flags; doors opening and closing; an ass braying, perhaps that was Mariette. The monastery was astir, preparing for the day.

Should he wake the abbot? Would he take kindly to being roused? No sooner had these thoughts passed through his mind than a bell tolled for the early morning prayers.

The abbot's snores broke off to be replaced by a series of coughs, and throat-clearings, and grunts. Within the sleeping chamber, the bed frame creaked, as the abbot rolled himself to the side of the bed, poked his feet from under the cover, and sat on the edge. With an effort, he stood up and clasping most of the blankets around him, tottered unsteadily to the door.

'God be with you, Master.' William stood up.

The abbot eyed the boy blearily for a moment or two, as though his memory too needed to catch up with actuality and then he nodded and mumbled, 'And with you.' The older man's hair looked like a straw-stiff ruff spreading out from the shaved crown. He disappeared back into the room and various sounds suggested a minimal toilet, and dressing activities.

'I'll do it properly later,' he said, more coherently now that he was dressed.

They left the guestrooms and made their way to church. The abbot took the position normally reserved for Roget, the incumbent abbot, and a place had been thoughtfully kept at his side for his young assistant.

Afterwards, they paused long enough at the refectory to order a working breakfast to be brought to the guest rooms. They then returned, lit candles and the abbot made good his intention of a more thorough wash, insisting also that the boy should follow his example.

Before breakfast arrived, they opened up the abbot's bag and arranged papers and pens and ink pots on the table in front of the window. He eased the shutters open a span or so, enough to glimpse the buds on the apple tree outside.

'Glass!' The abbot was impressed, he rapped his knuckles against the window; it was green and far from transparent but it held the warmth within and the cold without and still it let the light through. 'I'm willing to wager - if I were not in Holy Orders, and gambling was not the infernal sin that it most certainly is - I'd wager that this is a rarity. Probably the only window glass in the abbey, well, besides that in the church.'

With that, he threw the shutters aside and the work they had set out was lit by the clear glow of dawn, William pinched out the flames on the several candles.

'Master?'

'My boy?'

'Is it really necessary to start work before breakfast?'

The abbot chuckled and bent down to bring him closer to the boy. He adopted a conspiratorial tone. 'A good impression is most important,' he explained. 'Imperative.'

William raised his eyebrows inquiringly.

'I have ordered breakfast to be brought here. We shall make it known that we do not have time to spare for mundane things, our work is of the highest priority.....'

'So we must be working hard when the food is brought to us,' completed the boy.

'Just so. Just so.' The older man grinned at the youngster. 'Now, examine these notes of mine.' The abbot pointed to a long piece of papyrus, which carried a list of apparently unconnected jottings.

Cost excessive. Lobster? William read, the question mark, which had been underlined three times, loud in his voice. *Why not wooden dishes?* Again an emphasised question mark.

'These are the sort of notes I expect you to take down as I peruse accounts. These notes are for a kitchen's spending that I examined a month or two back; deception is apt to be more frequent in kitchens than anywhere else. Each query I note down must be investigated and a good and sufficient answer given.'

The youth nodded, but was saved the need to respond by the arrival of their breakfasts, carried in by a kitchen boy under the supervision of Brother Giles, headman in the kitchen. 'Where shall we put these, my lord?'

The abbot, who continued speaking as they entered,

feigned surprise at the interruption and waved vaguely to the table, while keeping his nose buried in the notes he was reading. William hurriedly cleared enough space, and the big wooden tray was put down.

'Enjoy.' Brother Giles beamed, winked at William and spun about to follow his own aide out of the room. The monk left behind an exhalation of hot winter soups and herbed dumplings, of beers and spices and new baked bread.

When the door was closed and the footsteps had died away, the abbot inspected the tray: oatmeal porridge, a small pot of honey, bread, a smoked fish of indeterminate species, and jugs of water, small beer. 'An excellent selection, my boy. Now...' He ladled porridge into a brown earthenware bowl and laced it thoroughly with honey. 'Ah, yes.'

The boy was about to follow suit. 'You might find it more wholesome to add salt.'

'Master?'

'Too much honey at your time of life can cause various ills to the undeveloped body. It makes young flesh spotty and greasy.' The abbot took his porridge over to the sofa nearer the fire and ate it slowly, savouring each mouthful. The boy compromised with a pinch of salt and somewhat more honey.

Both did full justice to the meal with the abbot claiming the fish on the grounds that he needed more food to keep his larger body active.

'Master?'

The abbot turned towards the boy, eyebrows raised.

'I think a succubus came to me in the night.'

'Now, this is not a fit subject for a boy of your age.'

'But Master, what should I do?'

‘A succubus? A woman, in the night?’

William nodded and scraped at his porridge bowl. ‘She had the likeness of the girl at the shrine. It was…’ he searched for a suitable word, ‘*terrible!*’

‘Hmm. And this, this likeness did terrible things to you?’

‘Well, no. She just looked at me and…’

‘Did you touch yourself? Hmm? Your private parts?’

‘Um, no, Master. Not than I can remember.’

‘Do not trouble yourself, boy. This is something growing boys experience. Wash your privates in cold water before going to bed, it will pass. Some more porridge?’

They were savouring their final mouthful, as the prior entered their room

‘Bless me.’ The abbot showed surprise. ‘The Lord bless you, Prior Josephus. We seem to have more visitors here than St. Peter’s on a warm summer day. How can I help you?’

‘It is I who have come to help you, my lord.’ He tilted himself to the right and pointed to the ceiling. ‘You expressed interest in Abbot Roget’s quarters. Up there.’

‘I did?’ The abbot was briefly amazed.

‘Indeed you did, Master,’ the boy prompted, nodding vigorously.

‘I did. The boy is my memory,’ he said, smiling. ‘Let us go at once.’

The prior led them through the abbey, along stone-flagged corridors, up a flight of stairs, along another corridor.

He attempted single-file conversation as they went. ‘So, now we have a new pope.’ His tone conveyed considerable satisfaction.

'Indeed we have, Prior. Simon de Brie, indeed. And what a deed.' There was that about the abbot's response that counselled caution.

'The election of Martin IV does not please you, m'lord?'

The corridors were lined with dark oak doors and several were open to varying degrees, though all the cells were empty. The abbot allowed several of these to pass by before he answered. 'A Frenchman? Elected only because two cardinals were imprisoned? Prior, this is the grimy end of politics. Twelve hundred and eighty years since our Lord was born and we have to use deceit to elect our Pope? Shameful, shameful!'

The prior had been gratified when the French de Brie had been elected; Abbot Roget had been pleased even though there had been a small contretemps among the electors. Abbot Rutilius did not share their enthusiasm. Mentally, the prior shrugged. *Such was life.*

Behind each of the doors they passed was a small cell with a narrow truckle bed, covered with a straw palliasse and a thin blanket. In most, there was a shelf carrying a crucifix and, perhaps, a religious motto. Which of the black-garbed monks occupied which cell was a mystery for the moment, but William felt a certain presence as they passed each one. Here, in his imagination, he saw a short, thin man with a sparse fringe of grey hair fanning out from his tonsure. There, another as thin as the first, but a head and shoulders taller, and with a long nose down which he looked, often with an expression of disdain. All the cells were steeped in widely varying natures, from the humorous to the saintly, from the spiteful to the benevolent.

Josephus opened a door, no different to a dozen others they had passed, ushered them through, and followed them in, still listing somewhat to the right.

Abbot Roget occupied three rooms: a reception, a study and a bedroom. A narrow garderobe opened off the bedroom, and a small alcove was furnished for private prayer with an altar and a kneeling block.

The sound of a bell and of a cart rolling over cobblestones drew their attention to a window of almost arrow-slit proportions. It was glazed with glass, somewhat clearer than that in the guestroom. The boy peered out of the narrow window, while the abbot leaned over him to see what was happening.

'Abbo,' the prior said, answering the unasked question, 'I sent someone to fetch the body up here.'

The abbot nodded. 'A well-run place, Prior Josephus. And all down to you, I'm sure.'

He was obviously pleased at the compliment, and then, uncomfortable at his own gratification, he scratched his chin, mortified.

The abbot continued his inspection, paced around the rooms, inching carefully between the furniture, observing everything. His expression remained carefully non-committal.

'Compact, my lord.' The prior spoke into the continuing silence, 'A little austere but the abbot is not one to favour soft living.'

'Oh yes, indeed, austere. Compact too; is there room for the two of us?'

'Master?'

'My boy?'

'It seems dark to me.' The acolyte hid his face from both of the adults. Amusement was not an expression to be shared at this point.

'Gloomy.'

'Abbot Roget always finds the light from the window adequate,' the prior said.

'Small and gloomy,' the abbot summarised.

'Master, it seems damp to me.'

'Papers must be kept dry. Vellum too.'

'Oh, we can have a fire going in here as soon as you like.'

The abbot looked at the fireplace. It was very small and had clearly not been used within living memory.

'I suffer from pains in my joints,' he said.

The prior sighed, nodded, sensing that it might be time to change sides. 'I do see that the guest suite is better suited to your, um, your requirements.'

'Indeed so, Prior.'

They left the small, cramped suite of rooms. The prior closed the door carefully and as he turned around, collided with his new abbot, who was looking up at the door lintel.

'My lord?'

'Such delicate carving. Quite beautiful.'

The prior looked back at the door frame. He nodded and pulled an earlobe. 'It is, isn't it? So many lovely things pass us by quite unnoticed after the years we spend here. Easy to forget what a beautiful place we have.'

They left the Abbot's suite and returned toward the lower floor.

'Prior,' said the abbot as they reached the foot of the stairs.

'My lord?'

'Could you arrange for the accounts from the kitchen to

be brought to my room, please?'

'Certainly. The kitchen accounts.'

'And those from the scriptorium. Who manages the scriptorium?'

'The Precentor, that's brother Willi.' He pronounced it in the German way.

'Surprised you have a precentor here, smallish for a copying room and overseer.'

'Brother Willi might take his talents elsewhere if there was no office of precentor,' the prior explained.

'And you do value Precentor Willi's talents? Excellent. We shall make a good start on those today.'

'The kitchen though, my lord Abbot?'

'As goes the kitchen, so goes the abbey. A truism, but nonetheless true for that,' the abbot pointed out with what seemed to him to be irreproachable logic. 'Exactly so.'

'Poor Abbot Roget,' said William after the prior left them.

'How is that?'

'What a dismal place in which to live. Except for his glass window, of course.'

The abbot looked sharply down at the youngster, but the boy was reading one of the lists with great concentration. The abbot pursed his lips. 'Well, you should realise that it is his choice to do so. Living frugally and uncomfortably helps some people to feel they are nearer to God.'

The boy nodded his head.

'I feel fortunate that I do not subscribe to this school of thought. Our Lord led a simple life, but there is nothing to suggest that He lived in deliberate discomfort or poverty. I do not believe that He asks that of me.'

Unconsciously, the abbot patted his well-rounded stomach. 'Holy thoughts come to the warm and the well-fed as often as to the cold and hungry.'

The breakfast things had been taken away during their absence and now the abbot rearranged his papers across the table.

'While we are waiting, go to the refectory or to the kitchen and see what is for lunch, will you?'

William left him and, while he was alone, the abbot took a second sheaf of papers from his bag and began to leaf through them. Judging by his almost detached manner, the occasional pause to reconsider a point more carefully, he was already familiar with the content. At length, he drew the papers back into a stack and, when a knock at the door heralded the arrival of the accounts for which he had asked, he replaced them in his bag.

'Come!'

The door opened and an altar boy entered, smaller and younger than his assistant.

'Papers, my lord.'

He tapped a bare patch on the table with his finger without taking his eyes from what he was reading. 'Set them down, my son. Here.'

The youth did as he was instructed, carefully arranging six sheets of paper covered in columns of minuscule writing and on top of these, a shallow box filled with scraps of paper. 'From the kitchen, my lord,' he said, indicating the box, and pinching the corners of the full sheets between finger and thumb, 'and the scribes.'

'Well done, young man. Thank you.' As the boy turned to go, the abbot looked up. 'Tell me, what manner of man is the head scribe?'

'Brother Willi?'

'The same.'

'Why, I suppose he's a bit fierce, sir.'

The abbot drew his eyebrows down in mock ferocity. 'Fierce?'

The youngster gave him a cheeky grin. 'Pull your ear for forgetting to bow. Paddle your backside for spilling ink.'

The eyebrows rose in amazement. 'Really?'

'There's no doubt, sir.'

'Then, I too must remember to bow and not to spill ink, I suppose.'

The lad gave him a broad grin and backed away. He bowed, grinning more widely. 'Will that be all, sir?'

'Indeed it will.'

The abbot sifted through the scraps of paper from the kitchen: receipted bills from suppliers; notes of sales; an IOU for money to buy cornbread from a baker in the village; several old menus; and a recipe for crisped duck in honey sauce. He would show the boy how to write up the notes as a set of accounts.

He turned now to the chief scribe's overly-neat records, peering at the minuscule writing. As intended, it was extremely difficult to read but the abbot had a remedy for such deceitful flummeries. He rummaged through his bag for a few moments and finally withdrew a rectangle of glass, a span or so in length. One side was flat and he laid this side down on the paper, the upper side had been ground and polished to a slightly convex shape, which magnified the characters sufficiently to make them clear.

The abbot read down the lists intently, not even noticing the return of the acolyte until he had finished.

'Ah, boy.' The abbot was in good spirits. 'What news?'

he asked, glancing up at William.

'Potato soup, Master.'

'Yes?' There was an expectant pause.

'Master?'

'What else?' The abbot laughed. 'Potato soup with what? *What* is there to *eat*?'

'Nothing, Master. Just soup.'

'This is a grave matter, boy.' The abbot's good spirits evaporated, his cheeks took on a darker shade. 'Arrangements must be made. We cannot be expected to work all day with nothing but a cup of soup.' He thrust a sheet of paper into the youngster's hands and a pen; he uncorked an inkpot. 'Take down these notes and then we shall see about soup.'

Using the magnifying glass again, and another pen, he marked certain of the entries on the account sheets.

'Item one. Write: one hundred skins sold to whom? Got that?'

Another mark. 'Item two. Write down: how many pens used in a month.'

Five more lines were accepted. Then, 'Item three. Write: four hundred and fifty sheets of best papyrus sold. To whom?'

The notes went on. The abbot dictated in a savage voice, query after query, until there were sixteen in all. 'Shake sand on the ink and place it beneath this book for privacy.' Evidently satisfied with his work, he rubbed his hands together. 'Soup for lunch. Rubbish!'

'Rubbish, my lord Abbot?'

The door had opened almost soundlessly to admit the prior.

'Ah, Prior Josephus, I believe I might have been commenting on the state of accounts from your scribe.

The fellow seems to be selling off materials to all and sundry.'

'Oh. We have an arrangement with St. Anione's. We get better prices if one of us buys a large quantity and then we sell half of it to the other.'

'Oh. Ah. Hmm. I see. The idea has merit though it should be made plain.'

'I'm sure, my lord. Actually, I came to ask you about a replacement for Brother Abbo.'

The abbot's face became grave. 'Yes indeed, I had thoughts about that myself. What is it that you recommend?'

'Two possibilities: Brother Anno, whom you have met, and Brother Sylvan, who has filled in from time to time at the shrine.'

'I'm sure that Brother Anno is good with animals, I saw the way he soothed our donkey last night, when the poor animal was so frightened by the thunder. Calmed the creature at once. Very like his kinsman in that respect, I imagine. Would he want to assume his brother's role, though? Hmm? Brother Sylvan, of course, is unknown to me.'

'Master?' And at the abbot's nod, he continued, 'He saw to our arrival, Master. Brother Sylvan brought us dry robes.'

'Ah yes, I do remember him. A zealous young man, I thought. Yes, zealous. Which do *you* recommend?'

Josephus chewed his lip a moment and made up his mind. 'I think it would be good for Anno, if he wished it.'

'Then, by all means put it to him, Prior Josephus. If he wishes it, let him do it.'

The prior went to the door and opened it. 'By the way,

my lord...'

'Prior?'

'Lunch has always been pottage, just pottage.'

'Is that so, Prior? Is that so?'

CHAPTER SIX

By themselves again, the abbot re-examined the accounting. 'Take the notes you have just made and scratch out items one and three. Cross out item six and um, item eight. And twelve.' He shook his head and checked through the list again. A certain inspiration took him. 'Add a last note. Say that third party names are imperative. Now dry the ink as before.'

The abbot looked towards the window. The sun was high in the sky. Only a narrow circular shadow surrounded the pedestal of the crucifix, which stood on the windowsill. 'Lunchtime.'

They placed books on top of their current work, a simple guard against persons with mild curiosity, and closed the door behind them. They turned left towards the main entrance. Six, seven paces further and the abbot came to an abrupt stop.

'What ...'

The abbot put a finger to his lips and shook his head. 'Listen,' he whispered.

The boy listened.

Faintly, from along the passageway came the sound of voices singing, a simple chant where each line hovered about a single note before finishing with the final words sung as a slow melody: plainsong.

'We'll listen for a little while before we go.' And the abbot paced along the cloister towards the sound. His assistant trailed reluctantly after. The voices, four or five men, perhaps as many as seven, were low and middle-register although the tones of at least one alto-tenor gave counterpoint at strategic places.

He was lost in the music. Tears ran down his cheeks, unnoticed. A priest swept by him into the church, unremarked.

Not so an altar boy who attended him a few steps behind. He wielded an incense pot, swinging it erratically and fighting to dodge the billows of smoke. He was the same boy who had come with the accounts. He grinned at William and held his nose, as a cloud of smoke erupted. William grinned back and nodded towards his master, rolling his eyes heavenward. The altar boy nodded, thrust a finger down his throat and mimed the act of retching which, after swallowing some of the bitter smoke, turned into a coughing fit.

Both stifled wide grins and parted company, perfect communication, perfect understanding.

At length, the chant finished and the abbot mopped his cheeks. 'Beautiful, beautiful,' he whispered. 'Eh, boy? Beautiful?'

William grunted and mumbled, plainly unimpressed.

They returned down the eastern cloister. 'Well, I'm sure you will find it so as you grow older. Not that I can sing a note, mind you. Can't hold a note in my head, never mind tell one mode from another.' They reached the entrance, the short flight of steps to the outside. 'Style is old-fashioned, of course.'

'Master?'

'Style. Old-fashioned. Gregorian in Rome now, though it's hardly likely to last.' The abbot looked at the sky and sniffed the breeze. 'Spring. It must be the best season of the year.'

Below stood the village, a small, more or less rectangular agglomeration of greater and lesser dwellings. A matter of no more than a few minutes' walk along a steep lane hedged with bushes of alder, ash, hawthorn. From the steps of the abbey, the eye was drawn, willy-nilly, beyond the village to the road that had brought them up from St. Jean de Fos. To either side were open woodlands with carpets of pale bluebells and patches of primrose-like yellow sunlight splashed across the green.

It was not possible to see the road dwindling away downhill without amazement at the long climb that had brought them here to this eyrie among the crags of Lange d'Oc.

Clearly the music had put the abbot in a good mood. He led the way slowly down the steps and out on to the road that led down to the village of St. Guilhem le Desert. Suddenly he stopped and bent, inspecting the gatepost.

'Look at this, boy. Just look at this wonder of God's invention.'

William looked. Embedded in the sandstone was a white, perfectly formed seashell of the type called whelk and about the size of his thumb. Wind and weather had worn away a niche, which now framed the shell. 'How did that get there?'

'The Lord put it there of course.' The abbot straightened up. 'When He made the world and all that is in it, He placed that shell there knowing that some quarryman would cut a gatepost and a mason fashion it just so and that we, and others, would see and marvel at His work.'

'Just for those few who would notice it?' William asked, a little awestruck.

'Exactly so. For people like you and me.'

The abbot's musing were interrupted by an unexpectedly insistent rumble from the abbot's own stomach; it returned his attention to lunch. 'Soup,' he said it with a disdainful curl to his lip. 'We cannot be expected to work on empty stomachs. Not when accuracy and fine judgement are so crucial.'

A warm sun had dried up much of the rain, although gutters and streams still ran full, and pools stood everywhere reflecting the clear blue of the sky. The abbot stopped at a corner just as they entered the village and regarded a small square house. Above the door, a bunch of greenery had been denuded to thin, broken stalks by the previous night's storm. 'Now that looks promising, young man. Very promising.' The abbot shook his staff at the place. They waited as an oxcart passed them by, then crossed the street in its wake, the abbot striding wide across the central runnel of storm water and the acolyte leaping behind. They entered the tavern.

Inside, it was a much smaller place than it appeared from outside. The main room was brightly lit by several open windows. New green rushes on the floor gave the place a pleasant, fresh smell. Above them in the shadows, several enigmatic cloth-covered parcels dangled from cords tied to the rafters beneath the roof thatch, and great bundles of dried herbs were hung to dry against future needs.

A score of patrons, both men and women, sat on benches ranged around the walls with a variety of tables close by. Most had goblets and jugs of ale to hand; a few had bowls of food or stew in front of them.

Two men were leaning on the serving bench and talking

to a third, who stood on the other side. The third one looked up and greeted the abbot and the boy, 'A good day to you, sirs.' He took note of the abbot's black habit and bowed across the bench. 'I am Jean Claude, your host.'

The other two, who were dressed in rather richer clothing than most, turned and looked the abbot up and down. Without a word or a nod, they walked down the room to a table at the far end. The innkeeper drew in a breath of obvious relief.

Jean Claude was tall for a commoner, tall and spare, with knees knobbly enough to be noticeable through his hose. Like his clothes, where seams had been re-sewn and worn areas darned or patched, the innkeeper had seen much use. His hands were horny from hard work. His teeth were eroded to yellow nubs, and he had lost one near the front. Hollow cheeks suggested that others too were missing further back. Even Jean Claude's eyes were a faded grey as though the sun had bleached out the brighter tones, and his hair, worn long without a hat, was thin and streaked with grey.

'They want the impossible,' Jean Claude said, nodding at the men, who were now engaged in their own conversation. He smiled, and the smile transformed him from the washed-out figure to a friendly, affable tavern keeper in a matter of instants.

The abbot warmed to him just as quickly. 'And will not be told no?'

'Who snared rabbits in the lord's forest yesterday? That is what they want to know. Rabbits! Do you think I'd say if I knew?' He left the abbot no time to answer. 'Enough of that, sir. We have good ale here, brewed at Gellone, and some mead, if you like a heavier drink, which is made to our private recipe.' He gestured to a bench close to the counter on which rested a huge barrel and a dozen jugs waiting to be filled. 'A seat, my lord, and young man.'

'Well, God be with you, innkeeper. Certainly, we'll take a draught of ale, though a small cup only for my assistant here.' The abbot sat himself down, with a certain flair, aware that many local eyes were watching, and that he would be judged by the figure he cut while he was here. 'Now tell me, sir, what have you to eat? We have been working hard since before daybreak and need something to build up our constitutions.'

'You have come to the right place, of course, perspicacious gentleman that you are. I can offer you a filling soup of potatoes and turnips, or a savoury stew.'

'I have just spurned soup at the abbey, innkeeper. I need something more substantial.'

'Then a bowl of stew it must be. And for your boy? The same?'

'Naturally. Pour the ale at once and bring on the stew as soon as may be,' the abbot told him in expansive tones.

These things were done with such a flourish and swagger that the abbot hid his amusement behind a hand. However, the ale was cool and crisp and bitter. The stew arrived and smelt most wonderfully. The abbot dipped a horn spoon, tasted… chewed. He dipped another spoonful and inspected the contents. A hush descended upon the tavern as everyone watched the abbot examining his food. He used the spoon to search through the contents of the bowl.

'Er, something wrong, my lord?' The tavern keeper's face showed concern. 'You have found something not to your liking, as it were?'

'Quite the reverse, innkeeper. On the contrary, something that I had hoped for is absent.'

'Really, my lord? I'm sure our other customers have been satisfied, what is lacking?'

'Beef, or mutton, or pork, or fish, or fowl. In short, innkeeper, meat of any kind whatsoever.'

'Well, my lord. I cannot help you there, not at all.' He looked around his other patrons and, fleetingly, at the two gentlemen now leaning on their table and listening to the exchange. Jean Claude spread out his hands. 'Meat is a commodity that we see only on rare occasions.'

'Is this true, sir? What occasions may those be?'

'When did we last have meat in our stew, Benoit?' Jean Claude asked one of his customers.

'Why, that would be when Edouard's ox died unexpectedly two month since, we had meat. Everyone in St. Guilhem had meat for a couple of weeks. And at Christmastide, Jean slaughtered his goat. We had both hind legs here, and then we sold sliced meat, and then minced, and then we made broth from the bones and the hooves, and I'm willing to swear that there's still a trace of it in the stockpot today.'

The abbot was appalled at the tale. 'No meat? Yet you all look healthy enough, strong and able. What do you eat instead?'

'Vegetables and barley, cabbages, leeks and onions. Bread.'

'No meat? I am amazed.' He turned to William. 'Are you not amazed?'

The boy shook his head, answered in a low voice. 'Here, meat will be scarce, Master.'

'Scarce?'

William nodded. 'This is not like the towns and the

cities you may be used to, Master.'

'In that case,' he said at last, 'the stew is excellent. I commend it and compliment the chef.' And he set to and finished the bowl before refilling his cup and settling back to drink in a careful and gentlemanly manner. A performance that the villagers watched with evident approval.

'We are near the lord's castle here, Master,' William explained in a low voice, when the villagers' attention had died away. 'You saw the two esquires when we came.'

The abbot nodded. 'And?'

'I would guess that the lord guards his rights jealously. Such meat as they have will likely be poached from the lord's land, or fish lifted from the lord's rivers.'

'And they have none of their own?'

'None that they can afford to turn into chops and joints.'

'Hmm. I have sometimes wondered why meat is scarce in one region, plentiful in another.' He drained his cup.

'That is the way of it.' The boy looked up. 'You have a visitor.'

As the abbot poured ale into his cup, an older woman got to her feet across the room. She chose a seat near enough to the abbot to talk to him in a low voice. 'May the Lord bless you, sir.'

'And you also, Mother.' He looked at her; the woman possessed a sense of faded glory that hinted at better times in her past.

There was an obvious determination to maintain appearances. Beneath her shawl, her hair had been hennaed to a passable auburn colour. Her bright blue eyes sparkled amid a spider web of fine lines, which suggested good humour. However, these were the only marks of age that the abbot could see; a skilful use of cosmetics had achieved an appearance more youthful than actuality.

'You may address me as Madame Brisenot.' She drew her cloak tighter around her shoulders. 'These others,' she nodded back towards the table, 'are some friends of mine. There is Dondo who, er, well, never mind, we were discussing business.' Dondo nodded to the abbot, as he was introduced. Rutilius smiled and nodded back while Madame smoothed the folds of her gown. This was made from heavy, blue-dyed linen, with a broad band of embroidery around the bottom, and another down the front of the kirtle. Although rich thread had been employed, it was now faded from washing. A pair of scuffed ankle-high boots peeped from beneath the hem of her gown.

'God's blessing on you, Madame Brisenot.' And again, he waited.

She tucked a few stray hairs back beneath the shawl and smiled coquettishly at the abbot then contrived a more motherly expression for the acolyte. 'Look at him, my lord. A pair of walking sticks wrapped in a bundle of cloth would have more fat to them.'

William scowled at her. 'I'm stringy, Madame, but strong.'

'He speaks the truth, Madame, I can vouch for it.'

'Perhaps so, my lord, but what a beautiful boy! Look at that face. I dare say there are angels who might be envious.' Madame Brisenot moistened her lips with little darts of her tongue, as though she were anticipating the taste of an almond pastry just cooled from the oven.

The acolyte suffered her to stroke his cheek but jerked

back his head sharply when Madame Brisenot would have pinched it. 'Madame!'

She grinned and leaned towards the abbot. 'On another matter, my lord, I am told that the cooking at my house is good. Excellent, in fact.'

'Well now, excellent, excellent.'

Madame Brisenot nodded. 'That is what I am told. I have buried three husbands and each one required six men to carry the coffin.'

The abbot nodded. 'Something of a record, I imagine.'

'Each one a fine figure of a man, at the end.'

'Naturally.' The abbot rested a hand on his stomach.

'I keep chickens, and a gentleman friend of mine knows how to set a trap for rabbits and partridge when the lord's gamekeepers…' she nodded towards the squires at a table by themselves, 'are engaged elsewhere. Do I make myself clear to you, my lord Abbot?'

The abbot guessed at her meaning and risked being wrong. 'Abundantly.' He leaned a little closer and lowered his voice to ensure confidentiality. 'I believe, for example, that for a certain consideration, you might provide a nourishing meal.'

Madame Brisenot nodded.

'At your own house, perhaps? A private arrangement?'

Again, she nodded.

'I accept with gratitude.'

No one but the acolyte could possibly have overheard their conversation but, for all that, the grins and the knowing looks suggested that all of the regular patrons knew exactly what bargain had been struck.

Madame Brisenot leaned back, satisfaction written large across her features. She glanced again at the acolyte. 'Bring him with you, my lord. He needs some flesh on him, though I dare say he won't eat much.'

'Boy!' prompted the abbot, when the other remained silent.

'Why, thank you, m'lady,' said William.

Madame Brisenot dimpled and looked this way and that, then leaned closer to the abbot once more. She spoke even more quietly, leaned even more closely. 'Perhaps also you could tell me about the murder?'

The abbot started with surprise, his cup thumped down on the table. 'Murder?' he tried to say but his mouth had gone dry, the word simply refusing to emerge. He tried again. 'Murder, Madame?' he whispered. 'What murder?'

'Brother Abbo, from the shrine to St. Jean de Fos, of course.'

Beside the abbot, his assistant's eyes opened very wide.

'Oh.' The abbot breathed a sigh of relief. Rumour had gone before and exaggerated the facts. 'There was no murder, Madame. No, no. Brother Abbo died of natural causes. I saw the body. Myself. I saw it.'

Madame Brisenot shook her head in a determined sort of way. 'Murder, my lord. Gilbert de Gignac. You know Gilbert?'

The abbot nodded.

'Gilbert organised the washing of the corpse, and I had it from Marie-Pierre herself. She and Benoit's girl did the preparation and she is very reliable.'

The abbot fanned himself with his empty bowl. 'Madame, I'm sure there is a mistake here. I sincerely believe that.'

Even though she whispered, Madame Brisenot's voice became a trifle strident. 'I suggest that you look into it, my lord. Murder, and no mistake.'

'Indeed, I will. Won't we, my boy?'

The acolyte's face was now a study in fascinated horror. 'Oh yes, Master. Oh yes.'

'In fact, we should take our leave, Madame Brisenot. We best return to the abbey immediately.' The abbot rose.

'Shall we say tomorrow, my lord? At midday, or would you prefer dinner?'

'I beg your pardon?' *What* was *the woman talking about?*

'Your meal, my lord. Lunch or dinner?'

'Oh … dinner.'

'Shall we say an hour after the vespers bell. Around seven?

'Just so.'

The abbot left coins on the table and saluted. 'Thank you for your hospitality, innkeeper.'

'Well, Master, who would have believed it?'

'Silly woman. Rumours.'

The abbot was bent forward, arms swinging in time to his urgent striding, sandals slapping at the hard-packed earth of the road, as the butt of his staff thumped heavily down at every other pace, the ruddy colours of his complexion mounting with exertion.

'Rumours, Master?' Young William followed on breathlessly.

'Gossip. Nothing more.' The abbot could not maintain his pace and, as it slackened, so his vexation died, he flicked his fingers in dismissal. 'Gossip and rumours.'

'Undoubtedly, Master.'

'I shall go to see Brother Willi this afternoon.'

'The scribe?'

Apart from the sound of heavy breathing, the abbot

remained silent for a while. They had come to the last part of the road leading to the abbey; steep, arduous, it required rather more effort than the abbot preferred to expend.

'Yes. Ah, the scribe, the chief scribe,' he answered, finally, having attained the crest and paused for a few breaths.

From the abbey, they could hear a bell ringing and the chant of monks in procession. They stopped outside the gates to listen. The acolyte turned to the abbot. 'It may still be wise to have this matter of murder investigated, Master.'

'I thought we were in agreement, my boy.'

Neither noticed the changing relationship. Despite his joking references to the boy as his memory, the abbot really was becoming dependent on the youngster, and the acolyte's opinion had come to matter to him. For the boy, on the other hand, there had been no one before who had valued his thoughts. This was something new, something exhilarating.

The abbot rubbed his chin. 'Not in our remit, boy. Fraud, theft even, yes, these are to be investigated, but murder?'

'But perhaps someone stands to profit from the Church, and we need to stop the rumour growing, Master. Whilst you are in charge.'

The abbot nodded. 'Aha, profiteering as well as murdering. Yes, put a stop to that, by all means. Yes, I can see that.'

They returned to the guestrooms, now irrevocably the abbot's suite, and he sat down to recover fully from the climb. The boy went to fetch a pitcher of cold beer from the kitchen to slake the abbot's thirst. 'It was the burial,

Master,' he said, on his return. 'They have buried Brother Abbo. That was what the bell and the psalms were about.'

'What? Before the corpse can be examined?' The abbot climbed wearily to his feet and set off along corridors in search of the prior, asking after his whereabouts each time he met one of the Brothers.

He was advised to look in the chapterhouse and there he found the prior, not in the chapterhouse but in a sort of arboreal cloister that opened from the chapterhouse. The prior was reading a treatise on cultivation and tending to a dozen or more pots in which flowering plants flourished.

'Aha, my lord. Come to see my orchids? They come from all over the world you ...'

'Prior. The body… of Brother… Abbo must… be exhumed… for examination,' he said, panting heavily at every other word.

'Calm yourself, my lord.' He scratched his right ear with the end of a miniature brass spade. 'Examine the body? Whatever for?'

'Murder. The village is alive with rumours of murder. The body must be examined so that the gossip can be refuted.'

'We are not compelled to listen to the tittle-tattle of the laity, my lord. Besides, the burial ...'

'I believe we should protect the name of the abbey, Prior. I am not anxious for the reputation of the Abbey of Gellone to be besmirched while its incumbent abbot is away. The body *must* be exhumed.'

'Exhumation is not needed.'

'Prior...'

The prior stuck his spade in an empty pot with a

deliberate movement, he pulled his nose hard, several times, his list became pronounced. 'My lord, please hear me. I was about to say that the burial has had to be postponed.'

'But the bell?'

'Was the moving bell. The coffin was brought back and is now resting in the church. The grave is waterlogged. Water is pouring out of it as though an angel opened a spring and commanded all the waters under the earth to flood the whole world again before vespers.'

It had been a long speech for the prior, now he drew in several great breaths to recover his composure.

'Ah. Blessed be the storm.' The abbot breathed a sigh of relief. 'God has foreseen all. Brother Abbo's interment is postponed; his body can be shown to be spotless. All will be well.'

'There is one other thing about which I should warn you, my lord.'

The certain knowledge that God had already arranged everything had brought tranquillity to the abbot's mind. 'And what is that, Prior Josephus?' He smiled down at the shorter man.

'Brother Sylvan seeks an audience with you.'

'Brother Sylvan?'

'You may remember his name was mentioned as a possibility for replacing Brother Abbo.'

'Of course. Yes. The zealot.' The abbot paused momentarily to remember the incident. 'We settled on Brother Anno, should he be willing.'

'Brother Sylvan reckons that he should be considered ahead of Brother Anno, since he has more experience of running the shrine, which, to an extent is true.'

'But we decided on Brother Anno. Have you chanced

to see him yet?'

'No, my lord. He is immersed in prayers for his natural brother.'

'Then there is nothing more to be said until Brother Anno decides.'

'Still, perhaps you will see him. To exert your authority?'

'Indeed. Of course.'

After a cupful or two of beer from the squat, round-bellied jug to refresh himself, the abbot took those pages from his bag that he had been studying that morning and checked that all were there. 'You may stay here and let any visitors know that I shall be back shortly,' he told the acolyte. Then, he picked up the six neat pages of accounts from the scriptorium and the notes that his assistant had written out.

'Names are imperative,' he read out and smirked.

The abbot had often wished that stairs could be made less steep and with better handrails, and not so far from bottom to top. He wished just those wishes again, as he headed for the chief scribe's *sanctum sanctorum*: the scriptorium.

It was on the first floor; a heavy oak door guarded the place from precipitate entry, and, inside, work went slowly. The scratch of pens on vellum was loud in the stillness. The inks, the coloured and the black and the gold and silver, dried slowly into brilliantly hued birds and impossibly twined animals, and plants curling and spiralling around the crisp letters.

The long roof was made of cedar boards blackened with age, the clerestory windows were filled with yellow sheets of shaved horn and oiled silk, with every fourth or fifth glazed with green glass. Great oaken pillars supported the roof and its weight of tiles, even the long scintillating beams of light peering through the windows seemed to uphold the great carved crossbeams with their burden of gargoyles and angels, malignant spirits and flowers.

'Brother Willi?' The abbot looked around expectantly to see which of the several quietly working monks would admit to the name.

The figure lounging indolently at the end of a long bench in the sun's warmth could be no other. The Germanic name fitted exactly with the crop-haired, four-square monk who looked up at the question.

Willi rose slowly to his feet. 'My lord Abbot.' He bowed, just a little.

The abbot looked around the long room, counting the monks who worked on, oblivious to their visitor. Along the top of each of the long lecterns was a piece of wood carved with a quotation from the scriptures, which exhorted the labouring monks to toil in the name of the Lord and to praise Him with fine works.

'What can I do for you, my lord?' The question came reluctantly, with a touch of puzzlement, as though he could think of nothing that the abbot might require of him.

'Two things, Brother Willi. I have made a preliminary examination of your accounting and there are points which need clarification; there are a few mathematical errors to be dealt with too. Also, I need this to be copied.' The abbot placed his own sheaf of handwritten notes on a lectern. 'As you will see, the work concerns matters of mathematics. Indeed, that is its title, *De Mathematica*.'

Willi nodded. 'Yes, I *am* fluent in the Latin, my lord. Quite practised.' He placed one of his great blunt hands on the manuscript, and the abbot wondered how such ungainly fingers could write a word of script at all.

'Very well, my lord. Copied. Parchment?'

The abbot could not have said why but he had been expecting some prevarication; it was the reason he had come prepared with complaints about the accounts. Now the wind had been taken from his sail, he felt – not that he would have admitted it, least of all to himself – but he did feel just slightly guilty. 'Parchment is exactly what I had in mind. When might it be ready? There are approximately sixty-three and one half pages to be copied.'

'Approximately? I see. Estimates of time and effort are difficult, my lord. I hesitate to give such an undertaking without examining the work more carefully.'

The abbot nodded, taking the news with bad grace. He debated whether to argue the case but said instead, 'I look forward to hearing from you.'

It was yet another thing that he would not have admitted to himself but brother Willi intimidated him and he would have given much to undo this encounter and try again on more neutral ground. Perhaps, with William behind him, for the lad was shrewd, there was no gainsaying that.

He turned to depart but stopped a moment to watch one of the scribes instructing a young boy in some exercises. He noticed too that most of the workers were arranged in pairs with an older monk instructing a younger in the craft. 'You spend a great deal of time on tuition, Brother Willi?'

'As and when necessary, my lord. Tuition has its place in all crafts. Yours too, I expect.'

'Hmm. That's so, I suppose.' Belatedly, he realised that

he still held the accounts and had still to discuss them. 'Ah, the accounts, Brother Willi.'

'By all means. Would you care to sit down in my office?' Brother Willi pointed to a kind of lean-to built within the workroom and at that point, there was a resounding crash as the heavy door, against all expectation, swung open and thudded solidly into the wall. The wind from its turning blew a sheaf of newly finished documents on to the floor.

'Master, oh Master.' The acolyte burst into scriptorium. 'Sorry,' he gasped, as the papers swirled around his feet. 'Master, you must come quickly, immediately.'

'I must?'

'Oh yes, indeed.'

He turned back to Brother Willi. 'I shall return.' Despite the noise and the disorder, Brother Willi's dark jowls spread in a serene smile. 'I am happy to wait, my lord.'

On the steps outside the scriptorium, the abbot grasped the boy's shoulder. 'Now, what is this all about?'

Inside the scriptorium, Brother Willi shamelessly pressed an ear against the closed door.

'Murder,' he heard, quite clearly.

CHAPTER SEVEN

Four hundred years before, perhaps a little more or a little less, for exactitude reduces history to no more than a ledger filled with dull numbers, the abbey in the valley of Gellone was built. Since then, new chambers had been added, a cloister had been built, an old kitchen pulled apart, a new infirmary built. The abbey changed and grew, like a living thing.

There had been losses, too. Beautiful carvings were hidden in dark nooks or covered by new plasterwork; forgotten windows looked out on blank walls with their lovely leaded glass pictures hidden in shadow.

The abbey was alive. It grew, pulsing with the seasons, breathing with the winds; its corridors and vaults were veins filled with monkish corpuscles.

And now, life had been wantonly spilled, a tragedy that could not fail to bring injury to the community.

Rutilius shuddered. A man's life taken, his chance to prepare for Eternity lost beyond all retrieval. The breeze was chill; he closed the window on the bright sun and turned away.

He had only just returned from viewing poor Abbo's corpse. It had been a melancholy duty. After he had given the order to examine the piteous husk that was so recently filled with Brother Abbo's soul, it had taken them an hour to find the tiny puncture in the back of the neck. When he went down to see what they discovered, it seemed no more than an insect's bite until he looked at the pin that caused the death.

He held it now, in the palm of his hand, no longer than his own little finger, as thick as a candlewick and an instrument of murder. The end, they pointed out, was broken off so that only the barest trace of the pin was visible. The other end, the pointed one, was bent at a right angle, bent with the force of the thrust against the bone.

'Murder, boy. There is no doubt, I'm afraid.'

'What has to be done then?' William asked, his humour a cross between excitement and horror at the furtive little weapon.

'It would be best if we can find the perpetrator before Abbot Roget returns. I…we… don't want to leave something like this unfinished when we go.'

'But the murderer could be anyone, from here at the abbey, Marcel or Gilbert, someone from St. Jean de Fos… Anyone.'

'You are right, but consider what the motive might have been.' The abbot sat down by the table and placed the broken pin in a small stone bowl. 'What reason could there be for killing a monk? Find a motive and we can find our man.'

William frowned in thought. 'We were robbed,' he said slowly. 'We might have been killed.'

'So, robbery. But there was nothing taken from the shrine.'

'Nothing we know of but we only know what Marcel told us.'

'But…' The abbot stopped and thought. 'You are right, of course. You seem to suggest that Marcel had a hand in it?'

'No. Not necessarily,' William replied slowly, 'though

we do not know him well.'

'I would be more inclined to consider Gilbert than Marcel.'

'There is nothing to actually suggest he was involved, any more than Marcel.'

'No. No, I know that, but he is an unpleasant man, sinister.'

William did not agree but offered no further argument. 'What about the villagers?' he asked instead. 'Perhaps, Brother Abbo argued with someone.'

'But I have arguments with people, with you sometimes. Do you want to murder me?'

'Well, that's different.' William grinned a little.

'No, no it's not. I don't think any ordinary person would kill a man of God.'

'In a fit of passion, he might.'

'But this wasn't done on impulse, boy. They found Brother Abbo slumped over a lectern, as though he had had a fit and had died while he prayed. That is planning, not passion. Mind you,' the abbot leaned back in his chair, 'you are still right, a villager cannot be ruled out, even though I'm reluctant to believe such a thing.'

Rutilius put an elbow on each chair arm, steepled his fingers together and closed his eyes. He tried to imagine someone thrusting a metal pin into someone's neck whilst they were at prayer, hard enough to bend over the end of the pin. It did not bear thinking about. 'Was that the bell for vespers?' he said some time later, startling William.

'I believe so, Master.'

'Then, supper cannot be far behind.'

After vespers, the prior touched the abbot's sleeve to draw his attention.

He stopped, and the flow of monks from the chapel came to a stop.

'I have a sort of message from Brother Abbo, m'lord.'

'From Abbo?' The abbot was startled. 'A *sort* of message?' wondering if the prior had received a spiritual visitation.

'Anno, m'lord. I meant Anno. He has some matters he must mention to you, something he discovered about the kitchen? You are looking at the conduct of the kitchen?'

'Yes.' The abbot moved aside and movement restarted. 'That's so. Tell Brother Anno he may see me at any time.'

'Thank you, m'lord. Er, have you any thoughts, um,' Prior Josephus bent at the waist like a reed in a gale and contrived to look up at the abbot, 'concerning the… er … killing.' He whispered the final word.

'Many thoughts, Prior, many. But they have to… to cook as it were, to stew before anything of importance is likely to come from them.'

'Well, of course, m'lord Abbot, naturally. Perhaps I might call by after the evening meal.'

'Perhaps you might, Prior.' The abbot smiled, as frostily as he dared, but it had no discernible effect on Josephus.

'Until later, then.'

The abbot returned to their room, where William was already tending to the fire and sweeping up the scattered ash.

Idly, he picked up some of the lists of kitchen expenditure that the acolyte had already written up and left on the table. Holding them close to a candle, he frowned over the neat writing.

'Side?' he frowned even more fiercely. 'Side what?

Boy! What does this say?'

William stood up and looked where the abbot pointed. 'Side of bacon? Yes, that's it – a side of bacon.'

The abbot shook his head. 'And this?'

'Repairs. To a kettle, I think.'

'Hmm. The light is too bad for this, it must wait until morning.' And having at last arrived at a reasonable excuse to postpone work until tomorrow, he sat down before the newly leaping flames, and gave a contented sigh. 'You have a way with fires, boy. A most satisfactory way.'

William smiled. 'They couldn't keep me away from them when I was young. A bonfire in the garden, a roast on a saint's day. I've always liked making fires...'

The boy's voice ran down, as memories caught up with him and presently, the abbot detected a quiet sob.

'Life often travels a path different to the one we expect,' he said, quietly. 'What plans the Lord has for us, we cannot know. Perhaps we are to learn something or to serve a purpose we cannot perceive at the time.'

'You cannot know,' William said, a tone of bitterness in his voice. 'I would have been lord in my father's stead. You have chosen to serve the Lord and your life is settled; you are content.'

'And that is what you believe, is it?' The abbot stood up and walked as far as the table, turned and walked back. 'That I chose to make accountings of money, to make sure that the Holy Father received his due?'

The abbot paced back to the table, waved at the piles of documents. 'To walk from one monastery to another, and search out those who would defraud the Church of its income?'

He came back again and leaned over the fire with both

hands on the mantle shelf. 'There was a time when I studied at the University of Pisa, when all that mattered to me, apart from young women, was the beauty and the elegance of mathematics.' The abbot's eyes were bright and looked into spaces unbound by the abbey's stonewalls. 'Numbers delighted me, the manner in which each would fit with another, and how they built into patterns, and ...'

There was a knock at the door, a creak as it opened.

'Aha, Prior. You are just in time to calm my enthusiasms.' The abbot took a deep breath. 'There now, I am composed again. I was telling the boy here, about the charms of mathematics, and getting quite carried away.'

The acolyte watched the abbot's performance with astonishment. In the bare week he had known him, William had never suspected that such a passion had lurked beneath the black habit.

'A chair, boy. For the prior.'

William dragged another chair closer to the fire and went to sit on a stool by the table. The prior sidled across the floor and seated himself, an action which seemed to bring him nearer the vertical.

'Now, Prior, how can I help you?

'Abbo.'

'Quite. Brother Abbo's death.'

'Well, rather the position left by Brother Abbo's death.'

'Ah yes. I see. We had rather decided on Brother Anno, had we not? Subject to his own desires in the matter.'

'Just so, Abbot. Brother Anno wishes to carry on his brother's work, he can think of nothing he would rather do. I use his own words, but he wonders if he is being selfish.'

'He knows of Brother Sylvan's hopes?'

'Indeed he does.' Josephus relaxed a little and tilted just slightly towards the abbot. 'Brother Sylvan is not a quiet person; he has certainly made his hopes known to me, and to others. Frequently, over the past days.'

'Then, in my judgement, Prior, I would say that he is not yet sufficiently submissive to authority to take such authority. No, the post should go to Brother Anno. Do you concur?'

'Certainly I do. I am pleased that we are of one mind on the subject.' They smiled at each other.

Encouraged by this, Prior Josephus leaned a little further from the perpendicular and scratched his chin. He continued, 'May I ask if you have had time to think about the um, the death or rather, its perpetrator?'

'Not exactly.' The abbot looked across at the acolyte. 'I… that is… we believe it possible that almost anyone from the village could have done it, yet we don't see why.'

Josephus pulled at an earlobe, twisted his little finger into the interior and twitched it up and down. 'Nothing was stolen?'

'Not that we can determine. Nothing was disturbed. There were no empty hangers around the icons, no empty spaces in the dust. Not that I suspected the villagers, you understand but…'

'A traveller?' suggested Prior Josephus, 'wishing to sleep before the altar, a beggar perhaps, some itinerant…'

'These are things we can inquire about in the village, though nothing was mentioned by Marcel.'

'But Marcel was no more aware of it being murder…' Josephus trailed off.

The abbot looked up thoughtfully. '…than we were.' Then, an expression of mixed doubts tinged with suspicion entered his eyes. This he hid from the prior by averting his head. He laid a hand on the other's arm. 'My dear Prior, what a clear head you have on those shoulders.'

The head tilted with surprise at the praise, and might have rolled off the shoulders were it secured any less substantially. 'We must return to St. Jean de Fos and speak again to Marcel and, of course, to Gilbert.'

'Ah, Gilbert.' There was a curious tone to the prior's voice.

'You know Gilbert?'

'Indeed, Abbot. A man of the world, shall we say. Why he gives any of his time to helping at the shrine, I don't know; perhaps to expiate some unknown sin.'

'Gilbert? Sins? Tell me, Prior, for I need to know his character.'

'Perhaps I go too far. He is a freeman. He used to be a merchant and came to live in St. Jean. Lord Girand de Fossard has no hold over him.'

'Well, that tells me a little, but as for sin and his immortal soul, that is in the care of his priest. Still, we shall keep Gilbert in our thoughts. What of Brother Abbo himself? Do you know of any quarrel he might have had with anyone?'

The prior sat back and grasped the arms of the chair, his mouth turned down. 'Brother Abbo probably made many enemies. It pains me to say this but, unlike his brother, he was not a likeable person, and he did not like his fellow man.'

'Oh dear, oh dear. There could be many people who would desire his end.'

'Perhaps not. He liked animals, he ministered to animals and had a great talent for it. It was the only reason he held the position at the shrine.'

The abbot nodded. 'He would have as little to do with men as was possible. I see. Hmm. Have there been any failures with his animal charges, I wonder? Marcel will know, I dare say.'

He rose to go. The abbot, followed by William, rose too.

'We shall make an early start.'

They reached the shrine well before lunchtime, a meal to which the abbot had been looking forward all morning. They tied the donkey to a doorknob and went inside, cool and almost Stygian compared with the bright day outside.

A young monk met them. 'God's blessing…oh,' he paused in surprise and then completed the phrase, 'be upon you. My lord Abbot and er, Brother, how can I help you?'

'God's blessings be upon you too, my boy. Tell me, is Marcel de Fos here today?'

'No m'lord. Gilbert is here although I've not seen him for a while. Can I not help you?'

'Not unless you were here on the night of the murder, and I don't think you were, were you?'

The young monk's hand went to his mouth. 'It *is* true, then. I heard it said but I didn't really believe it.'

'Who have you heard it from?'

'All sorts of people, from the village mostly, but I thought it was just gossip.'

'Hmm. Well, it's true enough. Do you know where Marcel lives?'

He nodded.

'What is your name?'

'George.'

'Brother George. If we mind the place for you, will you go and ask Marcel if he could spare me some time?'

Brother George nodded once more.

The abbot recalled the last meal that he and William had shared with Marcel and the pleasure of eating in the open air. 'In fact…' But the occasion had been altogether different, he shook his head. 'Ask Marcel if he will join us at the inn in the village, near the bridge.' He turned to the boy. 'And, William…'

'Master?'

'You may go with him if you wish.'

'Ah, yes, Master. Thank you.'

When they had gone, the abbot poked around the cave looking for any place or object from where the murderous pin might have come for anything that might confirm his suspicions. The tiny office space that obviously doubled as sleeping quarters for Brother George had been cleaned up and smelled fresher than the last time he had been there. At the altar to St. Jean, two new items were hanging: a silver model of a foot and a small lamp fashioned from silver-plated brass.

There was no sign of Gilbert at all, and the abbot hummed a tune to himself, wondering where he had heard it.

He wandered from place to place. He picked up a scrap of parchment and was almost startled out of his skin by the sound of a sneeze. He had assumed that he was alone and it took several long moments for his heart to settle down sufficiently to guess at the direction of the sound. An instant later he discovered in the small Lady Chapel that same young girl who had so taken William's fancy before. Here she was again, kneeling in prayer, apparently oblivious to the abbot's presence.

Presently, Brother George and the acolyte returned. 'Master Marcel will see you at the tavern shortly,' George reported. William had gone to sit by the river.

'And Gilbert de Gignac?' the abbot asked thoughtfully. 'Have you seen him while you have been out?'

The monk shook his head.

'Hmm.' The syllable carried a weight of disapproval. 'Very well. We will be on our way. God be with you, Brother.'

'Ah, Brother George.' It was the girl from the Lady Chapel. Instantaneously, she was the centre of all attention. 'Is Brother Sylvan to be made sacristan, do you know?' The voice was hardly diffident but then, her upbringing was surely the cause of that, thought the abbot, drawing nearer.

'It has not been decided yet, Mademoiselle,' he said and smiled. 'What was your interest?'

'Oh, nothing. Just curiosity,' she replied, and as Rutilius was about to ask something else, she added, 'I must go now. Good morning to you.'

William watched from the riverbank; each of them in his own way watched the girl as she walked down to the village and when she was gone, the abbot and the acolyte left in the same direction.

'I thought you might suggest a lunch like last time, Master,' William ventured after a few minutes.

'It had entered my mind, boy. I considered it, but the same bottle of wine cannot be opened twice.'

William was silent as they continued down the hill towards the village. 'Ah,' he said at length. 'The circumstances are different. Is that what you mean?'

'I do, boy. Just so. Today we are in a more melancholy mood; before was a celebration of spring.'

'My father's master-at-arms used to teach me to fight. He used to say, every attack is a new one.'

'That's as may be, boy. You must now think gentler thoughts; you should hope never to use a sword again.'

'Well, that's as may be, Master,' William repeated the abbot's expression. He remembered the excitement of facing a new opponent, testing the reactions, finding the habitual moves of defence and avoiding them. But all that hung on constant self-discipline. 'Without daily practice, the sleight is lost.'

They reached the inn and entered the long room, with its uneven tables and bearded landlord, who made a point of smiling affably at the abbot. There were fewer patrons at this time of the day and they found Marcel easily enough at a table that barricaded a small niche halfway along the room. He was talking to a dark-clothed man who stood up as they approached.

'Farewell,' he said to Marcel, nodded to the abbot, 'M'lord,' and ignored William.

'A friend,' Marcel explained.

The abbot nodded. A friend in muddy boots, with wet patches at the knees of his hose, Rutilius had seen him before. Recently, though he could not recall the moment.

'Now, Marcel. Perhaps we can ask you to order something to eat for us. And for yourself too, allow me to provide.' The abbot wished to get on.

With some dispatch, the landlord provided ale to drink and bread with a bowl of fruit to eat. 'My lord Abbot,' he grinned affably, 'you honour my small house yet again. I have pleasure in providing the best that our village can offer.'

Marcel raised his eyebrows and looked up at the roof where beams of brilliant sunlight pierced the balding thatch. Rutilius noted the door, how thick it was and how it was secured with a hefty piece of wood, which revolved into a securing socket by means of a pin.

'How can I help you?' asked Marcel, when all had eaten a mouthful or two.

The abbot cleared his throat. He turned the chair a little so that he was more or less facing the other. 'Marcel, doubtless you know that Brother Abbo was murdered?'

Marcel nodded. 'I heard, perhaps sooner than yourself, my lord.'

'After he had been washed and prepared for burial?'

Another nod.

'I heard that Gilbert made the arrangements for the preparation.'

Marcel shrugged. 'Gilbert favours his sister-in-law; she can always find a use for a fee, however small.'

'Do you have any idea who might have done this thing?' the abbot continued.

Marcel shook his head emphatically. 'No one from here, m'lord. I was with Brother Abbo until he shut the doors. He was treating that stupid animal, the goat I told you about?'

'I remember.'

'He led the animal into the shrine because the light was better. He let me out and secured the door behind me.'

'So he was alone? As far as you were aware?'

Marcel held out his hand, palm up. 'Certainly.'

'Could someone have been inside, in hiding?'

‘I suppose it is possible, but I saw no one come in to the chapel during the last hour or more. It was late. Young Brother Sylvan had gone. He would have been no help with the goat anyway.’

‘Brother Sylvan?’ The same Sylvan that wants Abbo’s position, Rutilius thought.

‘Yes,’ Marcel nodded, ‘he helps here now and then.’

‘I had heard that, too. So he went, when? What time?’

‘Mid-afternoon, perhaps. He had to be back for vespers.’

‘Gilbert? Was he here that day?’

‘Oh yes. I remember Gilbert being here. He comes and goes. Sometimes he does some work, sometimes he doesn’t.’

Suddenly, an idea struck the abbot. ‘The young girl who prays in the Lady Chapel…’

‘Yes, Lord Girand’s daughter. She is here quite often, since her mother died shortly after Christmas. I pray that God gives her peace.’

‘I suppose that there is no chance that Gilbert might… um…’ The abbot fluttered his fingers, hoping that Marcel would eventually take the meaning without his having to voice it aloud.

‘Gilbert? How do you mean?’

‘Um, well, you know, these things do happen.’

Marcel looked at the abbot blankly for several moments. ‘Ah!’ Eventually he grasped the idea. ‘Gilbert and Lady Anna-Marie?’ He shook his head and chuckled. ‘No. Oh no. I’m sure that Gilbert would prefer older, more, er, more robust ladies and the lady would prefer younger, more compliant men. No, put this from your mind, m’lord. Um…’ Marcel appeared uncertain then shook his head again, a little less firmly than before. 'No. I cannot imagine it.'

The abbot nodded, a trifle disappointed, and put the thought away, if not entirely out of his mind.

'Well. So there is no one whom we might suspect? No motives, no passing strangers to rob the shrine of its votive offerings?'

The other made a moué. 'Well, m'lord, there is me. I cannot prove that I left when I said I did. There is you, and there is the young acolyte, both strangers passing through.'

'Well certainly, I and the boy can prove our whereabouts for the time, but you? Surely your wife can vouch for you?'

Marcel shrugged. 'I live alone, my lord.'

'Then, as you say, you are the chief suspect for the moment.' Rutilius laughed a trifle too loudly, anxious not to suggest he was serious. 'You and Gilbert too.'

William, who had taken no part in the conversation, had continued to eat, and now his companions hastened to catch up. A little later, the abbot returned to his thoughts on the murder.

'How about Brother Abbo's work? Were there any problems, disagreements perhaps, when treatment of the animals did not go as hoped?'

'No, no, nothing like that, well, none that *I* know.'

'I would have liked to have spoken to Gilbert. It's a pity he was not there, at the shrine. Is there a possibility of his going there this afternoon, do you think?'

Marcel raised his shoulders and dropped them. 'Gilbert is a law unto himself. Who knows what he may do.'

'I saw Gilbert,' William said. 'He was driving a horse and cart, quite a small cart.'

‘A mule,’ Marcel corrected William. ‘In fact, the mule you have already met.’

‘*You* saw him?’ Rutilius asked, eyebrows raised.

‘When I was in the village with Brother George.’

‘Ah, I see.’ The abbot turned back to Marcel. ‘Brother George discharges his duties adequately, I hope?’

‘Adequately,’ Marcel replied. ‘We look forward to a more mature person, however.’

‘And there will be one, I promise you, shortly.’

The abbot paid the landlord and they left the tavern, walking to the bridge to gaze down at the turbulent currents below.

‘Vincent told me once, one day, at my father’s…’ William paused a moment, an unexpected lump restricting his throat. The abbot laid his hand on the boy’s arm briefly, and he continued, ‘My father’s court. He told me that most people who are murdered know their killer.’

‘Is that so?’ The abbot considered the words for a moment, raising and lowering his eyebrows. ‘If this is true, Marcel, our task should be somewhat easier, wouldn’t you say?’

‘Considering that Brother Abbo knew everyone in the village, m’lord, perhaps not.’ Marcel scratched his chin with rasping sound.

‘I think that when my assistant said *know* he meant something more familiar than a nodding acquaintance.’

Marcel gave a great Gallic shrug. ‘Ah, very well.’

‘Vincent?’ The abbot went back to William’s earlier words.

‘Vincent de Septa, my father’s master-at-arms.’

‘Aha, yes. De Septa, that’s a name from Pisa. You should probably have said “Vicente de Septa”. Almost a countryman of mine, in fact, I studied there, I told you, perhaps.'

William nodded morosely, refusing to be drawn from his melancholic mood.

'You are Italian, m'lord?' Marcel showed huge surprise.

'I am. I was born in a small village close to Venice.'

'That is surprising. I thought your accent must be from the court at Avignon, but now I see it is Venetian. Well, well, you speak French well, my lord. Not Occitan, of course, but French.'

'Thank you. I've been in these parts for a few years. About nine years at Avignon but here, I am a newcomer.'

'Mm.' Then, into the silence that followed, Rutilius murmured, 'Anna-Marie de Fossard.'

'The daughter of messier, Girand de Fossard,' Marcel added, when Rutilius did not continue.

'This is the same girl we saw the other night, the one that William found so interesting?'

William affected disinterest.

'Hmm. That's the one,' Marcel confirmed.

'Someone told me that she had been exorcised by Brother Abbo.'

Marcel smiled. 'Not that I'm aware,' he chuckled. 'Isn't that a job for a priest?'

'Indeed it is. You may imagine my surprise.'

Silence fell once more, except for the rushing of the waters, and the hum of insects, and the cries of birds.

'And so we are no further forward.' Marcel scratched his chin and was about to bid the others goodbye.

'Perhaps we, that is, er, you, could inquire among the villagers, to see if anyone might have a grudge against the good Abbo,' the abbot suggested.

'Well, I can talk to Gilbert first; see if he thinks of anybody.'

'Hm,' said the abbot. 'Gilbert?'

'He had someone in the cart with him,' William offered.

The abbot turned. 'Cart? Who, Gilbert?'

'When I saw him before lunch, he had someone with him, a lady.'

'His wife, perhaps.'

'Gilbert never married,' said Marcel. 'He often says that he has never felt the need.' He gave a small laugh of amusement, and envy too. 'It might have been his sister-in-law.' Marcel chewed his lip for a moment. 'He does spend a great deal of time with her.'

On the way back to the abbey, Rutilius thought again about the tavern door and the wooden bar that secured it. It swung up and down on a metal pin. What would happen, he wondered, if someone wrenched at it? Would the wood come away with the pin still in it? Was the shrine secured in like manner and, if so, was it still there, and could such an object be the murder weapon?

So many questions, so few answers. God would make everything clear in the fullness of time.

William was withdrawn all the way back, striding stoically up the steep hill.

The abbot washed himself and was about to enter his bedchamber when he realised that William was still hunched up in a chair staring into the last glowing embers in the grate. 'Time to get ready. Have you forgotten that we are to dine with Madame Brisenot today?'

The boy shrugged and the abbot perched himself

creakingly on the chair arm. 'What is it, boy? Your family?'

William nodded. 'My father, I suppose. And Vincent.'

'Ah yes, Vincent. You spent quite a lot of time with him, perhaps?'

William nodded. 'I practised every day except Sundays. More or less.'

'And what of your mother? I remember you saying that you had neither brothers nor sisters.'

William shrugged. 'My mother was the Duchess. Giving birth to an heir was her duty.'

'Oh.' The abbot was nonplussed. These words sounded far too old for a fifteen-year-old to utter. 'That sounds a little harsh.'

'It's what she told me.' William got up to go to the washroom. 'I remember exactly.'

'Oh.' And this time the abbot could think of nothing to say. He smiled when William returned. 'A clean robe, I think, wouldn't you say so?' The boy seemed recovered somewhat; he nodded.

'I've just remembered what you said about Vincent being Italian. He was. It's just that that's what everyone called him. You said he was your countryman.'

'That's so.' The abbot shrugged. 'I come from a village near Venice and attended the university in Pisa.'

'You said, but you don't sound Italian.'

'I have been in France a long time. Nine years since I came to Avignon,' Rutilius repeated what he told Marcel when that individual questioned his accent.

William upended the bag that contained his only possessions; a spare robe was rolled up in the bottom. 'Avignon, why there?'

'I was good at mathematics. A cardinal made the

mistake of confusing mathematics with arithmetic and determined that I should work in the counting house there.'

'And now you walk from one abbey to another, still counting money.'

'I used to dream of being famous as a mathematician, and I was not happy to be sent to the counting house. Still, I have become used to it; there are worse professions.'

'Did you learn anything new down there today? I mean, are you any wiser?'

Rutilius smiled. 'Learning is easy, one learns from books, people, happenings; using one's eyes and ears. Wisdom is something else again and can be likened to fishing with a net in muddy waters. One can cast in once and catch a net-full, or cast in a hundred times and catch nothing. Today shall we say there were a few titbits in the bottom of the net?'

'And so, by examining the titbits…?'

'Could make us wiser on the morrow, William. But now I think it time for a nap. These excursions take it out of one.'

Rutilius was normally a heavy sleeper, but not that afternoon. He kept dreaming of a metal pin, secured through a chunk of wood, whistling through the air and thudding into flesh. Then, the perpetrator wrenched at the wood breaking off the pin.

Over and over the dream repeated until the abbot was covered in sweat, despite the coolness of the chamber.

CHAPTER EIGHT

Inquiries in the village led them to Madame Brisenot's residence, a two-storey house with mortared brick between the timbers, and an impressively tall chimney at each end of the thatched roof. Before it was a space crowded with grasses and bushes grown wild and unkempt; a narrow path led through the shrubs to a front door of grey, unpainted wood, set near one end beneath a tiled porch. A handle on the end of a rusted length of chain was evidently the bell pull, though when William tugged, it refused to move, resisting solidly even when he swung his weight on it.

'There's no use in pulling that thing,' observed a voice.

Turning about, they discovered a miraculously thin and tall fellow peering round the edge of the opened door. His head was long, with pointed chin and forehead. To William, he looked like the man in the moon.

'Not worked in years. Now, you'll be the abbot I expect, and you,' he bent down, bringing his crescent-shaped face a little nearer to William's height, 'thin as a street waif, and eyes the colour of plum skins.' He smiled and stood back. 'Yes, you'll be the boy.' He swung the door wide. 'You'd best come in, if you want dinner.'

'Thank you,' said the abbot, stepping into a wide hallway. A stairway led up to a landing with doors visible at the back and an arched opening to the left. A chandelier held a dozen lighted candles to relieve the early evening gloom.

'Up the stairs, m'lord. If you will follow me.'

At the top of the staircase there was a narrow recess. In it, a table bore a small wooden bowl with a closely fitting lid. Their guide lifted the lid. Inside was a handful of coins, silver deniers, and gold coins of several varieties. 'Madame prefers not to negotiate recompense for her social evenings, m'lord, only trusted guests are invited. Whatever you might care to leave later is your own affair.'

'What an excellent judge of character Madame must be.'

They turned through the archway and along a corridor with openings looking down into the main entrance hall, which seemed from this vantage to have enough space for a ball. If the impression was correct, then musicians might well have peered from these same curtained openings in times past.

Fine decoration used to adorn the plaster walls but this was faded now, and only the shifting shadows invested the hall and corridors with a façade of its former grandeur. Here and there, as they walked on, the plaster was cracked or stained by mildew, some of the timbers were clearly rotting, and the atmosphere was one of slow decay.

This impression was left behind at the door to the dining room; beyond, a new world awaited them. Candles burned five at a time in wall sconces, and a candelabrum on the table spread light across the dark oak surface. The room was quite small, though the lofty ceiling was hidden in shadow, as was the farther wall, where a door was outlined by a greater light beyond, shining round the edges.

'My dear Abbot,' Madam Brisenot left the two

gentlemen she had been talking to and came towards them, hand outstretched, 'and the acolyte.' She treated them both to a daunting view of décolletage, a dress-style more normally seen at court rather than in a bucolic village setting. The abbot took a sudden interest in the décor; William was just overwhelmed. 'What *was* your name, dear boy?'

'William.'

Behind Madame's bright tones, the abbot managed a fragmentary 'God's blessings…'

'Isn't he a beauty? Does he sing?'

'No,' said William quickly, just in case his master developed ideas along those lines.

'Well. He's just delicious to look at. Let me introduce you to my other guests.' Madame Brisenot turned and gestured to them to follow, each movement wafting a heady perfume about her. 'Here is Jean Partuit, a physician of great repute. Jean, my Lord Abbot from the abbey.'

'Sir,' the abbot gave a small bow. 'May the Lord keep you.'

'My Lord.' The physician bowed too, a little deeper. 'A reputation in our small town is no great thing.'

'I'm certain you are too modest.'

'And this gentleman is our master cheesemaker. You will have a chance to judge his skills later. Gaston Ferrer, Gaston, my friend, the abbot.'

Gaston won the race to bow first. 'A delight to meet you, m'lord.'

'May God bless your cheeses, sir.'

'Actually, I am cheesemaker at the Château Fossard but I sell to Montpellier and Nimes, to the abbey too.'

'And to the townsfolk of St. Guilhem, very reasonable

prices,' added Madame.

'When there is some to spare.' Gaston raised his eyebrows to indicate that Madame Brisenot was being indiscreet.

'And allow me to introduce to you all, William who has captivated my heart.' Madame started to reach towards the boy's face, her finger and thumb ready to pinch his beardless cheek, but she noticed the look in William's eye and made a flamboyant gesture instead. 'We have one more guest to arrive and then we may begin.'

'Lucas?' Gaston asked.

Madame nodded. 'Lucas.'

'Always late,' he confided to the abbot, 'even on Sundays.'

'It is true,' Madame confirmed, '*especially* on Sundays. I think we will have some wine, teach Lucas a lesson. Georges …'

'Madame?' Georges, the servant, who had let them in, appeared from some dark corner.

'Serve a light wine. We are all in need of an aperitif.'

'For the boy …' the abbot began.

'Some apple juice for young William, Georges.'

'But, Madame, what if I am needed at the door?'

'He will have to wait. The wine, immediately!'

Georges hurried to fill glasses and pass them to the company, and then went to hover near a window from which he could see the path to the entrance. 'Ah,' he said, his crescent-shaped face moonbeaming 'He is arrived.'

A few minutes later, Lucas, evidently the local priest, joined them, accepted a glass of wine and was introduced to Madame's new guests. Madame twittered and brought the priest to the abbot. 'Perhaps you know each other already,' she said, 'our priest, our abbot.'

'The Lord keep you,' said the priest. 'Lucas Ferand.' Who fitted the picture of a small town priest in no wise.

'And His blessing upon you,' the abbot replied, finding something weirdly familiar about the man.

To Madame Brisenot, he said, 'No, we have not met before.' He eyed Lucas. 'A pleasure to meet you.'

'And this is my darling boy.' Madame squeezed William's arm and was interrupted by Georges sounding a small gong on the sideboard.

'Ah,' said the priest, rubbing long, finely manicured hands together. 'I am extremely hungry. For me, it has been a day of fasting.' They sat down, the two men of God side by side, William on the priest's other side, and Madame at the head of the table. Opposite, sat the physician and the cheesemaker.

'Fasting?' the abbot asked.

'My wife died on this day three years' since. I fast during daylight hours, out of respect. Now, I know what you will ask next, abbot: a married priest? Not so?'

The abbot bobbed his head. 'It crossed my mind.'

'I took holy orders after her death. I am tolerably well educated, tolerably well-off, too. I came to this out of the way place for peace and quiet, my lord, a place to sit quietly and think.'

'And what do you think about, Rector?'

But Lucas Ferand's attention had been caught by Jean Partuit, who asked him if he had visited a certain old man who was close to accounting to his Maker for his life.

The abbot drank a little wine and picked a handful of nuts from a small dish close by. The other conversation closed. 'Are you a regular guest at Madame's dinner parties?' he asked.

'Not as regular, as I shall be, now that you and your companion are here.'

'How is that?'

'Before … William?' The priest raised his eyebrows in question. The abbot nodded. 'Before William so obviously took her fancy, I'm afraid I was the object of her fantasies.'

'I can see that.' The priest's impeccable grooming, the dully gleaming black silk, the way it contrasted so effectively with the silver hair, which fluffed out like a halo around his head. 'Yes, I really do see that. Unfortunately, I am here only while the Abbot Roget is away.'

'Then, I shall have to make the most of your presence. And of the boy's.'

'Excuse me, m'lord Abbot,' the physician who, compared with the impeccable priest, was positively scruffy in his appearance, interrupted them once more. 'I was wondering what you intended to do about the murder?'

The abbot's world receded for a few seconds until he found William helping him back to his chair. He sat there panting for air, while the youngster thumped the abbot's back. 'Thank you, boy, but that was a trifle heavy-handed.'

'Your pardon, Master.'

'Nonsense, Abbot,' Madame was loud in her support for William's assistance. 'The boy knew exactly what to do. Now,' she proffered a brimming glass to the abbot, 'wine, refresh your throat and let us get down to eating, before everything is too cold.'

Madame stepped back and fixed the physician with a glare. 'And you, Jean Partuit, I would have thought you'd know better, springing such a question on him. You should learn to lead up to things gently; is this the way you tell a woman that she has become a widow?'

With a scraping of chairs, they resumed their seats and Georges finished serving the wooden dishes. The door from the kitchen opened and light flooded forth, only to be obscured for a moment as the chef brought out his work of art.

'Sardines,' he told them proudly. 'Slit along the backbone and the outside turned inside. Stuffed with ground marjoram, rosemary and sage, good spices, saffron, and the ground flesh of a few fish. Fried in oil.'

Georges brought a jug to the table. 'Lemon sauce,' said the chef. 'Enjoy.'

Georges followed the chef back to the kitchen and returned in a trice with a bowlful of dark, broken bread with which to soak up the sauce.

All fell to with a will and, for some little time, there was silence but for the sound of chewing and swallowing, and an occasional deep verbal expression of gratification.

'Madame,' the cheesemaker said eventually, 'this is truly a dish fit for angels. Your pardons, Rector, m'lord Abbot.' Both acknowledged the apology with mouth-filled mumbles.

Gradually, the pace of eating slackened and conversation resumed in fits and starts.

'Did you hear that that young sister-in-law of Gilbert's has gone off again?' someone said.

'Aha,' Madame Brisenot replied, as soon as her mouth was empty enough. 'Her husband has been gone for a year or more; she is left with a baby. Why should she not do as she pleases, eh? You men are worse than old women. You can forget your speculation because I tell you for a fact that she has only gone to her sister who is near her time. And…'

Madame stopped for breath and held up her hand to signal that there was more to be said. 'I also know that she has Fossard's permission to travel. Am I right, Lucas?'

'Indeed you are, Madame.'

'Aha.' A crust of bread waved beyond the candlelight and identified the speaker as the physician, Jean Partuit. 'But she has gone with … hmm, I forget his name, but she was seen.'

There was a pause as second helpings were taken.

'You must learn to guard that tongue, Jean. She has gone with her brother-in-law, who dotes on her and the child.' Madam Brisenot rapped the table with her knuckle. 'Georges, I believe we need some more wine here.'

Georges appeared at once, carrying a tall jug gleaming with condensation. 'Can I fill your cup, Madame?'

'Thank you, Georges. Then, you may leave the jug. Oh, William,' she laid her fingers on his hand, squeezed a little, 'some watered wine for William, Abbot?' She raised her eyebrows, somewhat darker and more definite tonight than he had remembered them to be.

'Why not?' agreed the abbot, rather more than mellow now. 'There comes a time when every boy must begin to grow to man's estate.'

Suddenly a little anxious, he nudged the priest and nodded to where Madame Brisenot's hand held William's. The boy could not remove his own without an unseemly kerfuffle.

Lucas Ferand glanced across and chuckled. 'Always,

she goes after the impossible, my friend, do not trouble yourself. Me, the boy, perhaps even yourself if you are here long enough. It is not the actuality she wishes for, you understand, but the illusion of pursuit.' He swept a piece of bread over the trencher, cleaning the remains of the tasty sauce. '*We* are safe.'

The abbot relaxed. The trenchers were cleared away, cups recharged, including William's, though without the water upon which the abbot would have insisted. Voices grew soft, even a trifle somnolent, as the wine worked its happy magic.

Georges brought in clean plates of olivewood. The chef brought in a bronze dish which was turned up around the edges; inside was… *something*. There was sugar on top, made from honey, warmed and dried and crushed to a coarse powder, beneath this was the source of a truly remarkable aroma.

'Well, Pierre. Tell us. What have you brought?' Lucas licked his lips. 'I have smelt nothing like this, ever.'

'Hmm,' Gaston Ferrer smiled to himself.

'Almonds,' said the chef, with a flutter of podgy fingers. 'A handful blanched and pounded as fine as it is possible. Sugar from honey, eggs, milk. Your mouths water, eh? Cinnamon, and as much salt as is proper and fresh cheese…'

'Aha,' Jean Partuit clapped his hands, 'now we know why Gaston was so pleased with himself.'

'This also is pounded until there is no need to pound it more. We mix these ingredients and put them in a floured dish set far from the fire, and when it is set, we sprinkle rosewater over it and sugar.'

When he was served, the abbot tasted his portion carefully. He closed his eyes and savoured it, let the spice tickle the surface of his tongue, felt the juices run into his mouth, and was lost.

Conversation continued around him, a low murmur, a background to the marvels that worked inside his mouth. When at last he finished that first morsel, he opened his eyes to see that his plate was empty; he had eaten every crumb.

'Abbot, a little more?' Madame was asking him.

'Madame, with pleasure.'

The abbot took a mouthful, swallowed, took another spoonful. 'Pardon?' he said, realising that a question had been asked and everyone was waiting for him to answer.

'Jean, I told you before; that is not fair.' Madame's defence of her new guest was sturdy.

'Come, Madame. The subject has already been broached. There is no need to approach the business in kid boots.' He turned back to the abbot. 'Well now, m'lord, what can you say to us?'

'Well, we do have a murder, it is true. We know how Brother Abbo was killed and we are making a study to find the man who killed him.'

'A man,' Jean Partuit leaned back. 'I understood it to have been a hatpin that was used on the poor fellow.'

'Well, that is the case, or something similar.' The abbot decided on openness, he might learn as much or more from these people than from any information Marcel might find. 'Does a woman have enough strength to force a pin into someone's spine like that?'

'Well, that's a thought. What do you say, Madame? Could you do such a thing?'

'Perhaps. If I were very angry. But this is a shabby

death and it was done by a mean and shabby person. I think it was a man.'

'Abbot?'

'I tend to agree. Tell me, does anyone know Gilbert de Gignac?'

'I do,' replied the physician.

'And I,' Madame Brisenot said. 'Why, surely you don't believe it was Gilbert?'

'He is known to like the ladies, so I have heard, and a young lady has been visiting the shrine for several weeks now.'

'Young Anna-Marie.' Madame nodded. 'So?'

'Perhaps Gilbert has been importuning and Brother Abbo reprimanded him.'

Madame shook her head. 'No, m'lord. It is true that Gilbert does like ladies but what you hear will be all blow and no porridge. And certainly he would not be interested in a flighty young thing like the Comte's daughter. What do you say, Gaston? I dare say she has been down to the home farm now and then.'

Gaston wagged his head. 'I have seen her, pretty to look at but… How old is Gilbert?'

'More than fifty, I would say,' Jean Partuit told him.

'No. I cannot see it.'

'There you are, Abbot. I dare say that our young acolyte would turn her head,' she reached for William's hand, 'but not someone like Gilbert.'

'Girls do not turn their heads for me, Madame.' William moved his hand quickly.

'But Marcel…' she went on, in a wondering sort of voice. 'I don't know that I would trust Marcel, you know.'

'Oh, Madame,' the abbot was quite startled, 'what

makes you say such a thing?'

'Marcel buried his wife over a dozen years since and has shown no interest in taking another. His son has married and lives behind the shop, so Marcel has his house to himself. He shows no interest in women beyond a certain good wife. I do not trust a man like that.'

'Gilbert lives alone, does he not?' Gaston asked.

'But Gilbert has never married. He has always been fancy-free. He fancies himself a ladies' man and men's gossip will likely bear him out, but really? Pfui,' Madam Brisenot nodded to herself.

This backward way of argument was too much for the abbot; he simply shook his head.

'What are you going to do then, Abbot?' Partuit, the physician asked. 'The Comte will hear of it soon enough and will demand the details so that his men can pursue whatever criminal is responsible.'

'I am sure that is so, Jean, but I hope to clear up the business myself. Call it pride if you will but I do not wish to leave this stain on the abbey's character for Abbot Roget to return to.'

'Time runs on swiftly,' Lucas said quietly. 'A day has gone since we tried to bury poor Abbo and failed; his soul is demanding justice.'

And the abbot realised where he had seen Lucas Ferand before. He had passed him as he had been listening to the chant on that first day, before there had been any question of murder. And, of course, it would have been Lucas who had led the burial party out to the grave and found it full of water.

'I am confident,' the abbot said in his most confident tones, 'that, with God's help, we shall find the perpetrator of this terrible act very soon. Our inquiries are going apace.'

'And that is quite enough of this grisly business, my friends.' Madame's words were uttered in a voice that brooked no disobedience. 'Our dinner party is not yet finished. Georges, some of that good red from last year.'

'Madame.'

The abbot smiled at Madame Brisenot and nodded his heartfelt thanks for her intervention. Smiling back at him, she patted William's hand.

With the good red from last year came a selection of cheeses from the Comte's home farm, courtesy of Gaston Ferrer. The diners grew yet more convivial, William included, so much so that he allowed and even enjoyed Madame Brisenot patting his hand and pinching his cheek. The final dish was served: grapes preserved in rich honey, with a clear white wine tart enough to make a gargoyle pucker its lips.

At length, the occasion wound to a close and the guests rose unsteadily to, in turn, kiss Madame on both cheeks and congratulate her on such a successful dinner party. As they tottered along the upper corridor and came to the niche, the abbot took out some coins he had already counted into a compartment in his purse and placed them carefully in the bowl.

William looked down into the hallway through the arched windows along the corridor. There was Madame being kissed again by the physician, and William felt a pang of an emotion that he would not identify as jealousy for several years to come. He was holding a vine stem that still held two heavy grapes. He pulled one off and flicked it out over the hall, watching it swoop down towards Jean Partuit. William's throw was almost perfect, but not quite. The grape tumbled out of the air and plunged into that dusky valley between Madame's breasts.

Shocked by his rash action, the acolyte dodged behind the partition wall, as their amazed hostess arrowed a glance upwards.

'Boy,' said the abbot, 'stop lurking back there, it's time to go.' He looked down into Madame Brisenot's astonished gaze.

Madame Brisenot's mouth curved into a wicked smile. She fluttered fingers at him. The abbot waved back and descended the stairs, crossed the hall. Behind him followed William, red of face, not daring to look. On tiptoes, Madame Brisenot offered first one cheek then the other to be kissed, a gesture to which the abbot was certainly unaccustomed. 'You naughty, naughty man,' she grinned, retrieving the grape from her décolletage and forcing it between the dismayed abbot's clenched teeth.

'What on earth was that all about?' the abbot wondered, blushing in the darkness as they walked back through the dark and silent town.

Wisely, the acolyte remained silent.

'I mean, what was that grape doing down the woman's front?'

They reached the abbey in time for the service of lauds. William was more or less sober but was suffering the penance of the worst headache he had ever had in his entire life.

The abbot was as mystified as ever and was still re-running the events in his mind in an attempt to make sense of them when a much disturbed Prior Josephus waylaid him, after the service.

'I'm sorry, Prior, what did you say?'

'I must speak with you! Urgently!' Josephus shifted from one tilted foot to the other.

'Really? About what?'

'I have heard about your dinner engagement. I really don't think…'

The abbot's eyebrows rose, he bent towards the prior, spoke in a low voice. 'Prior. The event is a thing of the past. Nothing will change before the morning. I give you leave to speak to me then.'

'It should really be discussed now…'

'No, Prior, it should not.' A shake of the head, a forceful shake of the head, a grim shake of the head. The prior capitulated.

CHAPTER NINE

The abbot poured cold water from pitcher to bowl and laved his face. 'Oh. Ah.' He scratched and stretched. 'Boy,' he called. 'Matins. Wake up and get dressed.'

William had, in fact, not undressed the previous night and was, therefore, ready before the abbot came out of his chamber.

'Ah, well done. How do you feel?'

'Miserable, Master.' William put a hand to each side of his head and pressed, the pressure giving momentary relief. 'My head will split apart.'

'Well, that's often the way we learn to be moderate in our dealings with wine. Now, there's the bell, it is time.'

On their way, the prior caught up with them. 'I must see you afterwards, Abbot.'

'Absolutely, Prior. After breakfast, that is. I will not be disturbed before then.'

William did not eat a hearty breakfast. Apart from two cups of water, the acolyte took nothing at all. The abbot more than made up for this lack of attention to the food. He enjoyed a bowl of cracked-oat porridge, several pieces of bread, some with cheese and some with honey, and two apples from the abbey's storeroom.

Exactly as the abbot instructed, the prior knocked on the door and entered the guestroom a few moments after the kitchen boy left with the tray. So prompt was he that the abbot was certain that Josephus had been waiting outside.

'Prior,' he acknowledged, a trifle gruffly.

'God's blessings, Abbot.'

The abbot nodded. 'And what can I do for you, Prior, as though I cannot guess?'

'I am surprised, no, scandalised at your visit to this woman's house last night.'

William at last took notice of what was going on. This had the makings of an interesting morning.

'Are you, Prior? Are you? And what is it in particular that scandalises you? The fact that she is a widow…?'

'Several times a widow.'

'Several times? And what else? Does she worship the Devil? Does she curse the name of the Pope? Does she act in a lewd and licentious manner, perhaps?'

The prior seemed to find difficulty in choosing between the several possibilities.

'Prior?'

'She is a woman; she has a certain…' Josephus wiggled his fingers as he tried to find a word, '…let us say, a certain reputation which will not do you any good.'

'Well now, she is a woman, this is a fact that cannot be denied. I believe almost half humankind to be women, so we cannot hold that against her. What reputation does she have? Hmm?'

'She likes men.'

'Aha. Now we are getting to the nub of the matter. Boy!'

'Master?'

'Go and ask for the accounts from the keeper of the infirmary and from the, er, hmm,' the abbot thought a moment, 'from the maintenance people.'

'Maintenance, Master?'

'Upkeep. Masons, carpenters, that sort of thing.'

William, disappointed, left to go about his errands.

'Please be seated, Prior.' The abbot sat down heavily on a hard chair. 'Prior, I am sad to see you so prejudiced.'

'Prejudiced, Abbot? Me?'

'You.'

Silent, the abbot looked at him for some moments. 'Unless she acts in the manner of a whore, Madame Brisenot commits no sin in liking men. I like women, not all of them but some of them. Their view of life is different, that view is often valuable. Sometimes it is amusing.'

The abbot rose and moved to a more comfortable seat. 'I think that as much as anything you disapprove of me, Prior.'

Josephus opened his mouth but the abbot's raised forefinger forestalled him. 'I am not humble like your Abbot Roget, I do not live an ascetic life. I do not hide myself away from the world within a monastery. You may think of me as one who has licence to meet with the laity. I must mix with the community. Even within the cloister, my duties excuse me from following the normal regimen. I work on my accountings while others study. I may sleep during the recitation of the Divine Office, or eat meat and converse in the guest dining hall.'

The abbot leaned back and deliberately smiled to ease the atmosphere.

'Nor do I believe that deliberate discomfort makes me holier than the next man, so I enjoy good food and soft chairs.' He patted the cushion on which he leaned. 'I do not believe that cutting myself free from the laity makes me somehow purer, and so I can enjoy intelligent and amusing conversation. Some of it with women.'

Again, he paused. 'Do I make myself clear?'

The prior nodded.

'This is not to say that I decry the simple life that Abbot Roget obviously practises. He has the right to his own views and preferences.'

'I am sorry, m'lord Abbot.'

The abbot shook his head. 'It doesn't matter, Prior; you and I differ. I now have to spend my life trudging from one abbey to another and come into regular contact with ordinary people, and you spend your life here, in holy works. Beyond our love of God and our worship, it would be odd if our views coincided.'

The prior, a little dazed, nodded.

'And one other point: let it not be forgotten that the knowledge of this murder came to me from Madame Brisenot. If it had not been for her, Brother Abbo might have been buried for weeks before the fact became known to us. If ever.'

The prior's eyebrows rose. 'That is true. I hadn't thought of that.'

'Last night, I dined with Madame Brisenot in the company of four other gentlemen, and we discussed who might have been guilty of this heinous crime. As it happened, there was no firm conclusion, but I came away with a warning.'

'Warning? Of what?'

'That if we do not find this murderer soon, the Comte de Fossard will get wind of the crime and will take over. Do you want his heavy-handed men trampling all over the shrine and the abbey?'

'Absolutely not.'

The abbot stood up. 'Exactly. Absolutely not.'

Prior Josephus got up too, and headed for the door. 'Oh, Abbot?' He stopped with his hand on the latch. The abbot looked up. 'Brother Anno will be leaving to work at the shrine in the next day or two, as soon as he has things tidied up here but Brother Sylvan is pestering me to let him go instead.'

'Brother Sylvan? Our number two choice? That one again?'

'That one.' The prior scratched his ear vigorously. 'The very one.'

'Tell him that if he persists… No. If he persists,' the abbot grinned, 'if he persists in pestering, tell him to come to see me. That might well settle the matter. Oh, and ask Brother Anno to see me before he goes, I'd like a word with him, to wish him well, and so on.'

Alone, the abbot poked at the fire then sat back, as the flames leaped a little higher. The conversation with Prior Josephus had gone better than he had expected. In fact, he seemed to have made an ally rather than an opponent.

He allowed his mind to turn to more mundane things, the list of receipts and disbursements from the kitchen. There had been something odd there. Now, what was it?

Noisily, William entered the room and the misgivings that had been on the verge of recall were gone, at least for the time being.

'Well? Where have you been?'

'The infirmary. You asked for their receipts.'

'Oh yes. That's right. And the masons?'

'And the carpenters who work at opposite ends of the same yard.'

'Is that so? And the receipts? I see you have nothing with you.'

'Brother August, from the infirmary, will bring them

this afternoon. They are not quite ready. The carpenters were too busy and the masons didn't know what I was talking about.'

'Then you'd better teach them.'

'Me?'

'Who else?'

Lunch came and went. A box of receipts came from the abbey's medical department, and the abbot added these to the growing piles of paperwork that were filling the room. He had compiled the cooking lists from the box of receipts and notes brought by the boy, Claude.

William had gone to the carpenters and the stonemasons to try to explain the idea of costs and records.

The abbot scratched his head, something in the lists had come to mind earlier in the day but it was proving difficult to remember what it had been. And then he had it, his eye rested on the line of neat writing, checking the item before going to the box and selecting a numbered bundle.

He untied the string and went through the notes. It was the fifth one, soiled with something oily and smelly. He put it to his nose. *Fishy. Now why would Madame Brisenot buy three-brace of pheasant from the abbey kitchen?*

The abbot looked at the half-legible note for some time and then looked for more of them. He found seven for the past year. The items included a smoked ham, a dozen doves, carp and the three-brace of pheasant. Each one was enough to provide for a small dinner party such as the one he had enjoyed the previous evening.

As that thought came to him, he realised that these were not receipts after all, they were records of food being sold or got rid of. It was clear that all the goods had either been given away or sold for a purely nominal amount. Some of the notes carried memoranda: stale, substandard; the words 'fly-blown' had been scrawled on the note dealing with the ham.

The abbot drummed his fingers on the table. Was the kitchen making a profit from selling spoilt food? Had he and his fellow guests, in fact, consumed inferior food dressed up with spices? Another thought came to him. Was the kitchen subsidising the widow Brisenot with perfectly good food?

He came to a mental halt. *If that were the case, he had already aided and supported this nefarious activity. Perhaps now was the time to pray for guidance.*

The carpenters and the stonemasons shared a long compound at the back of the abbey. Both ends had been roofed with long rafters and thatch to protect the craftsmen while they were working.

At the carpenters' end, several projects were underway. William had introduced himself to this particular man before; his name was Jean. Jean had been working the upper end of a long two-handled saw while another man, almost invisible in the dark pit below, had been toiling at the lower end. The result of their labour, the boy assumed, were the long rafters into which two monks were carving words of Latin scripture.

Brother Jean was now working a piece of dark wood, the size of his head. With a wooden mallet and a variety of chisels and gouges, the monk was turning the hard close-grained wood into a tiny hill of flowers and leaves. When the two rafters were placed, this mound of foliage would cover the joint where they crossed.

'Well, William, back so soon?' Brother Jean put down

his tools and stretched his arms until the joints cracked. 'I thought we'd not see you before tomorrow or the next day.'

'My master was insistent.'

'Aha. The new abbot drives all before him, eh? Like fallen leaves before a gale.'

'Well, only a little. The abbot is good to me.'

'Then I am pleased for you. So what was it your master believes is so important?'

'He must make a reckoning of everything bought and sold since the middle of last year.'

'That's a lot of work, young man. I seem to remember another coming last fall, and he asked the same sort of questions.'

'Ah,' said William. 'You will know what is necessary already then.'

'Well, not as such,' Brother Jean replied. 'Only in principle. You want bills of sale and notes and receipts and things. Is that the way of it?'

William nodded.

'Here we come upon our first difficulty.'

The acolyte's brow creased. 'What is so difficult?'

'There is no one here who can read.'

'This is a problem with which I can help,' he said with enthusiasm. 'Show me where you keep these things. I can order them and list them for my master.'

'Or write,' added Jean when the opportunity occurred.

'Ah. Yes, I see.' William chewed his bottom lip and thought. 'Give me a little while and I will think about it.'

'Think on, young man, there is as much time as you want.'

William nodded and stood back as Brother Jean took up his mallet and chisel again. With seven light taps of the mallet, he shaped a leaf, and then put down the tools. He selected a different chisel and smoothed the edges, scooped hollows into the surface, made a lacework of veins that seemed to be already there in the wood, just waiting for his skill to expose them.

'Wonderful,' said William and, as Jean looked up, smiling at the appreciation, 'Where will it go?'

'These and six more, and the rafters are for a new ceiling in the scriptorium.'

'Is the roof leaking?'

'These are for the greater glory of God.' Jean's eyes gleamed with an amusement that belied his solemn words.

'I see. Well, I shall see you tomorrow.' He wandered outside.

Here, two boys of more or less his own age were building a small porch to go over an outer door. The framework was finished and they were nailing shingles to the framework.

'Where will that go when it's finished?' he asked them.

'Over a door. Where do you think, tickle brain?' sneered one of the boys. The other one laughed.

'There's no need to be rude.'

'Lackwit.'

The acolyte was indignant. 'I'll report you to the prior.'

'Oh dear, the prior!'

The other boy giggled again. 'What do you think the prior'll do? We aren't prissy little monk boys. There're plenty of other jobs to do, we don't have to come here.'

'Now push off, po-head, and leave us alone.'

William shook with anger. As the son of a duke, he had grown up amid a certain measure of indifference. Being at the receiving end of scorn was a new experience, as was someone who both considered him an inferior and was free so to say. With great difficulty, he turned his back and started off towards the gate leading from the yard.

Still laughing hysterically at their own wit, the two boys started discussing what duties a po-head might carry out.

'He'll have to carry out the abbot's pisspot in the morning.'

'Have to hold it, while the fat man uses it.'

'A bum-bailey like him probably has to lift the back of his robe on order when the abbot feels like a bit of …'

It was as far he got. A tremendous buffet to his ear put a stop to his invention. He clapped a hand to the side of his head and rounded on his assailant.

'By God, you're going to rue that, monk boy.' His fist shot out, though the intention had been too clear from the start. William sidestepped, while the other all but lost his balance. 'You'll need to be faster than that, flap-mouth.' William smacked the boy's ear with his hand slightly curved. It had the effect of a clap of thunder going off just inside the ear. Half-deafened, half-blinded with tears, the lad came at him again, picking up a pole from the ground and swinging it wildly.

William was perfectly familiar with the rough and tumble of fighting. His coordination and skills in hand-to-hand combat had been perfect by the time he was twelve. At fourteen, he was well on his way to becoming a swordsman. Skipping backward, he found another length of wood and held it out like a sword.

His assailant snarled and came at him again, trying to hit his legs below the knee. William poked the other in the chest and sprang back another foot or two. His attacker came on again, holding his own weapon a bit higher. William lunged; the other moved to slap it aside. William dropped under the clumsy parry and drove the pole hard into the lad's ribs, knocking the breath out of him.

William had forgotten there were two of them. Just as the first sprawled on the ground, he was seized from behind and lifted off the ground in a bear hug. Grinning at last, the fallen boy scrambled to his feet and came in with his fist back ready to slam forward into William's face.

William lifted his legs up in front of him and drove them both into the already badly bruised ribs. The other fell again, coughing and spluttering. Dropping his feet now, he kicked his heels back against the shins of the one who held him. There was a yelp of pain, and he was suddenly free. William stamped down on a foot and shoved himself away with a backward blow from his elbow.

He put his back against a stack of timber and took a deep breath. 'May your name be scratched from the book of life, bumpkin,' William said in a pleasant conversational sort of voice, while he straightened out his robe. 'May your flesh be tossed to the birds of the air and the beasts of the earth.'

'I don't think there's need for that sort of thing, lad.' Brother Jean had come around the timber, now he spoke in a low voice from his side. 'It'll be some time before they're likely to bother you again.' The two monks who were with him chuckled and several others from the masons' area watched with interest. 'That's if you haven't put them off working here.'

One of the others grinned. 'They'll be back again

tomorrow. The abbey pays too good a wage, and there're only fetching and carrying jobs anywhere else. And, I dare say, the story will be all round the village by suppertime.'

'Even so,' said Jean, 'go now, and pray the Lord will forgive you for letting temper get the better of you. Anger is a great sin and must be rooted out.'

William was not convinced of this reasoning. Anger had saved him from harm on a number of occasions. However, he knew when to play a convincing part. 'Yes, Brother,' he said, meekly. 'I will go at once.'

Brother Jean nodded. 'And then come back in the morning and we will remember whatever we can while you write it all down.'

'I will, Brother.'

Monks working in the gardens, or as William had been, in the maintenance areas, could enter the church by a side entrance. Boot scrapers were provided and there was always a thick layer of fresh rushes to catch the dirt from outside before it could be trampled into the main hall. William stood for a moment waiting for his eyes to adjust to the darker interior. The church was deserted for once. William still could see no logic in asking God to forgive him his anger but, on the other hand, there was such a thing as gratitude. He should thank his Maker for success in the fight and for finding a way to make out the abbot's lists.

William was not the only visitor to the church just then.

The main entrance to the church was in the north cloister, opposite the abbey doors in the south. A short hall, floored with marble, separated the church from the cloister itself, the rest of the abbey could be reached from the four-square cloister. The abbot came to the church this way, his eyes staring unseeingly at the floor as he battled with his problem. He reached the threshold.

'Boy?'

'Master?'

'I have come to pray for guidance.'

'As have I, Master.'

CHAPTER TEN

'Now, what should we do this morning?'

'I have work to do with the carpenters, Master.' William explained the problem and the solution. 'They are quite busy, a new ceiling for Brother Willi, the precentor they said, to glorify God.'

The abbot nodded. 'Very good, boy. Excellent, in fact. There is one other thing.'

'Master?'

'At noon, you are to go into the village and look into the tavern there. If you see Madame Brisenot …'

William pursed his lips.

'You are not fond of Madame?'

'She keeps pawing at me.'

'You seemed to enjoy it the other night.'

William blushed. 'You were saying, Master?'

'If she is there, tell her that she must wait until I come, and then you are to return and let me know. Tell her that it is about a very serious matter, understand?'

'Yes, Master.'

'Good.'

And so it went.

Between them, William and Brother Jean concocted a list of expenditures for the abbot until a little before the noon bell tolled, they were finished and William left. He took the gateway from the yard and walked around the side of the abbey where brambles and nettles hemmed in the narrow cart track. He spied a well-trodden pathway through a patch of alder and guessed that this was a shortcut. He was well within the jumble of houses and almost completely lost by the time the bell sounded.

'Sir,' he said at last, stopping a young man perhaps five years older than himself.

'A good day to you,' said the other, turning and looking him up and down. 'From the abbey?'

'That is so. Can you help me please? I'm looking for the inn.'

'You, a young boy from the abbey?'

'I am running an errand for my master, the abbot.'

'The abbot is your master? You are the one named after our saint?'

William had no answer to the question and he frowned as he tried to understand.

'St. Guilhem,' said the villager, pronouncing it in the Occitan manner. 'And William,' this time in the French-style, 'they are the same.'

'Well yes, now I see what you mean. I never realised it before.'

'So, the William who bested young Louis yesterday then?'

William was cautious. Was this friend or foe? 'Well, perhaps he slipped, or maybe he tripped.'

'Not from what I heard, young man. Fair and square is what I heard, and you could not have chosen a more deserving little scoundrel.'

'Oh, I didn't choose him, sir.'

'Well no. I heard the story. But Louis is going to be a lot less sure of himself for a little while. Now, the tavern, which one did you want?'

'Um, is there one with a landlord called Jean Claude?'

'Ah yes, that one …' and his supporter gave him directions.

William put his nose round the door and inspected the patrons. Sure enough, there was Madame; in front of her was a cup of ale.

Timidly, he entered the tavern and sidled along the wall until he was as near to Madame Brisenot as he could get without being noticed. 'Madame,' he called, hoping to engage her attention without anyone else hearing him.

It was a forlorn hope. Madame heard him. She turned and beamed. 'William, my precious.' She held out her arms. 'Come here my beautiful boy.' She turned to her companions. 'He has come to see me. Is he not the most beautiful boy you have ever seen?'

'Not only beautiful, Madame, but the most courageous of young princes.' And as she impatiently gestured William to her, the landlord went on with a lurid account of how William had set about trouncing the bully, Louis.

'Such a gallant little prince,' and Madame bestowed kiss after kiss on his face.

'Madame, please! I bring word from my master, the Abbot.'

To William's relief the effect was magical. She desisted at once. 'The Abbot?'

'I am to ask you to remain here until my master comes. He has to discuss a most serious business with you.'

Madame's hand flew to her mouth. 'A serious business?'

'I have to return and tell him that you are here.'

'Fly, young prince.' She took a kerchief and wet it on the tip of her tongue. She dabbed at his cheek where some of her rouge had left a mark. 'Tell your master that Adrienne Marguerite Brisenot awaits his coming. I will be here. Now go and quickly.'

William went, and as quickly as he was bid. Out of breath, panting and hardly capable of putting one word after another, nevertheless, the abbot grasped the situation quickly enough.

He had had the foresight to order that a donkey be brought for him. Now he realised that he could hardly require William to accompany him, he patted the boy on the head. 'Catch your breath, young man, and thank you for your haste.'

He left the guest quarters and bustled outside. There, he mounted the animal and, once settled into the saddle, spoke to the youngster from the stables. 'Well, come along then, young fellow. You'll be escorting your abbot today. Hurry now.'

'Abbot,' said Madame Brisenot, smiling and rising to meet him halfway across the floor. 'Rutilius,' she said somewhat more quietly, 'dear Rutilius, such a pleasant surprise. What is this serious matter that our acolyte mentioned?'

'Let us sit over here,' said the abbot. 'Wine?'

'If it pleases you.'

The abbot signalled to Jean Claude who brought them two cups of red wine.

'Thank you, landlord.' Then, when they were alone again, 'Madame.'

'Adrienne, please.'

'Adrienne. I believe I have mentioned that one of my tasks while I am at the abbey is to make an accounting of monies paid and received. Have I told you this?'

Madame Brisenot nodded.

'I find that the kitchen has been selling off meat and fish, perhaps even giving stuff away that has begun to smell rather too highly.'

Madame shrugged. 'There are enough poor people in this place to appreciate such kindness.'

The abbot paused. This was something he had not considered. He knew about the poor, of course; he prayed for them often, made provision for alms in his budgets, but Madame's words opened up a new perspective. Here he was, so to speak, in the midst of poor people.

'I'm pleased that you pointed that out, Madame.'

'Adrienne.'

'Adrienne. There is a note in the kitchen receipts with your name on it.'

'Mine? How would that happen?'

'If you had bought or received food from the abbey kitchen.'

'But that's a preposterous idea. Georges always bought for my pantry.'

'Georges? Hmm. Would he also buy for your dinner parties?'

'Well no, that would be Sebastian.'

'The chef?'

Madame nodded. 'He is under chef to the Comte de Fossard.'

'But not you, yourself, ever?'

'Certainly not.'

The abbot leaned back and folded his hands on the table. Madame placed hers on the abbot's. 'You have been worried about this?'

'Well yes, I have. Your reputation was in danger.'

'Dear Rutilius.'

'It may be that you and I and your other guests have unwittingly become involved in a deception. It may be that Sebastian will have to be reprimanded.'

'There, then. It is not as bad as you feared, hmm? Why not have something to eat while you are here? I thought perhaps there was something else you wished to say to me.'

The suggestion was tempting. He nodded. 'A youngster from the abbey is holding my donkey. Is there somewhere he can take it, do you think? Then he may have something too.

'Um, something else?' he asked, belatedly taking in what she had said.

Madame shrugged delicate shoulders and smoothed the linen surcoat over her knees. 'A woman likes to be complimented,' she said, with downcast eyes, 'by someone who regards her well, even if his station means that nothing may be done about it.'

'Madame, Adrienne, I…'

The abbot did not dine well at the evening meal. Concern ate at him, anxiety gnawed. More investigation had shown him that the deception had been going on as far back as he had looked – three months before. What was he to do? He had to assume that the note with Madame Brisenot's name was false, but revealing the fraud might well implicate himself. And Madame Brisenot, and the boy. He was going to have to broach the subject with Brother Giles and it would have to be this suppertime too. And what if disciplinary actions had to be taken? A kitchen without its kitchener? It would be a heavy price to pay.

The prior signalled the end of the meal with a prayer of gratitude that did nothing to dispel his mood. Nor did his foreboding grow any lighter when Josephus beckoned to him on his way out, and led him aside into his indoor garden, beyond the chapterhouse.

'We shall not be disturbed here, I think,' Josephus said. 'Quite private.'

'What is the privacy for?'

'Brother Anno was to have gone to the Shrine of St. Jean tomorrow morning. I had arranged for him to see you tonight.'

'Well, why all this past tense? Why can he not go now?'

'Because he has disappeared. No one could find him this afternoon.'

The abbot frowned. 'No one has seen him?'

The prior shook his head and scratched his ear, then his nose.

'Perhaps he has gone early then. Perhaps he has gone to the shrine this afternoon.'

Prior Josephus brightened. 'Indeed, Abbot, perhaps he has.'

'So you must send someone down there first thing, at first light. Right?'

The prior nodded, practically bolt upright, relieved at the abbot's conjecture. 'I thank God that you are with us, Abbot. I would have drowned in a sea of despair this afternoon but you are our…' The prior swept his hands through the air as he tried to think of a suitable simile. 'Our rock, our Pharos on the rock.'

'That's good of you to say so, Prior.' The abbot smiled as the other clutched so enthusiastically at this straw. He turned to go. 'So pleased.'

It was a pleasure that lasted only long enough for the abbot to return to his guestroom and sit down.

The acolyte threw the door open and rushed in. 'Master, oh, Master.'

'What on earth is the matter, boy?'
'Brother Anno, Master.'
'I know. He has disappeared.'
'No longer. He has been found... In the stables, Master.'
Strictly speaking, it was not the stables but the storeroom beyond where feed and animal remedies were kept. The building was stone and had a tiled roof, and was much drier than the stables themselves.
Brother Anno lay on his back in the middle of the central aisle just beyond the entrance, his feet towards the closed door. On his forehead was the imprint of a five-petalled rose, swollen and dull red against the blue-black skin. Looked at closely, it was possible to see that the skin had been broken, though there was little bleeding.
'Had no one looked in here earlier?' the abbot asked of those who now stood around the body, for body it was. Anno was most certainly dead.
The brothers shuffled, some shook their heads, others coughed. One novice thought that another had looked but no one, it seemed, *had* actually looked in the storehouse.
'So, our brother forgot to duck under the lintel, in his hurry.' Prior Josephus had quietly joined them and was now leaning slightly towards the corpse.
Eyes turned towards the lintel, which had the likeness of the exact same rose carved into the stone slab. One of the monks raised his lantern to reveal a smear of blood on the stone petals.
'No,' said the monk who had discovered Anno's body when he had gone for oats. 'Brother Anno ducked at every doorway whether it was big enough or not. It was a habit.'

‘Even habits are forgotten sometimes,’ Prior Josephus said thoughtfully, tugging an earlobe and leaning first one way, then the other. ‘We shall have to arrange another funeral, inter him next to his brother. It will be a double burial. How very, very sad.’

‘You know,’ William said later when they returned to the guestrooms. ‘His forehead had bled from the left-hand side of the wound. And the blood on the lintel is on the left-hand side of the rose.’

‘Good observation, boy,’ said the abbot. ‘That’s all right, then.’

‘No, it isn’t.’ The acolyte tried to explain, ‘The blood should have been on the right-hand side of one of them.’

‘How do you mean?’

‘If Brother Anno’s head had hit the lintel, the blood should have been on the opposite side of the carving.’

The abbot was a little impatient. His stomach hurt and the food he had eaten rested there like a lump of uncooked suet. ‘Well, it seems all right to me, boy, and anyway, perhaps you didn’t look properly.’

‘But it…’

‘No *buts* at the present, boy. I have urgent need…’ And the abbot, somewhat whey-faced compared to his normal colour, left the room quickly.

William looked around for some way of explaining things to the abbot when he returned. He found a candle stub and with a penknife, cut it into the rough likeness of a rose. From the mantelshelf, he took down the head of John the Baptist, which had been fashioned from a piece of oak. A drop of scarlet sealing wax gave the Baptist a bloody wound on the forehead. All was now in readiness.

The abbot’s return however was deferred. In fact, it was

the better part of half an hour before he came back and William, taking one look at his master, helped him quietly to his bedchamber.

'Thank you, boy,' he whispered painfully. 'Your kindness is a blessing. Pray for me will you for, although I shall do my best. I am in some pain and holy thoughts do not come clearly.'

'Of course, Master.'

William did as he was asked. An abrupt knock at the door surprised him. 'Brother Giles,' he said, as the kitchener entered.

'Supper for your master and for yourself.'

'The abbot is feeling unwell,' he told Brother Giles. 'I will take a small piece of bread and some of that infusion he likes so well, juniper was it? It may soothe whatever is wrong when he wakes.'

'A nice thought, young William. Take what you need and I shall return in the morning.'

'Thank you, Brother. I shall see you later at prayers.'

But he didn't. Without the abbot to wake him, he slept through the tolling of the bell, and woke only when the abbot himself awoke the following morning with groans and loud prayers for help from Above and assistance from William.

The abbot sent the acolyte to notify the prior of his illness. He performed ablutions, said prayers at the small shrine in the main guest chamber and returned to bed. He refused breakfast except for a jug of water, and left William to his own devices.

The acolyte decided that he would visit the masons. Brother Jean had introduced him to Brother Christophe and explained what the young acolyte had been charged to do. In the event, the task was quickly finished. The abbey was not large enough to warrant a mason capable of making an accounting; stone and lime were delivered as required but generally in large enough quantities to require payment made directly by the prior or the resident abbot.

Their work had been accompanied by the continual ringing of chisels on stone and, when William asked what was going on, Brother Christophe donned his leather apron and took him into the covered part of the yard. Here, two junior masons, both hired servants from the village, were cutting an elaborate leaf pattern along a pair of square columns.

'There is to be an extension to the cloister. These will be the door posts of the new entrance to the dormitory stair; there are others, still to be cut, for the new rooms under the dormitory.'

'The carving is very fine and I have heard my master compliment the work.'

'That is very gratifying.'

William stepped back, as one of the craftsmen gathered up his tools. The boy's foot caught on something behind him and he fell backward across some stonework lying on the ground.

'Whoops!' said Christophe. 'Are you all right?'

William nodded and clambered back to his feet.

'The abbot would not compliment us on this.' Brother Christophe bent and picked up the creamy coloured stone, with a central boss. 'This should be stacked with the others. Out of the way of people's feet.'

'It was stacked yesterday, Brother. I hadn't noticed that it had been moved.'

'Who would move it but one of us? Hmm?'

William caught sight of the stylised rose at its centre

point, 'Just a minute, that's a lintel, isn't it? For a doorway?'

'It is. All the doorways are made to the same pattern.'

'And look,' William grew excited, 'the carving has blood on it.'

'Blood?' said the craftsman, who denied moving the length of stone.

'Have you hurt yourself ?' Brother Christophe asked. 'Your hand, perhaps?'

'No, no. It's not my blood. And look there, the end has been broken away.' The edge of the lintel was crushed, as though it had been hit with another piece of stone or had, perhaps, been dropped. 'I think this may be important, I shall have to speak to my master.'

'We can make another, young William.' Brother Christophe was anxious. 'Surely the abbot need not know.'

'I think this has something to do with Brother Anno's death.'

There were three sharp intakes of breath.

'Can you keep this safe? Put it in a store place and cover it, perhaps? And I must ask you to say nothing of this until the abbot has seen it with his own eyes.'

'This is not a foolish jape, is it? Not a youngster's joke?'

'I promise, Brother Christophe, I am as serious as you.'

'Then it shall be done. The abbot has to see it, you say?'

William nodded and looked again at the lintel, imagining it being positioned just so and then being dropped on to Brother Anno's forehead.

William left them to hide the stone lintel from casual view and went to the kitchen. It was time for the midday meal but he did not want to go to the refectory; he felt a little intimidated by the idea of going there alone. Besides, the abbot should really eat something however badly he felt. Some pottage, perhaps.

He put this to Brother Giles, who nodded. He was busy, and tapped the shoulder of one of the monks appointed for temporary assistance, asking him to get whatever William thought to be best.

The abbot was awake and bleary-eyed. He staggered into the dayroom, with his hair looking even more like a bird's nest of straw than usual. 'Thank you, boy. A spoon or two of pottage is just what I need.'

'More than a spoon or two, Master.'

'You may not have noticed, boy, but I do carry around a certain amount of emergency rations.' The abbot patted his stomach and William knew then that the other was on the mend. 'Whatever else, starvation will not carry me off.'

They ate in silence. William considered what he thought to be the growing evidence for a second murder. The abbot also deliberated on his discovery of a fraud in the kitchen.

'What have you done this morning?' the abbot asked, at length.

William described the routine part of his activity.

'And this afternoon?'

'I don't believe the infirmary records have come yet. I think I'll go and see if I can hurry them up.'

'We really are going to make an examiner out of you, aren't we, boy?' The abbot patted his stomach gently. 'I think it's only a case of bad indigestion. The meal disagreed with me last night. I could feel it at the time. Perhaps you could ask for a physic, when you see the infirmarian.' The abbot rose from the table and returned to his bed after the unusually meagre lunch.

William went off to the infirmary, which he had visited early the previous day in search of bills and stock lists. Here, he looked up the same individual and greeted him.

'And what is it this time? More records? I don't know when I shall be able to get them. I'm really busy with Brother Anno.' Brother August shook his head gloomily.

'Well, this has nothing to do with the abbot, I mean, the abbot's records and things.' The other brightened considerably. 'What I, that is, we need to know is how tall was Brother Anno.'

'How tall?' August frowned. 'Why ever do you need to know that?'

'I suppose it's just for my master's records. He wants to know for sure whether Brother Anno could or could not have hit his head on the door lintel.'

'That seems sensible enough, but I don't have a measure or anything like that. You could try the carpenters, they're sure to need that sort of thing.'

'Have you a length of cord, maybe?'

Brother August nodded and led William into the small sickroom where Brother Anno's body was laid out all but naked, ready for washing.

William, who had envisaged them each taking an end and holding it alongside the body, suddenly found that he could not approach the corpse. It wasn't that he had not seen dead men before; there had been hangings, deaths in the jousts, and only recently Anno's twin, but this was different. A naked corpse on a hospital bed was too much.

'I can't,' he told Brother August. 'I can't make myself go near.'

'Hmm.' Brother August was used to such things and treated the dead in much the same fashion as the living, in a businesslike manner. He was, however, used to squeamishness in others. 'I can't do it by myself. You'd better come back later. Or, no, I have the answer.' August tied a knot in the cord a yard from one end, 'Take this end and hold it so the knot is over the top of his head.'

William found this was possible. August took the string and holding it taut, made another knot directly above Anno's toes. 'There, now you have the exact height or perhaps in this case, we should say length.'

'There is blood on the sheet here, Brother August.'

'Oh really? There's a wound on the back of the head, where he hit the ground as he fell backwards, I imagine. Just a moment,' Brother August lifted the head carefully and placed a wad of linen beneath the skull.

William thanked Brother August, asked that he say nothing about this until the abbot gave him leave, and turned to go. 'Oh, the abbot would also be grateful for the records,' he added.

'Tonight, young man. After the body has been prepared, I will bring them along. There really is only so much that one man can do, you know.'

'And one last thing. My master has the stomach ache, have you a simple that would give him ease?'

'Hmm. I will have something through there.' He nodded to the outer area, beyond the sickroom. Outside, he led the way to the back of the room, along which was a set of shelves as tall as a man, filled with stoneware jars and jugs, small glass bottles of tincture, packages of old yellow paper.

'Now, marjoram with mint, I think.' August took down a stoppered bottle from among many and poured a small amount into a glass vial. He corked this and gave it to William. 'Tell him to take half tonight and the remainder tomorrow morning. If the problem persists, he could try a tea of camomile leaves for a day or two.'

'Thank you, Brother August, we really are most grateful for your help.'

William hastened to the stables, careful not be caught running, he went on through to the back. He could hear mice in the hay and made a mental note to tell Brother Sylvan before he left for the shrine.

Now, the acolyte needed something on which to stand, a box or… He noticed a ladder leaning against the wooden stage where hay had been stored. He moved it across and found it long enough to reach up above the doorframe. The boy climbed up and, taking the ball of twine from his purse, let it unravel, suppressing a curse when it tangled and hung halfway to the floor.

He clambered down again and found a harness ring in the stable that he could tie to the end of the string near the lower marker knot. Up the ladder again and, this time, he let it down more slowly. When the weight reached the floor, the top marker was barely a finger's width above the lower edge of the lintel.

He climbed down and walked more slowly back to the guestrooms. If Brother Anno had rushed through the door without ducking properly, he might have grazed the top of his head, nothing more.

From the hayloft came two long drawn-out sighs and a burst of giggling.

'What *was* he doing?' Anna-Marie asked.

Brother Sylvan shook his head, brushing his nose against a perky nipple as he did so. 'Don't know, don't care,' he said, 'but this…'

And they became engrossed in other things.

Later, after they were dressed and were pulling hay stalks from each other's hair, Brother Sylvan stopped abruptly. 'God's bones. The stupid child has left the ladder against the doorway.'

'So? Oh, how are we going to get down?'

When William returned, it was to find the abbot sitting in front of a smoky fire with the small bottle he carried in his bag for emergencies. He took a sip, as the boy entered, and smiled a little uncertainly. 'Feeling a little better now.'

William approached to tend to the fire, achieving a cheerful blaze that brought some warmth to the room. 'He sent this for you, Master, for your stomach.'

'That's good of him. What is it?'

William frowned. 'Um, something and mint. Marj-something and mint. You're supposed to take half tonight and half tomorrow.'

'Well, I believe I'll try it. Half, you say?'

'That's right,' said William, as the abbot drew the stopper and took a sip from the vial.

'God's mercy, boy,' the abbot's lips were so pursed he had difficulty speaking. 'That's as bitter as gall and wormwood.'

'Perhaps you should take it with water, Master.'

The abbot glowered for a moment. 'No. I'll see how I am tomorrow. Perhaps I shall try again if I am still as afflicted. Now, what of the infirmary records?'

'They're not quite ready, Master,' he said, bending the truth to help Brother August who had helped him. 'He will bring them tonight.'

The abbot shook his head. 'There is not the respect for

seniority that there used to be, boy. Time was when…' He sat bolt upright and clutched his stomach.

'Master?'

'Have to go! The privy! Really, really have to go, I may be some time.'

He rose to his feet as fast as his condition would allow and hurriedly pulled his robe about him. 'Those sales receipts that we were talking about last night, sort them out into two piles, will you. One for stuff that was sold and one for where it was free.'

William watched the older man go with some concern, and then began the task the abbot had asked of him. It was soon finished, there were about twenty notes, fourteen recorded small sums of money, six did not. These, he noticed, the free ones, were for flour or oatmeal, some bread that had gone stale, and one for a jug of pottage. The others were for fish or meat.

The abbot had still not returned and, bored, William looked at the bundle of papers that recorded kitchen purchases back to more than half a year past. Perhaps the abbot had meant him to go through them all. He addressed the larger task and again, it did not take as long as he had anticipated. Soon, he had tripled the number of notes regarding sales and gifts. Again, they were in roughly the same proportion.

Still with time on his hands, William took his length of string and removed the link ring he had used to weight it before re-rolling it and putting it away. Suddenly, he saw in his mind's eye the ladder he had left against the doorway to the storeroom in the stables. Annoyed at his blunder, he was about to go and put matters right when the abbot returned.

He was in a somewhat better humour than when he had

left, and William told him of what he had found. His master nodded. 'That's good. You know, on occasion, being shut in the privy can be a useful thing. I have a theory that many of the keenest insights come at such times.'

'You seem to be feeling better, Master.'

'I am, boy. We shall have to see about something to eat in a little while. But for now...' The abbot looked through the two piles of notes. 'Interesting... Jellied pigeon, a small ham, carp, eggs, and so on, and in the other, flour and bread mainly. And the ones with money are all ordinary sorts of meat that are on hand here except for that one mention of pheasant, and all sold for a small amount.'

He looked across at William. 'What do you think?'

William shook his head. 'I don't know. Perhaps the pheasant was a mistake.'

The abbot grinned. 'Exactly, boy. The name of Madame Brisenot, too. I have come to the same conclusion. I don't know what it's all about, not yet, but I do know that it had nothing to do with Madame Brisenot.'

The answer pleased the abbot for, if it had nothing to do with Madame Brisenot, it was clear that he, himself, was not implicated in consuming illicitly obtained food. The indigestion had gone.

'Obviously, there's a fraud going on here but it's hard to see what it is at the moment.'

At the abbot's bidding, William went to the kitchen to request a supper tray. However, he detoured by way of the stables and was puzzled to find the ladder back where he had found it.

'But...' William scratched his nose.

'Now what do you want?'

Turning, he saw Brother Sylvan sitting on the floor with one foot across his knee, massaging the ankle. He seemed to be in some pain. William was quite surprised at how good it made him feel.

'I'm so sorry,' William said, keeping the grin off his face. 'I know it's dark in here, did you bump into the ladder? I know I shouldn't have left it so untidy.'

'For sweet Jesu's sake, go! Just leave me be.'

'Well…'

'Go! Go!'

William went, beaming.

'The abbot feeling better now?' the kitchener smiled down at him.

'Oh yes, Brother Giles. Much improved, thank you.'

Giles gathered together a selection of food. Some chicken, bread, and cheese. He dropped some herbs in to an earthenware jug and, from a kettle simmering by the fire, he dipped some hot water into the jug.

'Thank you, Brother.' William reached for the tray but Giles held it up out of reach.

'You go ahead and open the doors for me, young man. I will carry this.'

With unusual tact, William knocked on the door when they reached the guest rooms.

'Come, Prior,' the abbot said from inside.

'It is me, with Brother Giles and the supper things, Master.'

'Oh, thank you, Brother.' The abbot remembered his earlier misgivings. 'Brother, a timely visit.'

'M'lord?'

The abbot lurched to his feet and searched through the notes he had been looking at all afternoon. 'Ah, now, here it is. This note, can you explain it to me?'

Brother Giles put the tray down on the table and took the parchment. He held it arm's length and peered for a moment, he shook his head, then went nearer to the light and tried again. 'No, m'lord, I need longer arms and bigger writing. My eyes are getting old.'

'Here, then.' The abbot brought out his cure for old eyes: the rounded glass slab. 'Try that.'

Brother Giles tried and laughed. 'Truly, a gift from God.' He read the note. 'Three-brace of pheasant, overhung.' He turned and looked at the abbot with raised eyebrows.

'A little more. Read on.'

He bent over again and laboured over the letters. 'Madame Brisenot. One denier.'

He chuckled. 'I don't understand, m'lord Abbot. What is it about?'

'The note says these are pheasants sold to Madame Brisenot at a very cheap price.'

'So?'

'From the kitchen, here, at the abbey.'

'That's ridiculous, if you'll pardon me for saying so, m'lord.'

The abbot nodded. 'I thought so too but tell me why.'

The kitchener straightened up, and perched a buttock on the table. 'We don't have pheasant here. We hardly have meat at all unless it's for an invalid, or someone like yourself, m'lord.' Giles smiled. 'Tonight, I found a little chicken for you but usually, it's more likely to be pigeon, from the cote.'

The abbot brightened. He nodded.

'And also, we wouldn't sell food.'

'Really?' The abbot raised his eyebrows, 'Not even cheaply, to the poor?'

'We'd give it away. And a woman like Madame Brisenot wouldn't buy it from here, anyway.'

'Perhaps her servant?'

'Georges is more particular about from where he buys than Madame is.'

'Perhaps you recognise the handwriting?'

Giles shook his head. 'Been too long since I could read anything, m'lord. Certainly not handwriting. I leave that to Edouard, from the village.'

'Aha, a servant, is he?'

'That's so. But it's all absurd, m'lord. Why should we be selling stuff? And pheasant isn't the sort of thing we'd ever have.'

The abbot nodded. 'You're right, of course, it *is* absurd. I shall have to think about this. Thank you for your help. And for our supper.'

'Don't take too long, m'lord. That verbena tea won't stay warm for long.'

When Giles had gone, he picked up the still-steaming jug and poured a measure into an empty beaker, he carried it back to the chair in front of the fire. 'Mystery, mystery, mystery. All at once.'

The abbot was almost asleep in the chair when another knock on the door heralded a visitor. William opened it quietly with a finger to his lips, asking for silence.

'Ah, Brother August,' he said in a low voice. 'The abbot is not too well, we will not disturb him.'

Brother August came in with a bundle of papers in either hand. 'Purchases,' he said, waving one bundle, 'And sales,' brandishing the other. 'We sell to physicians both here and down in St. Jean as well.'

'Who's that?' The abbot's voice came to them.

'Brother August, Master. From the infirmary.'

'Thank you for your help, Brother, spending all this time for us.' The abbot sat upright and turned to look at the infirmarian.

'Not at all, m'lord. It's just that there has been so much to do, you know. Brother Anno's death added more work, and the measuring, of course. I hope it told you what you needed to know.'

'Measuring?'

William ground his teeth.

'His height, m'lord.'

'Ah. Height! Yes well, it all adds up, I'm sure.'

When Brother August had gone, the abbot heaved himself to his feet. 'I am going to bed, boy. I feel that I shall sleep much better tonight.'

'Goodnight, Master.'

'You can tell me all about it tomorrow.'

'Tomorrow?'

'Brother Anno's height.'

CHAPTER ELEVEN

William lay awake for some time that night, listening to the distant chant of prayers for Brother Anno's soul, a melancholy sound, but as he drowsed and eventually rested, a comforting one.

He dreamed he was back at his family home in Castres, walking through an orchard of plum trees. Mixed white and pink blossoms were all around him and the sound of bees visiting those still on the trees was loud and insistent, while the grass beneath his feet was soft with the fallen blooms.

He came to a trio of trunks growing from the same bowl. A seat had been woven from young saplings springing direct from the tree's roots and here, where William played as a child, sat Vincent his tutor in the matter of weapons training. Across his knees were two full-size swords, their tips bound with leather secured with pitch.

'Today, William, we are going to study the *envelopement*. Not easy for a youngster but I think you'll master it by lunchtime. If not, we go hungry.' He stood up and tossed one of the weapons to William.

William snatched the blade from the air and swept it back and forth once or twice. He lifted the sword. 'Come at me then,' he laughed, eager to begin.

'Wait until I've shown you the move…'

William was not to learn the parry on this occasion, however. His waking was abrupt.

Suddenly back to health, the abbot rose from his bed for nocturnes and took William, who had become just a little laggard in his prayers over the past day or so, along to the church. A little while later, they returned and were on hand as Brother Giles and the kitchen boy brought their breakfast.

'M'lord Abbot? Feeling well today?'

'Truly, Brother Giles, I am haler today than when we arrived. Down to good healthy food, I dare say.'

Brother Giles raised his eyebrows. 'And not all from our kitchen, so I hear, m'lord.'

'It is better to say nothing about those matters, Brother Giles; the prior is a sensitive soul. Now, the servant you mentioned, the one who writes your accounting of expenditure, his name is?'

Giles's expression became more serious. 'Edouard, m'lord. Edouard. A servant who can write is uncommon, he is a useful fellow.'

When Brother Giles had left them and their meal was well advanced, William broke the silence. 'Brother Giles was a little disrespectful, Master.'

'Well now. Perhaps he did overstep the mark, just a little. But if all of us were to guard our self-respect with diligence, nobody would be speaking to anyone within a day.'

'Hmm.'

'Now, about Brother Anno's height, boy.'

William confessed his investigations.

'And you believe that it would be impossible for Brother Anno to have struck his forehead on the lintel?'

'Absolutely, Master.' William remembered the preparations he had made two evenings before. He fetched the candle-stub-rose and the head of John the Baptist.

'Also, the blood on the doorway was on the left-hand side of the rose, here.' William rotated the wax rose until the wick was on the left. 'And the blood on Brother Anno's wound was also on the left.' He pointed to the sealing wax on John the Baptist's head and then brought them together.

'But it *would* have been on Brother Anno's left…'

'On *his* left, yes, but not on the left, as you look at it.'

'Ah, yes.' The abbot now saw what William had seen. 'Hmm.'

'The two parts with blood on do not match.'

'Thus, the blood was put on the door lintel afterwards.' The abbot nodded.

'After the wound had been made in the mason's yard.'

'Some more investigation?'

And again, William related his findings.

'So he could have been killed almost anywhere and carried to the mason's yard and then to the storeroom behind the stables.'

'There was quite a large wound on the back of his head. Brother August thought it must be from when he fell backwards after he struck the door lintel.'

The abbot pursed his lips and made an uncomplimentary noise.

William had a further thought. 'There may be a bloodstain on the floor somewhere.'

'May well be, boy, but I'd guess it's been cleaned by now if anyone was likely to find it. However, *I* am satisfied that this has been another murder, and that is all that matters. The first thing we need to do is to have Gilbert de Gignac come here to give us an account of his movements over the past few days.'

'Gilbert?'

'Shifty fellow. I have had my suspicions about Gilbert for some time. But now,' the abbot rubbed his hands together, 'it is high time my little treatise was copied. There has been time to do it three times over. You go and speak to the precentor, what was his name?'

'In the scriptorium? Brother Willi?'

'Willi. Go and bring back the work he has done for me. I shall go and find the prior and talk to him about Gilbert de Gignac, and the evidence that you have unearthed.'

William did not like the sound of the abbot's suspicions concerning Gilbert. As far as he could see, there was nothing to link the man with this second murder and precious little to make a connection with the first. As he climbed the stairs, the boy tried to think of ways in which the murderer could be exposed.

He came to the scriptorium above the chapterhouse and pushed open the door, more gently than the last time. No one looked up from what they were doing, he was ignored, as though he had been a cricket on the windowsill, yet he was certain that everyone must be aware of him. He cleared his throat; no one took notice. He coughed. Nothing. 'Precentor Willi,' he said out loud, and was at last rewarded by Willi's supercilious stare.

'Well?'

'I have come for my lord Abbot's treatise on mathematics.'

'Then you shall have it without delay.'

Willi had been sitting by a window, looking out over a stretch of open land to the vistas in the south. He stood and took down a small bundle of papers from a shelf above his head. 'There.'

'Thank you.' William riffled through the pages. 'These are the originals. He will want the copies too.'

'The copies are not ready.'

'Well, there is no point in taking these. When can I come for the copies?'

'You may come whenever you wish to do so, young man. Whether the copies will be ready is something I do not care to reckon.'

'The abbot will wish to know how much has been done.'

'Nothing. The copying has not yet been started.'

'The abbot may…' William thought better of what he had been about to say. 'I will tell the abbot.'

Now everyone felt free to look at him. Some smiled sympathetically, others smiled with malice, for even in a place devoted to the love of God, conceit grows by example.

William returned to their rooms and, while waiting for the abbot, tried to clean the sealing wax from John the Baptist's head. He was not wholly successful even by the time his master returned.

The abbot was not in the best of tempers. 'I had some difficulty in explaining my conjectures to the prior. He didn't seem able to accept Gilbert as a logical choice. In the end, I had to order the thing done. Can you imagine it coming to that?'

William could, and in view of the abbot's mood, forbore from telling him about Brother Willi's lack of progress.

Lunch came courtesy of Brother Giles. The kitchener had taken it upon himself to provide meals in the guest chamber, an arrangement the abbot found most acceptable, and which Brother Giles hoped would guarantee a favourable report of his qualities when Abbot Roget returned.

The abbot, replete and in a better mood, remembered the errand he had given William. 'And how has the copying gone, boy? Nearly finished?'

'Um, no, master.'

'Halfway?'

'They are not yet started.'

'Not started?'

From calm and equable to angry and raging in the space of a single breath. The abbot carefully put down the knife with which he had been slicing cheese. He stood up. 'Come with me.'

'Are you sure, Master?'

'Sure?'

'Would it not be better to see Brother Willi here, in private?'

'I would prefer the whole congregation to watch Brother Willi tormented with a plague of scorpions but,' the abbot took a deep breath and then another, 'no doubt you are right, boy.'

'Tell the precentor to come and visit me here. Immediately.'

Glumly, William nodded and left the room. He slowly climbed the stairs and went into the scriptorium. Brother Willi, was sitting as before, gazing across the countryside. Again, the same faces watched him with commiseration and spite.

'Precentor.'

Willi looked round. He frowned.

'The abbot would like to speak to you, Precentor.'

Willi raised his eyebrows as though surprised. 'Very

well. I am available whenever he wishes.'

'He wishes to see you now, Precentor. In the guest suite.'

William left. He had no desire to be in the same room with Brother Willi and the abbot, or even to listen at the door. He descended to the cloister and walked across to the church but it was already in use, a requiem for Brother Anno echoing among its lofty arches. He returned to the courtyard enclosed by the cloister and sat by the fountain. The sun was warm and relaxing.

At first, he was certain that he was dreaming. The face that he saw was that of Anna-Marie de Fossard. It had been in his dreams since they had come to the abbey and once he had been reassured by the abbot, he determined to enjoy her ghostly presence. She stood with her back to a pillar a few yards away and was talking to someone not quite visible. The discussion was urgent; every nod, every gesture was sharp. Though too far away to hear what was said, William knew those full lips were pouting, the eyes flashing with fury.

'Soon…' He heard and the figure of Brother Sylvan came into view. 'If not then…' And again, further words were lost.

'It will be. Now that Anno…' that was Brother Sylvan.

Anna-Marie leaned forward and, had it not been a dream, William would have been scandalised to see the two of them kissing. A moment later, the girl strode off and he was appalled all over again to see that she wore hose and hunting boots, and a man's vest. With a single glance behind her, the Comte's daughter left the cloister by a small gate in the far corner.

For a minute longer, Brother Sylvan stood looking after

her and then he too, turned to go. He came along the western colonnade and William took his gaze from the gateway just in time to see the monk exit into the main hallway.

Was he dreaming or waking? Had he been seen? William didn't know, but even if it was a dream he had rather Brother Sylvan had not seen.

Brother Sylvan and Anna-Marie! It was a great blow. He had begun to idolise the girl, to imagine that he might have had the place the young monk obviously occupied. Now, without her imaginary presence, his mind felt cold and empty, lonely.

But then there was a comprehension. The Comte's daughter was consorting with a monk, she wore men's clothing; she was not the unsullied woman he had imagined. In fact, she fell far short of the ideal that the troubadours sang about. Unworthy.

Another sort of confrontation was about to occur in the guestrooms.

'God be with you, m'lord Abbot.' Brother Willi bowed.

'May His blessings be upon you, Precentor.' The abbot gestured to a chair and he himself sat down next to the table where the accounts were stacked.

'You wish to see me, m'lord?'

'I wish to see my treatise copied, Precentor. I am told that the work is not yet commenced.'

'That is correct,' Brother Willi nodded.

This was going to be like extracting teeth, the abbot thought. 'Why?'

'We have no paper, m'lord. You did suggest that parchment be used.'

'Actually, Precentor, *you* suggested parchment. You must have known at the time that you had none. Why did you not tell me this and why have you not purchased some?'

'I…' Brother Willi chewed his bottom lip for a moment, 'I was not sure of the stock at that time, m'lord, and we have no money to purchase more.'

The abbot referred to his list of queries for the scriptorium and then leafed through the record of sales and purchases. 'I see you sold a large quantity of parchment to St. Benedict's last month.' He went through the list again. 'Also, two months before that. Can you explain why this was done and where the money from that sale went?' On familiar ground here, the abbot knew what questions to put and how to phrase them. This was his profession. 'You might also explain why there is no money to keep the scriptorium in the necessary materials for work?'

The first time that these two had met, the abbot had only just heard of the rumours of murder, rumours that he had disbelieved, until they had been rather bluntly confirmed later. It had not been a good day. Both had made assumptions as to the other's character; Brother Willi now wondered if he had drawn his own conclusions a little prematurely.

'We have a purchasing arrangement with St. Benedict's at Aniane,' he said. 'St. Guilhem buys parchment and vellum in the first part of the year and sells half on to St. Benedict's; during the second half-year the position is reversed. We get a better price, that way.'

The abbot nodded. 'That is quite reasonable. So you have used up all the parchment purchased since the beginning of the year?'

'Not exactly, m'lord. We did not purchase our half at these times.'

The abbot considered this for a moment. Something that William had said came to mind, though the details escaped him. 'Something to do with renovations perhaps?' The abbot was fishing without knowing if the bait was right or even if there were fish in the pool, but the hook snagged something.

'Um, well…'

'Tell me about it.'

'Our workshop needs improvement,' said Brother Willi.

'The roof leaks rain?' The abbot suggested, 'Bats' droppings ruin your work?'

'Hmm. There is a higher purpose…'

'Oh yes, I know all about that. This is to the greater glory of God. Is that it?'

Willi did not like the weariness expressed in the abbot's words. 'You have it exactly, my lord.'

'And you sought permission and gained it from the Abbot Roget, before he went on his pilgrimage, naturally.'

'It was certainly mentioned, my lord Abbot.' Brother Willi chose his words with care.

'If not from the abbot, then from Prior Josephus?'

Brother Willi, no longer able to maintain the demeanour of Precentor, held his hands out in unconscious supplication. 'The scriptorium is a plain room, m'lord. We work to make beautiful things, to perpetuate them down the generations. The more that God's glory is made manifest, the better are we able to express it in the beauty of the script, in the colours of illumination…'

'Yes, Brother Willi, I do get the picture. Yet how are you going to produce these wondrous examples of your work without paper?'

'There are other media, m'lord.'

The abbot saw the hunted look. 'You have vellum, then?'

'Not exactly, m'lord.'

The pitfall yawned. 'Papyrus?'

Brother Willi shook his head.

'Chalk and slates? No, don't bother. You have put all this money into timber…'

A final desperate attempt. 'Best quality timber, m'lord.'

The abbot ignored it. 'To make you a more beautiful ceiling so your scribes now have nothing to work with, they are idling their time away practising on scraps while you… what *do* you do, Brother Willi?'

'I contemplate, m'lord. And plan.'

'Go away, Brother Willi, while I contemplate on what you have done, quite apart from the lies you have tried to tell me.'

The precentor stood up. 'M'lord…'

'Go.'

The abbot remained seated as Brother Willi left, and he slowly willed himself to relax. He really did hate to use anger in his dealings and, on those occasions when it appeared to be necessary, it left him exhausted. He massaged his stomach, hoping that the disorder would not return.

Eventually, he heaved himself to his feet and went off in search of the prior. Josephus was not in his tiny conservatory nor had anyone seen him. Quite by chance, the abbot met him, as the service in the church finished. Rutilius had quite forgotten the service for Brother Anno and thoughts of the murder now displaced the recent unpleasantness with Brother Willi.

The prior smiled at the abbot, determined to be polite despite being bullied earlier on into sending for Gilbert. 'M'lord.'

'Well met, Prior, I have been looking for you.'

The prior bent slightly backward at the waist, as though the abbot's expansive personality were pressing on his chest. 'And now I am found.'

'Suppose we just sit over here.' The abbot gestured towards the garth.

They walked across the rough turf and, on the steps of the fountain, discovered the acolyte asleep in the sun. The abbot gently shook his shoulder. 'Well, boy, you may return to our room now and begin checking the infirmary records. I shall be along directly, as soon as I have had a word with Prior Josephus.'

The older man took William's place.

'Some more bad news, I'm sorry to say, Prior.'

'Oh? What is it this time?'

'Did you know that there has been no work done in the scriptorium over the past three months?'

'Oh come, m'lord, surely you're mistaken. I've been up there a number of times and everyone appeared to be busy.'

'Practising on scraps of paper, nothing more.' And the abbot went on to tell him about the precentor's grandiose scheme to redirect money for writing materials into the purchase of timber.

Josephus was horrified. 'I don't know what to say. Abbot Roget is going to be most upset when he returns. He will blame himself, I know, as indeed I blame *myself* too.'

'Blaming yourself is not going to put matters right, Prior. First of all, the carpentry work needs to be halted and secondarily, copying needs to be restarted.'

'But if the roof is in bad repair…'

'There is nothing wrong with the roof. The work is of a decorative nature only. I forget; how many monks work as scribes?'

The prior shook his shoulders and scratched under his chin. 'Eight, normally.'

'What work do you do to bring in extra income?'

'Nothing really, we are self-sufficient in most things, any insufficiency is made up by our benefactors. In fact, the scriptorium undertakes outside work and usually contributes quite a lot to the abbey over the year. There's the shrine, of course, it brings in a reasonable amount.'

'The shrine, of course. And we have eight scribes and brother Willi with nothing to do.'

The prior frowned and clasped his hands together. 'I don't follow.'

'I feel it is time that St. Jean went to meet the people, Prior. Designate four of the brothers from the scriptorium as a bearer party, plan a route that will take in several of the villages between here and, say, Montpellier. Arrange to show the effigy at each church they pass and to stay the night there, the monks can take bowls and solicit donations.'

Josephus nodded slowly. 'Recoup some of the losses.'

'Exactly.' He was fired with enthusiasm. 'Let them spend a fortnight before returning and then plan a second route up towards Nîmes for the four other brothers. Let the precentor do the planning, at least he will do something useful that way, and it may teach him that lying to his abbot is a sin.'

Now that his actions had been signalled to him, Prior Josephus became rather more eager, almost enthusiastic, to right the wrongs that the abbot had pointed out. Rutilius left to return to the guestrooms.

'M'lord.' The greeting was brusque, to say the least.

The monk who had hurried past him in the corridor was vaguely familiar. 'God's blessing upon you, Brother.'

Back in the room, William looked up. 'Ah, Master. Did you see Brother… Sylvan? He said he'd wanted to speak to you.'

'I passed someone. He did not stop. Sylvan? Oh yes, we shall have to send him down to the shrine, I suppose. Now that we have lost Brother Anno, he seems the logical choice.' The abbot pulled a stool up to the table and drew the kitchen accountings towards him. He began to look at the notes that William had sorted out.

'Actually, that's what he wanted to see you about, Master, going to the shrine.'

'Well, that will be organised in due course. How are the infirmary records?'

'Detailed, actually. Every bottle, every pill used. Every packet of herbs, tincture and powder bought.'

'Excellent. Let us hope that this efficiency does not cover deficiency. Everything is written up? The liabilities and the assets balanced?'

William looked up to make sure the abbot was serious. He shook his head. 'There are scores of records to total. This will take a good part of tomorrow as well as this afternoon.'

'Ah well, I had expected that would be done already. Never mind.'

The two of them were silent except for the scratching of William's pen and the occasional sound of the abbot chewing and sucking his bottom lip in thought. At last the bell tolled.

'Good. I'm feeling quite hungry. I've had a vigorous day. Brother Giles should be along shortly.'

William was annoyed. He had been working for hours and now the abbot simply ignored his efforts, while the only labour he had seen his master perform was an idle browse through the kitchen notes. William had yet to appreciate the energy that might be expended simply by exercising authority.

He seethed quietly for a few minutes, then, 'Have you mentioned Brother Anno's murder to the prior yet? I have heard the rumour going about already.' He was perversely pleased to convey the bad news.

'Is that so?' Rutilius was content. 'One of your informants, I suspect. A pity.'

'I suppose it must be, no one else would have known.' To find that he, himself, was implicated in the gossip only added to William's irritation.

'Except the murderer himself, of course. Not that he would be here still.' The abbot shook his head. 'No, no I didn't mention our new evidence to the prior.'

Our evidence! William bristled.

The abbot continued, oblivious to William's mood. 'We discussed brother Willi's unfortunate plans for the scriptorium. I really wanted to speak to Gilbert first but I can't delay telling him very long.'

'Surely Gilbert would have no reason to do away with Brother Anno.' The boy's tone was more reproachful than he had intended.

The abbot raised his eyebrows. 'Criminals,' he said, 'use a logic that is foreign to us. The trick is to understand it. Do that, and you are well on the way to exposing them.'

'But, Gilbert?'

The abbot did not respond. Instead he carefully laid down one of the notes from the kitchen records. 'Now, here is just such an example. See here, the one concerning Madame Brisenot, compare it with these others.'

William looked. His eyes were tired and the handwriting was little more than a scrawl. 'I don't see what I'm comparing'

'Surely you must, it is a different hand.'

William was not convinced, another whimsical idea of his master's. 'And what can you deduce from this, Master?'

'At this moment, boy, not very much. But like Gilbert de Gignac, whoever is doing this will make a mistake; possibly he has already done so. I shall catch him.'

And with that, there was the knock at the door and the genial Brother Giles entered with their evening meal.

They went to vespers and, throughout, William worried about the abbot's theory on the murders. If his master accused Gilbert of murder how, in the face of such authority, could the lay worker refute the allegation? As others recited the prayers, made the responses, he formed a plan to force the real murderer into the open. Now that the rumour of the second murder was about to be confirmed, he would be able to put it into effect and let facts prove their worth over daydreams.

At the door to the guest room, the prior was awaiting their return.

'Ah, Abbot.'

'Prior Josephus, how pleasant. May the Lord bless our sleep.'

'May He protect us through the hours of darkness.'

The abbot saw that his clever references to sleep and to

time were disregarded. 'Come inside, Prior,' he invited, at last. 'What can we do for you at this late hour?'

'Our Brothers Abbo and Anno will be interred tomorrow, m'lord. Their clothes were burned today and one of the brothers found this.' The prior held out his hand, a blue enamel butterfly lay there. 'It fell out of a fold in Brother Abbo's habit. I think it might be the other end of the pin that was used to murder him.'

'Merciful God.' The abbot picked up the decoration and examined it. 'The pin, boy. It's in the pen box, wrapped in a scrap of paper.'

William went to the worktable and found the little parcel. Inside was the pin, as long as his index finger. They compared it with the stub, which protruded from the centre of the butterfly ornament, both ends showed the same sort of twisting and breakage.

'It certainly seems like it, Prior, it's a cloak pin, isn't it? The sort women wear. Compliment the brother on his observation, will you?'

'I will, but mind you, I can't see what use it might be.'

'No one can say. It may be of no use at all, it might be crucial.' Rutilius shook his head slowly, Nothing to do with a window bar or a door, at all. Nothing from the shrine, then. A woman's cloak fastener, one of the circular kind.

'You know,' William said, with some satisfaction, 'I think Marcel was a jeweller.' But the abbot ignored William's remark.

'I have also had word that Gilbert de Gignac is not to be found,' the prior went on.

'There,' said the abbot, 'an admission of guilt as clear as you could wish for.'

William groaned under his breath.

CHAPTER TWELVE

After breakfast, the abbot took coins from the small leather poke he kept at the bottom of his travel bag. 'I'm going to see Brother Willi.'

'Very good, Master.'

'I'm certain you can find something useful to do while I'm gone.'

The abbot spoke evenly, matter-of-factly, but William felt a weight in the comment that came entirely from his imagination. He seethed.

He too was certain that he could fill the time usefully. When the abbot left, he went out in search of Milos, the youngster who acted as altar boy when Rector Ferand officiated at the abbey, and who would be the perfect, if unaware, accomplice. He ran him to earth in a tiny garden behind the infirmary, planting out cuttings of herbs.

'Were you in church for Brother Abbo's requiem?' William asked.

Milos nodded and coughed. 'Really likes his incense, you know?'

'The priest?'

'Mm. Thinks he's no end of a gent, does the priest. All black silk and fine white linen.'

'Did you know that Brother Anno was murdered?'

Milos's eyes opened wide. 'Don't believe you. How would you know?'

'My master knows everything, he knows how and he

knows who, same one as killed Brother Abbo. What do you think of that?'

'Well, why doesn't he lock the murderer in the crypt then and call the Comte de Fossard?'

'He'll do what he wants when he wants. Just remember that.'

'Bet Smokey knows, anyway.'

'Smokey?'

'Rector Ferand.'

William squatted next to Milos, a faintly discernable scent came to him. 'What's this?' He touched a finger to a grey-leafed tuft of foliage. 'It looks dead.'

'It'll come, it's just the colour of the leaves makes it look dead. That's lavender.'

William smelt his fingertip. 'Ah. Yes, of course.' The smell gave a powerful jolt to memories. In his mind's eye, William saw again the young woman in the Lady Chapel when he had first gone to the Shrine at St. Jean de Foss. The air had been full of this same perfume then. He remembered that fall of dark hair, the delicate ear just visible, the slender ankles… And then he thought again of that meeting he witnessed in the cloisters. There was no comparison between the Anna-Marie he saw there and the girl who visited his dreams. The meeting had been real, he had no doubts. William turned back to Milos.

'Shall I tell you who it is?'

'The murderer?' Milos's eyes shone with excitement, 'Who?'

'Brother Sylvan.'

***

'Ah, m'lord Abbot.' Brother Willi had recovered his

composure. 'How can I help you?'

The abbot sat down on an empty bench seat. 'Paper, Brother Willi. I want you to buy some parchment immediately and set to work on my treatise.'

'*De Mathematica.*' The precentor, who was not at all sure now how long he would keep the title, nodded. He spoke carefully, his voice neutral. 'I thought that we understood one another, m'lord. We do not have the material.'

'Here is money to purchase enough to do the work I require. Go to St. Benedict's and buy some.'

'It will be done as you require, m'lord.'

'And when will it be completed?'

Brother Willi put his head back and closed his eyes. 'Sixty-three and one half pages.'

The abbot was impressed by the other's recall, though he gave no indication.

'In one week. That gives me time to send for paper.'

'Why not go yourself, brother? The weather is fine. It will do you good to get out of this dusty room. My profession requires a lot of travel, much of it on foot. I assure you that you will feel better for the exercise.'

On his return to the guest rooms, the abbot found William in an angry mood. 'Why, whatever is the matter, boy?'

'That monk, Brother Sylvan, has been here again, wanting to see you. I suggested that he wait but he hadn't the time, he said. He had time to try to poke his nose into our records, though.'

'How do you mean?'

'He was looking through the records. I looked up from what I was doing and there he was, reading through the notes. The kitchen ones, I think. He wouldn't move when

I told him they were private. I had to push him away before he moved.'

'How very curious. He saw me last night but chose to say nothing.' The abbot sat down and closed his eyes. 'We must lock the door when we leave, in future.'

'Oh, and a letter was delivered for you, Master.' William took the folded paper and passed it to the abbot, who opened his eyes at this news.

'A letter.' He inspected the outside first. 'Had a word with our Brother Willi… More tractable now, deferential almost.'

The abbot flaked off the sealing wax with a thumbnail. He read the small neat handwriting. 'Aha, from Madame Brisenot. Well, there's a pleasant surprise.'

'Master?'

'Madame Brisenot is having a small evening repast at the priest's suggestion for just the three of us. A man of excellent discernment, obviously, but I wonder what he has in mind.'

'I wish you every enjoyment, Master.'

The abbot was just finishing the letter, he held up his hand to stop any further conversation. 'Apparently, the invitation includes you too. Madame writes that I should bring you as a chaperone, since she does not wish to put me in a compromising situation.' He chuckled. 'I do believe she is making a joke.'

The acolyte did not know whether to be pleased or annoyed.

'Goodness!' The abbot's eyebrows climbed.

'Master?'

'Tonight. She means us to go tonight. It leaves us little time.'

Brother Giles and his kitchen boy brought lunch, for

which the abbot thanked him extravagantly. 'Brother, I wonder if we could come to see your kitchen at some time?'

'Of course, m'lord, though why would you want to do such a thing?'

The abbot smiled. 'If I was content just to work with the records, just to check accounts written down on paper, I would be a very inept examiner, indeed. I have to watch a place working so that I can picture it alive, with people there, a part of the whole congregation.'

Brother Giles smiled, pretending to understand this, although it was clear that he considered the abbot's wits to be a little befuddled, a conclusion that did not trouble the abbot at all. Having secured the invitation, both of them spent the rest of the day working at the abbey's records of monies, although Rutilius spent rather more time in examining the suspect notes from the kitchen than in checking accruals.

'I'm certain this is a forgery,' he said at length. 'The writing is so poor in both cases that I can't say it's a different hand. But the lines are thicker, as with a different pen and the ink is of a different colour.'

William sat back. 'But why?' he asked. 'What purpose is served?'

'I don't know... or perhaps I do. I've just had an idea.' The abbot stood up and paced back and forth as he filled out his first thoughts. 'Suppose someone in the kitchen knows a fraud is being committed, regularly, over a long period. But the previous examiner doesn't notice it. He thinks to himself: *this time, I'll put something into the records that they cannot ignore.* So this is counterfeit, not real; it's there to alert us to what is going on.'

William's annoyance continued to wax, and he was hard put to keep the note of scorn from his voice. 'That's interesting, Master, but would someone go to so much trouble?'

'People will go to enormous lengths to defraud Mother Church, William. Absolutely immense. So I see no reason to doubt that a more honourable person might take such trouble. Perhaps he dare not say anything to Brother Giles and this is his only way of exposing it.'

There came a knock to the door. 'Come,' called the abbot. A pause, nothing happened. 'Well, come in, whoever you are.'

The latch was slowly raised, the door opened and the small but robust figure of Brother Sylvan entered. 'God keep you, brother. I have heard that you wished to see me.'

He did not look as if he wished to see the abbot. His eyes darted here and there, examining everything in sight. 'I, er…' His eyes locked with the abbot's for a heartbeat, looked away again.

'Come on, Brother Sylvan, what is it?'

Then, his words coming in a rush, 'Now that Brother Anno is dead, when will I be able to take up the duty of sacristan at the shrine?'

'Ah yes. Has the prior said nothing to you?'

'Only that I will probably be chosen, though there is still need for someone to see to the livestock here.'

'I think the prior has stated the situation exactly.' The abbot frowned a little. 'What else can I say?'

'But when will it be decided? There really needs to be somebody there with an understanding of animals.' Again, Brother Sylvan's eyes were anywhere but on the abbot's face.

He leaned back in his chair. 'Why such urgency, brother?'

'Um. The shrine is well known for its husbandry, m'lord. It would be a shame to let the reputation lapse.'

'Come and see me tomorrow, when your work in the stables is done for the day. In the meanwhile, I shall speak with the prior when I see him. If he is satisfied that you can go, I will give my permission.'

A great relief seemed to flood across Brother Sylvan's face. 'Thank you, m'lord. Thank you.'

The abbot held up a hand in warning. 'I may not be here. There are other more pressing demands on my time. If that is the case, you must return later.'

'I will, m'lord. Certainly.'

When he had gone, the abbot turned to William. 'There is more there than meets the eye. Something that Brother Sylvan does not wish to discuss.'

William sniffed. 'He believes himself far more important than he is.'

'That's a common failing, one of which we are all guilty at some time or another.'

Again, William was sure that this was an allusion to himself.

That evening, they arrived at Madame Brisenot's house and were shown, not to the grand dining room they used before, but to a long room on the ground floor that had a glassed-in window giving a view on to a garden area. Decorations consisted of armour and swords, and tattered banners far too high for Georges to clean off the dust of decades.

The dinner was by no means as splendid as the previous

affair. The four of them ate from a low table on which Georges served a pottage and savoury pastries. This was followed by fruits preserved in honey with a board of cheeses to refresh their palates.

'Gentlemen,' Madame Brisenot looked from the rector to the abbot and back again, 'Lucas tells me he has important matters to discuss. I think William and I will take a walk and return later. Hmm?'

Lucas stood up, bowed a little. 'Madame, I am most grateful to you.'

Madame waved her hand at them. 'Not too long, do you hear?' With her arm about the boy's shoulders, she took him away from the men.

The priest gestured to a pair of chairs. The window had been opened, and through the opening they had a view over an expanse of scrawny garden where the remains of a half-dozen vines were draped across fallen posts and broken struts. The view was to the south-west and fingers of red sunlight cast long shadows from the mounded vegetation.

'I hope you didn't mind this sudden summons, Abbot.' Lucas Ferand rubbed his hands together, perhaps a trifle nervously.

'Of course not, Rector. I rather looked forward to seeing you again, in a non-official capacity.'

Lucas nodded and sat down; he cast about for some common subject to open the conversation. 'Well, now we have a new pope, my lord. Have you heard the news?'

The abbot's lips tightened. 'Indeed so. Rector…'

'Please, call me Lucas. Surely we are friends?'

'Lucas. And of course you must call me Rutilius. Lucas, I must mention that I am from the Venice region, you may imagine how I feel that two cardinals had to be imprisoned to ensure the election of Simon de Brie.'

'Ah.' Perhaps not such a good opening gambit.

Lucas was silent for a few moments. Despite the fact that the rector and his countrymen felt it unlikely that God's will was served by a succession of Italian popes, he knew himself to be far from impartial in the matter, he put it to one side. 'I can indeed imagine, Rutilius. Let us leave the matter alone.'

The abbot drew a great breath and nodded. He, however, would never even realise that he was similarly prejudiced, let alone admit to the possibility.

'And back to our own affair. I have news for you, which is not so good. I let you into a secret – I am a distant relation to the Comte up there in his château, if it can be called such, a distant cousin of some sort. It is why I suggested we meet away from the abbey. I would prefer that Girand not know about it.'

The abbot nodded.

'My wife died three years ago and I wished to get away from the world. I had a little money and, in the right place, it bought me an ordination.' He bent towards the abbot for a moment. 'I don't like him much but I persuaded my cousin to let me have the living here and,' he shrugged, 'here I am. Actually, it was a surprise when I discovered that I also had duties at the abbey.'

'A quiet retreat from the world?'

Lucas smiled. 'Just so. Anyway, the news I mentioned,' Lucas carefully interlaced his fingers, 'Girand will be at the abbey tomorrow, probably first thing in the morning, hoping to catch you unawares and scare the daylights out of you.'

'Girand? The Comte?'

Lucas nodded. 'I heard it from…from one of his servants.'

'But why? What does he want?'

'Ah, of course, I should have told you this first.' Lucas shook his head and pulled his hands apart. 'He has heard of the murder. Just the one, the first. Since he is responsible to – whom? Will it be the Duc de Montpellier or someone like that? I do not pay much attention to this sort of thing nowadays.'

The abbot shook his head this time. 'No, nor do I.'

'Anyway, Girand believes you are trying to cover up the situation, and I suppose it is not an unreasonable assumption from his point of view.' Again, he threaded his fingers together and slowly parted them, as the abbot digested the information, and compressed his lips. 'No, I suppose not,' he agreed finally. 'I was hoping to have it all cleared up before he heard of it. As you know, of course.'

'Indeed. I'm afraid you've run out of time, though, and he needs a suspect to put in one of his cells, for the look of the thing, if for no other reason.'

Lucas stood up and returned to the supper table. 'There is a little wine left, Rutilius. Would you care for some more?'

'Does wine help the mind to think? Never mind, it is an excellent idea in any case, my friend.'

Lucas brought the jug over, and two cups. He poured the rich red wine. 'It seals friendships, Rutilius, and to my mind, friendships are what matter in this life.'

The conversation moved to other subjects.

***

'My late husband was a captain. Did you know that, my dear?'

William shook his head.

Madame pointed out the flags that hung, still and dust-laden along the length of the room. 'He brought these home from his campaigns. That's his uniform there, and his sword. What do they call it in the infantry?'

'A sabre?'

'A sabre. That's right, William. He looked very splendid in his uniform, with his sabre.'

They walked on through the hall of memories. On tables, beneath the banners and pennants, were pieces of armour: helmets, breastplates, many of them dented or damaged more seriously; there were also spearheads and swords, often broken ones.

'Were they his, Madame?' William pointed to the armour and weapons.

'Oh no. These belonged to his enemies. My captain only ever took one injury, the one that killed him.'

'I'm sorry, Madame.'

Madame Brisenot ruffled his hair, 'It was a long time ago, now. He was my favourite husband, though. So dashing, so grand on that huge horse of his.'

They reached the end of the hall. The abbot and Lucas were shadows at the far end, barely visible against the red sky beyond the window.

'How long will the abbot be at the abbey, do you think?' Madame Brisenot asked.

William shook his head. 'A few weeks perhaps, until

Abbot Roget returns from his pilgrimage.'

'A dear man. Quite infatuated, though he cannot show it, of course. What of you, William? Do you intend to become a monk?'

'Well,' said William, suddenly aware that he might have a choice in the matter, 'um, the Master would be most disappointed.'

'That's as may be. But there's no doubt that you are more beautiful than sweet Rutilius. It would be a pity to hide such charm away. You should find a young woman and make babies.'

This was not really the order of events that William had understood to be usual. 'Girls take no notice of me. I don't believe I appeal to them.'

Madame Brisenot looked shocked for a moment. 'I find that hard to believe, William.' She turned him to face her. 'Well, hmm. How old are you?'

'Fifteen years, Madame.'

'I think you look much younger than that. Your skin is so fine, those great eyes you have, you look no more than twelve, sometimes.' She nodded. 'That is what it is. Look, not a trace of beard yet.'

She traced a finger along his chin. 'Wait a while and things will change, I promise you, William. Young ladies will discover you and faint with pleasure.'

'Should we be going back now?' he asked, scratching his chin where Madame Brisenot's finger had left an itch.

'Probably. Slowly, anyway.' They turned around. 'I can guess that this conference,' she gestured towards where Lucas and the abbot were now lost in the gloom, 'is about the murder. How do you think Rutilius is managing with that?'

William did not reply immediately. 'Don't tell him I

said this, Madame, but I think he is after the wrong man.'

'And who is that?'

'He seems to believe that Gilbert is responsible.'

'Gilbert? Gilbert de Gignac? I remember him thinking along these lines before.'

William nodded.

Madame snorted in an unladylike manner. 'He should look closer to home than Gilbert; that is what I think.' They walked on and presently she spoke again, 'Oh no. Not Gilbert. You must stop him.'

'I have tried. He made me very angry.'

'I suppose the abbot is not easy to persuade?'

'Not easy at all.'

'And his beliefs? As a man of God? Very staunch?'

'Very,' William nodded firmly. 'Some are not as usual as I'd expect though.' This observation changed the subject.

'Really?' Madame Brisenot sounded interested. 'Tell me.'

'Well, like here. Did the Abbot Roget ever come to dinner here?'

'Well, no.'

'Does he drink wine, eat meat?'

'I see what you mean. You mean that Rutilius is a little unorthodox. Hmm. Well, now I wonder.'

William and the abbot returned to the abbey, both tired, both in a thoughtful mood. Having been told by the abbot of the Comte's expected visit, William found himself unexpectedly looking forward to meeting the man. Here was a man in a similar position to his own father before... The boy avoided finishing the thought. There would be a few retainers, perhaps his master-at-arms would accompany him…

The abbot, for his part, ruminated on how to handle the Comte. Should he perhaps throw him the suspect or would it still be possible to avoid this until everything was explained?

He slowed his pace and turned to William. 'Boy, if I let this Comte have Gilbert, then we cannot question him about the second murder and I'm not willing to inform the Comte about that. Can you think of a way out?'

William looked at the abbot with such disbelief that his master raised his eyebrows and stepped away. 'Is something wrong?'

'You cannot give him Gilbert, Master. I am certain that Gilbert had nothing to do with it, I would swear to that on the Holy Bible.'

'But… on the bible, eh? Hmm.'

The abbot prayed for help before going to bed and afterwards, slept fitfully wondering what Gilbert's involvement might really be. If not Gilbert, then what linked the two murders?

***

They returned to the guestroom after matins to find several unwelcome visitors. There were armed guards at the main entrance, two more outside their room and one who, judging by his arrogant stance and impatience, could only be the Comte. Behind him was another, in whom William recognised a master-at-arms.

The Comte was tall and broad, with shaggy eyebrows frowning down over intense brown eyes. His nose would have been handsome had it not been for a break that had tilted it to the left. His mouth was an angry line mostly hidden by untidy black whiskers. He smelled of old linen and horses, and other less identifiable odours.

William was repelled. This was no brother gentleman to his father. This was a lout, a ruffian. The master-at-arms was only a little better; a man with a long saturnine face and small bright eyes like pebbles of obsidian. The boy stayed in the background as far as he could, drawing as little attention as possible to himself.

The abbot needed no introduction. 'Well, I see you have found me,' he said in as brisk a tone as he could manage. 'What can I do for you?'

With the master-at-arms in tow, the Comte followed them in to the room. Here he untied his cloak and tossed it over a chair. 'You aren't Abbot Roget.' He shook the loose chain mail shirt and propped his backside on the table. He folded his arms.

'I have to admit that I am not.'

'Then who are you?'

'I am Abbot Rutilius, special envoy from the Council of Cardinals, at Avignon, with responsibility for the financial running of the abbeys, monasteries and priories to which the Council appoint me.'

'Wounds! That's a mouthful but it doesn't seem to cover withholding evidence of murder.' The Comte grinned, and his breath would have extinguished the holiest candle in the abbey. 'Does it?'

'No evidence has been withheld. All is documented.' The abbot's stomach groaned. 'And can't this wait until a more civilised hour? I've not yet breakfasted.'

'It will do you good, Abbot. God's wounds, fellow, you'd look a lot healthier if Lent lasted six months.' He was about to poke the abbot in his paunch but thought better of it. 'Very well, then. This murder, tell me all about it.'

With deliberate movements, the abbot seated himself as far from the Comte as possible and related to him all that he knew of the murder.

'The weapon has not been found?'

'Indeed, it has. Boy,' the abbot called to William, 'be good enough to show the murder weapon to my lord.'

William went to the table and found the twist of paper with the broken pin inside it. He unwrapped the pin and showed it to the Comte.

'That's it? That's all there is?'

The abbot tapped the back of his neck. 'Between the vertebrae. Quite sufficient. Death would have been nearly instantaneous, I'm told.'

'Hmm. And suspects?'

The abbot met William's gaze for an instant. 'There are no credible suspects at the moment.'

'No. I can't say that that's surprising. Between getting down on your knees every quarter-hour and confessing each other's sins, you'd hardly have time to find a suspect, would you?'

The abbot bristled. 'We do not confess each other's sins, my lord. That is between the priest and the brother.'

'Well, names, Abbot. I want names. Anyone at all connected with the business.' He looked at the broken pin he'd been given, and tossed it back on to the table with a grimace of distaste. 'Any women involved? This sort of killing looks like a woman's work to me.'

'No women. There are two lay workers at the shrine.' The names of Marcel and Gilbert would quickly become known to the Comte; it would serve no useful purpose to pretend he did not know. He gave the names. 'If you want a woman to question, your daughter prays there regularly.'

The Comte de Fossard was momentarily taken aback. 'God's wounds, Abbot, is that where she prays? We've a chapel at home, no need for her to tramp all that way.'

Rutilius shrugged. 'That's all I know.'

'It's precious little. From where do they hail?'

'The lay workers? From St. Jean de Fos.'

'Both of them? Well, we'll take them and get the truth out before you can recite your catechism, Abbot.' The Comte picked up his cloak and swung it around his shoulders despite the warmth of the early morning. 'Ramon, get the men together. I want to go down to St. Jean at once and find these people.'

He turned back to the abbot again. 'My daughter praying, you say?'

Rutilius nodded.

'Doesn't sound like Anna-Marie.' He shook his head. 'Abbot, doubtless we'll see each other again.'

CHAPTER THIRTEEN

'What an unpleasant man,' said the abbot, when they were alone again. 'Open the windows and the door. Let the air blow through and clear this reek.'

William finished wrapping up the broken pin, and hurried to let the wind sweeten the place.

'And check that breakfast is on its way, boy. That fellow has made me very hungry. Oh, and boy.'

'Master?'

'Do I seem fat to you?'

'Fat, Master? You?' William's tone was one of such amazement that no more needed to be said.

Brother Giles waited until the Comte and his men were well clear before bringing along the food. The abbot and the acolyte ate heartily as they considered what should be done next. The abbot drummed his fingers among the crumbs of breakfast. 'The Comte has no conception of priority, boy. Murder may be serious but this abbey still has to be managed.'

'Of course, Master.'

'I think we shall see the kitchen this morning and talk to the people there. We shall need the records, of course, some paper, ink, pens…'

Thus, they followed in Brother Giles's wake as he took their empty tray back to the kitchen, beyond the refectory, William as laden as the kitchener.

The kitchen was a cavernous space with a hearth large enough to heat a half-dozen kettles at once. The air was steamy and warm, a mélange of smells and aromas and taints, a chronicle of the countless meals made here over the past four centuries, a richer version of the waft exuded by Brother Giles's habit.

There were three people there in addition to Brother Giles himself and the youngster who had accompanied him to open doors along the way. He introduced them one by one. 'This is Francis.'

Francis was a plump monk with gravy stains down the front of his habit, and a perpetual smile on his round face. 'M'lord,' he said, his smile widening briefly to a grin, a chuckle and then a smile once more. He scratched his pate through the fringe of curls and continued with his task of chopping leeks.

'And this, Edouard, who comes each morning from St Guilhem. Now, Edouard will interest you, m'lord, because he is our record-keeper. He writes up all our purchases and our few sales, records victuals, which occasionally have to be discarded. That sort of thing.'

He turned back. 'M'lord Abbot is engaged in accounting for all our dealings, so your work is rather important.'

Edouard raised his eyebrows. He was an older man, early fifties, and appeared frail enough to need a heavy stone in his purse against a chance gust of wind blowing him away. 'The day-to-day things,' he offered by way of explanation.

'This is Matthias. Matthias is our baker. He has already done most of his work before we attend matins.'

'And is Matthias from the village too?' the abbot asked, taking in everything.

'Certainly not,' Brother Giles responded. 'Beneath this dusty smock is a habit as black as yours, my lord.'

'Well, thank you for acquainting me with everyone here. I shall relish my food all the more. However, I think there is one more person to meet.'

'Ah.' Brother Giles's eyebrows rose. 'Of course there is. Young Thomas.'

'Another from the village?'

'No. A novitiate. Came to us last year, around this time, actually. Does a little of everything.' Brother Giles turned to Edouard. 'Where will he be at the moment?'

'The refectory. He usually manages to spend an hour in cleaning the tables.' Evidently, from the tone, there was a certain discontent in the kitchen.

Brother Giles shrugged his great shoulders. 'Claude, will you go and fetch Thomas, please?'

The kitchen boy nodded and disappeared

'Thomas does tend towards laziness, I'm afraid,' he admitted, sadly.

'Bone idleness is the phrase I would use,' Edouard sniffed.

'And I think it unlikely that he will ever become a monk.'

The abbot smiled. 'Not everyone is suited to the life. Now, Brother Giles, when there is anything to give to the poor, do you do that?'

'No, not me.' The kitchener shook his head. 'Usually, it's Brother Francis.'

Thomas entered behind Claude. He wore a long apron over his habit, which was a little large for him, hiding his hands from sight. The abbot looked at each one. Of them all, Edouard was the only one who appeared nervous.

The abbot took up the stack of bills that William had sorted out, and laid it on an empty table. 'These are all for food either donated freely to the poor of St. Guilhem, or sold at a very low price.'

All of the old kitchen staff nodded. The abbot divided the pile into two parts at a marker he had inserted previously.

'The larger bundle is for bread, flour, corn, that sort of thing. All free.' He put that bundle down and brandished the other. 'These are for meat and fish, all with a price, not a high one, but a price.'

'I'm sorry,' Brother Giles interrupted, 'I don't think I get the point, my lord. Meat and fish?'

'Meat and fish, Brother Giles. Surprising quantities.' He turned to Brother Francis. 'Brother, how often do you give meat and fish away?'

'Why, not very often, my lord.'

'When was the last time?'

Brother Francis tried to remember, with frowns of concentration marring his moon-like face. 'No, my lord, I can't remember any.'

'No. It doesn't seem likely.' The abbot turned now to Edouard, the servant who kept the records in his spidery writing. 'You keep the records, Edouard? Can you shed light on this?'

'I write what I am told to write, m'lord. Five loaves, a bushel of corn… Whatever is disbursed.' Edouard's tone was defiant.

The abbot read from some of the notes. 'And a dozen carp, a whole basket of chickens, plucked, a little rotten. Do you remember those?'

'I can't say I do, m'lord.'

The abbot shook his head. 'The carp were recorded two weeks ago, the chicken five weeks since.'

'Not by me, my lord.'

'Well, there is an easy way to tell who is responsible.

Edouard and Thomas can write. Who else can?'

'I can, if I write big enough,' said Brother Giles.

'William, if you please.'

William handed out a small piece of paper to each of the three.

'Now, each of you; write the word *carp*, please.'

He watched carefully as they wrote. The novice, with his tongue caught between his teeth, and obviously labouring, Edouard, in two quick scrawls, Brother Giles trying to write small enough to fit on to the scrap of paper.

'William.'

William collected the three samples and laid them on the table. The abbot laid several of the suspect bills alongside. Both of them compared the results.

'Brother Giles's is obviously different,' William said in a low voice. 'Even apart from the size, the letters are shaped differently.'

The abbot answered in the same low tones. 'As I feared, I can't tell between the others, both are too untutored. Did you see how hard it seemed for Thomas to write, though?'

'Yes, not an easy task.'

'Or he did not wish it to seem so.'

'You think he was acting?'

'We'll see.'

They turned round. The abbot looked at them all in turn, lingered on Thomas, as he asked, 'Well, Edouard?'

'My lord?' The words came out as a sort of gasp and the abbot blinked in surprise. Edouard had not been his suspect, he had been using Edouard to cover his observation of Thomas and, indeed, Thomas had taken in a huge breath of relief at Edouard's apprehension.

Now he was at a loss. He shook the bunch of notes. 'You admit to forging these things?' Behind him, he heard Brother Giles's intake of surprised breath.

'No, my lord. I do no such thing.'

This was not turning out as he had expected. He believed Edouard's denial. 'You're sure?'

'Absolutely. Of course I'm sure.'

'Well, Thomas, what about you?' And this time, the abbot knew that his first instinct had been correct after all.

'What? What do you mean, my lord?' He might well not have spoken a word. The sheen of sweat on his brow, the shaking of his fingers as he fiddled with the pen; these spoke far louder than words.

'Still, there is just one thing that puzzles me.'

'My lord?' His voice became a little stronger, as though the abbot admitting to being puzzled improved his chances of escaping retribution.

'Why such an obvious falsehood as this one?' He put a single record down on the table where Thomas could read it.

Thomas looked at it, reading the words slowly. 'Madame Brisenot? Who is that?'

'You don't know? Surely you do, from the village? Why use a name at all, anyway? All the others are unnamed.'

'That has nothing to do with me. Nothing at all.'

'Come, Thomas, admit it. Why did you try to bring the name of a citizen into disrepute?'

'I don't admit it, the others may…'

But it was too late. The trap had been set, Thomas had sprung it.

'I'm sure you know what I mean, Thomas. These are

your fabrications, aren't they?'

'Not willingly done, my lord. I was made to do it.'

'Really? Why? Explain to me.'

'It's Master Dondo, he takes game from the Comte's lands and brings it here.'

'And...?'

The abbot took Thomas to the pantry and extracted the full story. Afterwards, when he was locked in the crypt until his fate could be decided, the abbot explained it all to an astonished Brother Giles.

'There is a poacher, perhaps more than one, who takes game or fish from the Comte's estate. He brings it here, to Thomas who exchanges it with your food stocks; chickens, carp, pigeons.'

Brother Giles was aghast. 'All this right under my nose?'

'As you say, under your nose.

'The poacher goes away and uses the food or, perhaps, shares it with his friends. Thomas then sells the more valuable food to wealthier citizens. He has a small list of customers. He will tell you if you ask him.'

'Well, my lord. In my own kitchen! He obviously has no intention of joining the congregation, of professing.'

'No, you were quite right about that. It's odd really, if he had not tried to fix the records, it might have been much longer before anyone noticed that livestock was disappearing.'

'Too much spice in the sauce?' Brother Giles grasped the abbot's meaning. They both laughed, a little ruefully.

'What I am not sure about is this one: the one with Madame Brisenot's name on it. I thought at first that it was, perhaps, Edouard who had put it in the records to make me notice that something was going on.'

'I don't think he would think of such a thing.'

'Having met him, I don't either. It's this note that is puzzling.'

'So, that one will remain a mystery?'

'Exactly so, or perhaps Thomas over-egged the pudding?'

Brother Giles placed his hands on the table and pushed himself to his feet. 'A novice's error, my lord. So, Thomas and the poacher were using us to, sort of, clean up their dirty business, weren't they?'

'A laundry for thieves, Brother.'

'Brother Francis,' said Brother Giles. 'There are some pies just come out of the oven this morning.'

'Yes, Brother, I recollect.'

'Bring two of them, will you?'

Brother Francis did as he was bidden and brought two of the hot pies.

'Oh, m'lord…' Brother Giles pushed them towards the abbot on a little wooden tray. 'Just in case you should feel hungry during the day.'

He looked up. 'And something to wrap them in, Brother Francis. The gravy is leaking.'

'How thoughtful. How very thoughtful of you. Boy, perhaps you would carry them for us. Would you?'

Francis found a scrap of muslin and wrapped the savouries before passing them on to William.

'Hmm. I think that was quite satisfactory, boy.'

'Master?' William was still sullen, when he remembered to be.

'Edouard is not a happy man, though. I'm sure it was he who put that note concerning Madame Brisenot in the records.'

'Master, I fear that we shall never know.' William's

voice definitely carried a tone of disinterest on this occasion.

'And careful with those pies, boy, you're dribbling gravy everywhere you go.' The abbot looked at him long enough to convey his resentment and sorrow.

Accompanied only by their shadows, they walked through the cloister in silence. Gradually, William's scorn receded, the abbot's ire cooled.

'I'm sorry, Master. I have been angry and I had no cause.'

The abbot pursed his lips and took time to think about a reply. 'Let the matter rest there then, my son. We need speak of it no more.'

They walked onward, taking comfort in each other's presence.

'Abbot, my lord Abbot!' It was the prior, labouring to overtake them with one foot taking a longer stride than the other, giving him a lopsided gait.

The abbot stopped and turned to face him. 'Prior Josephus. A beautiful morning.'

'No doubt, no doubt, my lord Abbot. My lord, I hear a rumour concerning Brother Anno's death.'

'Well, Prior, I have to say that it is no longer just a rumour. It is fact.'

Josephus's face seemed to somehow crumple in on itself. 'Another killing? Was there something terrible about those two? Twins, a black and a white child from the same womb?'

'At the same time! No, Prior, I don't think so, unless God has made a commandment that forbids such a thing, without my hearing of it.'

This was sufficiently near blasphemy to jolt the prior out of his sudden despair. 'Abbot, such words!'

'Then, let us not think such thoughts, Prior. The "something terrible" is the person who did this, and I fear he has gone and we shall never bring him to justice now.'

'You know who did it? I have heard it said that you know this, too.'

'Have you? Well, proof is hard to come by, but I feel Gilbert de Gignac is the one.'

The prior was silent for some time. He put out a hand to lean on the nearest pillar, and shook his head. 'This is why you wished to see him? You didn't say, you know.' He took a deep breath. 'Gilbert. I can't believe it. I hear you say it but I cannot believe it.'

'Well, we shall see. God will disclose all in His own good time. Now tell me about something else. Come over here and sit in the sun, just where we sat the other day and we can talk.' He looked at William. 'Boy, you are leaking gravy, go and put Brother Giles's gifts somewhere cool; on the windowsill so that the whole place does not smell of pigeon pie.' The abbot felt through his purse. 'Here's the key.'

They sat down while William hastened off with the pies.

'Pigeon pies, Abbot?'

'I know, I know. Brother Giles has conceived this idea that if he feeds me at every opportunity, I shall make a special report to Roget saying what a very fine fellow he is. He forgets that I am a frugal man and that I eat only enough to keep me going.' The abbot shook his head.

'How the world misunderstands us, Prior.'

Prior Josephus decided to say no more on the subject. 'You wanted to talk about something?'

'Yes. Brother Sylvan.'

'The prior threw up his hands. 'I am tired of Brother Sylvan.'

'And I am quite sick of him. Is he good enough to send down to the shrine?'

'He is an average sort of monk. Certainly, now that Abbo and Anno are with us no longer, he is the most skilled in dealing with domestic animals.'

'Then I am tempted to tell him to go, and be done with his tiresome inquiries; get him out of our way. Still, there is one other thing.'

'Hmm?'

'There is something on his mind that he prefers to keep to himself. He is evasive.'

'An understatement, my lord.'

'Well. I think we'll let him go, but I'll send a letter to Marcel to keep an eye on his behaviour. We might find what it's all about then.'

'Marcel?'

'The lay brother, or whatever he is, at St. Jean de Fos.'

'Ah yes, that Marcel. Neither one thing nor the other, at the moment. He has enough put by to pay for burial and prayers, he intends to enter our congregation when he becomes infirm.'

The abbot nodded slowly. 'This is none of my concern, but I take it the Abbot Roget is content with the arrangement?'

'Quite so. So, back to Brother Sylvan. We let him go?'

'Agreed, Prior.'

The abbot entered the guestrooms to the sound of recriminations.

'Master, praise God you're here.'

'What is going on?'

'When I got back, Brother Sylvan was going through our boxes of records. When I tried to stop him, he pushed me away, and the pies from Brother Giles are all over the floor.'

'It was an accident.' Brother Sylvan stood with his arms at his sides with hands tucked up inside his sleeves. 'And only one pie fell to the floor, the other is there.' He pointed to a slightly battered pie on the table.

The other pie was slowly collapsing into a gravy-coloured mud in William's hands.

'Get out, Brother Sylvan. You may come to see me later when I am calm enough to make no rash decisions.'

'But you said to come to see you.'

'I said after you have finished the day's work. It still lacks two hours to midday. But now, I want no further disturbance, do you understand?'

Brother Sylvan scuttled out of the room and closed the door quietly.

'He must learn that this abbey does not dance to his tune.'

William smiled. 'It might diminish his conceit a little.'

'It might,' the abbot agreed cautiously. 'What is the matter with the fellow, anyway? Did he just lose his reason?'

'Master, I came in and found him looking through our boxes. There were stacks of notes all over the place. Look! I was trying to put them back in some order when he managed to knock the pie off the table.'

'Well, you'd better wrap that one up again and put it out of the way.'

'Yes, Master. Can you see the wrapping in which I brought them?'

They looked on the table, among the boxes, on the

floor. The cloth was nowhere to be seen.

'No, it's rolled under something. Here, use this paper. I'm sure a bit of ink won't harm our innards.'

And when the pie was set aside and the boxes tidied up, the abbot sat down heavily. 'I really don't know what that was all about. Perhaps Brother Sylvan had some sort of fit. I shall be pleased to see the back of him and I know the prior will as well.'

William wiped up the last of the gravy from the floor where a dozen ants had already discovered this insect manna from heaven. 'You'll let him go to the shrine?'

'The quicker the better, boy. I've agreed with the prior to get him out of the way and send a letter to Marcel with instructions to keep watch on him.'

The rest of the morning passed tolerably well, the only annoyance was the loss of the decorative end to the pin, which he had wanted Madame Brisenot to see and to comment upon. It was nowhere to be found.

'It will be in one of these boxes, I expect. Never mind.'

Finally, Brother Sylvan reappeared. A knock, and a face around the edge of the door. 'Er, my lord…?'

'Brother Sylvan.' The abbot looked up over the sheaf of papers he was reading. 'I am still in two minds about letting you go; indeed I wonder about the state of *your* mind. You seem to me to lack the temperament for a task of this kind.'

Brother Sylvan's face reflected a number of emotions. 'I assure you, my lord…'

The abbot ploughed on. 'However, I have discussions planned for this evening. My assistant,' the abbot nodded towards William, 'has evidence that must be examined and deliberated upon – possibly with others. So there is no possibility of a decision in your case, not until after that.'

'But…'

'No buts, Brother Sylvan.'

Brother Sylvan withdrew and closed the door.

'Evidence and discussions, Master?'

'I'm sure there will be things to discuss tonight, boy. Let Brother Sylvan realise that we are busy people and that our business is more important than his. I shall let him go but it will do him no harm for him to kick his heels for a while.'

'Ah, m'lord Abbot,' the prior poked his head around the door and knocked simultaneously. 'We have two visitors come to see you.'

'Visitors? Not that awful Comte again?'

'No, no. Marcel and Gilbert. You will remember that I made inquiries about Gilbert and he had, it was said, left the village?'

'I do remember. And they have come here?'

'I have put them in the novices' day room. It seemed most appropriate.'

'Well thank you, Prior. Thank you, indeed. I will go there at once.' He turned to William, who was still at work on the records. 'God works wonderfully, does He not, boy?'

The abbot departed. Once out of earshot, he hummed a few lines from one of his favourite chants. He hummed it very well and he smiled. *Now we shall see*, he thought and rubbed his hands together.

Marcel rose as the abbot entered the low-ceilinged room and gave Gilbert's shoulder a tug so that he got to his feet too.

'How nice to see you both this fine day. Please, please

be seated, both of you. What brings you here?'

'We came to see you, m'lord,' said Marcel. 'The prior had sent to the village for Gilbert to come and speak to you, but he has been away. It seemed a good idea to come as soon as he returned.'

'Of course. I do remember.' He turned to Gilbert, beaming at him. 'So you've been away? And just returned?'

'Mm,' answered Gilbert, rather less ebullient than the abbot. 'Came back last night, well, afternoon, really.' Gone were the frowns and glares; in their place, the man had an asinine grin on his face, his mouth squashed into a long line as though all his teeth had come out.

The abbot still did not like Gilbert and feared he might be over-compensating in his manner. 'May I ask where you've been?' he asked more sternly than before.

'You may ask, m'lord. I may tell you. In fact I went to Gignac.'

'Gignac, your home. Far away?'

'An afternoon's ride. My sister still lives there. She has just borne her third child. A daughter.' Gilbert grew quite animated. 'Things went very well, Marie-Louise was with her, and now I have another niece.'

'Marie-Louise?'

'Ah. My friend.'

'Is she still there?'

'No, I brought her back yesterday.'

'Would Marie-Louise be able to confirm your movements?'

Gilbert grew suddenly hostile. 'Why should my travels need confirming? Have I been accused of some terrible act while I have been away?'

The abbot put out his hands, palms down, and made

soothing gestures. 'Gilbert, calm yourself. No, there has been no accusation but the Comte has heard of the murder and was out looking for you and for Marcel this morning.'

'With his guard?' Marcel asked, his eyes suddenly wide, his voice squeaky with apprehension.

'Exactly.'

'We saw them. We were at the tavern when they came.'

'And they interrogated you?' the abbot asked.

Marcel shook his head. 'We left by the back way and hid under the Devil's Bridge.'

'Well, somehow, we must establish your innocence before they do find you. Can this Marie-Louise vouch for you, Gilbert?'

'I don't want her interviewed. The neighbours would make assumptions and imagine the worst.'

'Surely, to clear your name…'

'No. Marie-Louise is not to be involved.'

The abbot sighed, shook his head. 'It may make things more difficult for you.'

'I have nothing to hide, nothing. The Comte cannot take me if I have done nothing wrong.'

'I hope you are right, Gilbert. Now,' he turned to Marcel, 'we are sending Brother Sylvan to remain at the shrine. I understand he has some experience of work there?'

'Some,' nodded Marcel.

Gilbert murmured something under his breath.

'No, no,' Marcel replied. 'I'm sure you're mistaken,' he said to Gilbert.

'What was that?' asked the abbot.

'Little reprobate,' Gilbert's scowl suggested he had said something much worse, 'Fussing around that girl who prays all the time in the Lady Chapel. Told me he had to exorcise her once.'

'Brother Sylvan exorcised her?' The abbot had forgotten about this until now but remembered that he had the impression of Brother Abbo being responsible for that episode.

'I can guess what he meant,' William said in quiet voice, 'and it wasn't exorcism.'

Gilbert nodded. 'There goes a wise head on young shoulders.'

'I saw them in the cloister the other day; they mentioned Anno.'

'Here? In the abbey? A woman?' The abbot could hardly believe his ears.

William nodded.

'We shall discuss this shortly, boy. However, I cannot believe he had anything to do with exorcism.'

'That's just it, Master, not exorcism but…'

'Enough. I do have reservations about him. He seems over excitable…'

'Excitable? Excuse me, m'lord,' Marcel's eyebrows rose towards the brim of his hat, 'we are discussing Brother Sylvan? Shortish, fierce eyes?'

'Now you mention it, yes. A very intense gaze. But that's the one. Unreliable, rude too. Perhaps excitable is the wrong word, short-tempered.'

'Aha, yes. That's him. Short-tempered when he can't get his own way.'

'Well, Marcel, we'll see how it goes. Unfortunately, he is the last of our monks with anything like practice with animals. Keep an eye on him and let me know how it works out.' The abbot stood up. 'For now, you must stay here. I'll speak to Prior Josephus about a safe place for you both. Marcel…'

'M'lord?' Marcel stood too.

'Walk with me.'

A small distance away from Gilbert, he spoke again. 'Marcel, I tell you this in confidence, I am not altogether happy with Gilbert's story. He had the opportunity to murder, and we hear that he has a partiality for women; possibly he has been importuning that young girl we spoke about, I can imagine Brother Abbo having to reprimand him and incurring his wrath.'

'Gilbert?' Marcel shook his head. 'No, no, m'lord. This womanising you hear of is just talk. There is only Marie-Louise and the infant.' Afraid that he had said too much, he added, 'Not that there's anything improper, of course, nothing at all. I'm sure there's nothing at all.' He lifted his hat and scratched his head. 'What of this second murder? Of Anno. He cannot be implicated in that, can he?'

The abbot paused. *What was the reason for that?* he wondered. *There must have been a reason. Ah!* 'They were twins, Marcel. What Abbo knew, he would tell to Anno. Gilbert – I mean *whoever* killed Anno – could have come here and lain in wait for him.'

Marcel frowned. 'When would Abbo have come here to the abbey, or Anno gone to the shrine, for that matter? They might see one another on a saint's day but that would be all. I do find this difficult to believe but,' Marcel nodded to himself, 'you are a clever man, my lord Abbot. Who am I to cast doubt?'

'Just be on your guard, Marcel. We are dealing with a violent man, whoever he is. Now, I will give instruction for you to be hidden in the crypt.'

They walked slowly back to the guestrooms. William

bristled with anger. He would prove Brother Sylvan guilty, and he knew just how to do it.

As the abbot walked, he wondered about William's story and about his appraisal of Gilbert. Could he have been mistaken? The concept was difficult to accept. *Tomorrow, they would go to St. Jean de Fos and speak to Marie-Louise whether Gilbert desired it or no,* he told himself, *that would settle the matter once and for all.*

'I do beg your pardon.' The abbot rebounded from his collision with the rector. 'Why…'

'Rutilius. A pleasant surprise, if rather a bumpy one.' Lucas Ferand smiled. 'How are you today?'

'A little rushed, but otherwise coping, thank you. I hadn't realised you would be here.'

'Nor I until my housekeeper reminded me at breakfast this morning. Confession. For Prior Josephus.'

The abbot nodded. 'And has he much to confess? Perhaps I shouldn't ask.'

Lucas rocked his head from side to side. 'Not as you or I might think of it, but he is a simple soul. A hurtful remark is as serious as an argument might be to one of my villagers. All is relative.'

'Exactly.' The abbot shook his head. 'Were everything as simple. However, this chance meeting is very timely. Do you have plans for this evening?'

'Nothing out of the usual, really. I might go to the tavern, it is often easier to speak to my flock there than at the church.'

'Now that is an excellent idea, Lucas. May I meet you there and seek your advice?'

The rector agreed, and they parted.

Later, William returned to the guestrooms. 'Ah, boy, where have you been? It's almost time for prayers.'

'I hadn't forgotten, Master.' And he smiled. A chance meeting with Brother Sylvan had cleared William's surly mood, he recalled their conversation and his smile became a grin…

'I saw you and Anna-Marie, you know.'

Brother Sylvan looked both ways along the corridor and took a bunch of William's habit in his fist. 'What are you talking about?' he grunted and pushed the other back until he came up against the wall.

'In the cloister.'

'It would be good for you to forget what you saw, little pig. Else you'll end up sausage meat.'

'I have to speak to the abbot tonight. He's expecting me for vespers now, but after the evening meal I have to talk to him then. Don't you remember?'

William was shaking when he got away, but the feeling was distinctly satisfying. *Watch him wriggle now*, he thought.

After vespers, the abbot and the acolyte made their way towards the village.

'You have them hidden, Master?'

Rutilius nodded. 'In the crypt. They can look after our kitchen fraudster.'

'I thought you were certain that Gilbert was the murderer.'

'And so I am… nearly. This is abbey business, though. Nothing to do with the Comte de Fossard. If he comes calling again, I don't want either of them discovered.'

By starlight and the noise of merriment, they found their way to the tavern. Inside, it was crowded but Jean Claude noticed them at the door and welcomed them. When they asked after the priest, he took them through the throng to a small alcove occupied by Lucas Ferand and two men of the village.

At sight of the abbot, the rector stood, asking the villagers to leave so that he might speak to the abbot but Rutilius gestured them to remain. 'It may be that these two worthies can help me,' he explained.

They sat, and Jean Claude brought them great leather cups of sweet ale. 'Your healths,' he said to the abbot and to William. 'Hmm, I hope I have not given the boy more than he can manage.'

'Don't worry,' grinned Lucas. 'I'm sure we can find someone to help him out if necessary.'

All of them drank and the two village men looked questioningly at the abbot.

'Do either of you know Gilbert and Marcel who attend to the shrine at St. Jean de Fos?'

'Gilbert de Gignac?' asked one. 'Lame and rather puffed-up?'

The abbot nodded. 'The same. Perhaps a little puffed-up. Just a little.'

'Yes. I know the man and Marcel; yes, we know him too.'

'These two are our guests at the abbey.'

The two men and Lucas all showed surprise.

'The Comte Girand de Fossard is anxious to interview them.'

Consternation showed in the villagers' faces.

'I would rather he didn't.'

'Aha, it's a hidey-hole you want?' said the talkative one of the pair.

'Exactly so.' The abbot drank deeply and wiped the froth from his upper lip. 'A hidey-hole. Can one be found?'

They looked at each other. ‘The caves?’ asked one of the other.

‘The caves,’ agreed the other.

‘Deep caves,’ they explained. ‘Give them food and candles and a warm cloak, a warm cloak each…’

‘Two warm cloaks each because the cave is cold.’

‘The Comte could search until the last trump is sounded and would never find them.’

The abbot looked across at Lucas. ‘That sounds excellent. Tomorrow, we must put this plan to use.’ To the two villagers, ‘I’m grateful for your advice, gentlemen.’

All five of them drank to the success of the plan to hide Marcel and Gilbert. They drank again, to a lack of success for the Comte. A third time to the abbot’s health, to … well, they drank to the priest, to the prior, the innkeeper, the quality of the beer. Just to be certain, several toasts were drunk twice, perhaps more than twice.

CHAPTER FOURTEEN

The abbey was a blaze of light in the darkness as they returned from the village; candles were alight behind every window. Movement was everywhere; even outside, monks were going about in twos and threes with blazing links.

They ran the last few yards, the abbot puffing and almost managing to keep up with his acolyte. The gate was shut; a burly monk stood guard.

'What's happening, Brother?' The abbot waited while the other peered into his face to identify him.

'Oh, m'lord. It's young Milos, someone took a pole to him and nearly killed him.'

'Milos?' The abbot could not place him.

'The young boy,' William said. 'You know him, altar boy when the priest comes.'

'Oh merciful God in Heaven. Why? Do we know anything?'

'Nobody knows, m'lord. He's unconscious, he may yet die.'

'Let me in, Brother. William, go to the house of Madame Brisenot and get Georges to take you to the rector. Bring him here to give last rites, in case, you know…'

For once, the abbot's size was a help rather than a hindrance. He hurried along the cloister to the infirmary where he assumed young Milos would be; brothers and servants moved quickly out of his way without a second thought. He thrust through a heavy door into the small sickroom and there was the boy, his head in bandages, his face held no more colour than the sheet he lay upon.

Brother August sat at his side.

Rutilius halted and panted at the bedside. 'The poor boy.'

He regained a little breath. 'Can anyone tell me anything about what happened, and why is everyone rushing around like this?'

August shook his head. 'If he recovers, he may tell us something, but often such an injury drives away the memory of it.'

'And the brothers… oh,' the abbot had realised, 'they are searching?'

'For an intruder, m'lord. Yes.'

'There is nothing I can do elsewhere, I will pray. I shall be more use that way than any other.'

The abbot eased himself down on to his knees. 'Brother, something to kneel on, please. The stone is very hard.'

Brother August reached across to another cot and pulled a bolster off it.

'Thank you.' The abbot clasped his hands and shut his eyes, but still, he saw the pale, waxy face, the bandage with the tiny trickle of blood and, when he was able to calm himself enough to speak to his God, his first word was *why?*

Half an hour passed by and he was disturbed again.

'Your pardon, Rutilius, I'm sorry, my lord Abbot. I came with William, as you asked.'

'The boy, Rector. You know him, I think.'

The abbot rose and put the bolster back, while the priest washed his hands and otherwise ordered himself. He would give extreme unction and perform the last rites so that the boy would be properly prepared should the Lord decide to take him.

William came soon after the priest had completed his work and sat on the other side of the cot from Brother August. His eyes were red with tears, he looked wretched, and his mood was beyond the abbot's understanding. Time passed slowly and Milos's condition remained unchanged.

'Is the rector still here?' William asked.

The abbot nodded. 'In the church. You wish to see him?'

William nodded and got up. 'Do you mind if I leave you for a while?'

'Of course not, boy. At a time like this, you must seek whatever help you may.'

At the back of the church, William spoke to the priest. 'I need to confess my sins.'

The rector nodded and sat down on the end of the bench. 'Tell me what sins you have committed.'

'I have caused injury to my friend, Milos.'

'I don't understand. Both of us know that you were nowhere near here when this awful thing was done.'

'Rector, I was the cause. My pride was the cause.'

Lucas took one of William's limp hands into his own. 'William, you are going to have to explain this so that I can understand.'

'I told Milos of my suspicions about the murderer.'

'Why did you tell him this?'

'I thought that Milos might spread the story a little and the murderer would do something stupid. My master says that God wills criminals to lose their reason, so that we know them.'

The priest thought about this for a while. 'And young Milos's beating was the something stupid?'

William nodded.

'So, why should the murderer beat Milos? He was only telling what he'd heard.'

'He was mistaken for me, I think. I also reminded Brother Sylvan that I had to talk to the abbot about evidence tonight.'

Lucas pinched his lips together and tried to make sense of William's confession. 'So this beating was to stop you telling Rutilius anything?'

'That's right.'

'Brother Sylvan, did you say? Why tell Brother Sylvan that, about your meeting?'

'Because it is he who is the murderer, not Gilbert as the abbot thinks.'

'Come, come now. I agree that Gilbert seems unlikely for several reasons, but Brother Sylvan? Why ever for?'

'He is having this *thing* with the Comte's daughter. Um, you know; an affair.'

'Goodness, are you certain?'

'I saw them kissing. They met in the cloisters.'

'This gets more preposterous by the minute, William. Let's just concentrate on what we know.'

William shook his head and showered tears across the rector's clasped hands.

'If whoever it was beat Milos thought he was you, then that is not your fault. Even if this was the same person who murdered the twin monks, it was not your fault. Milos's injuries are not your responsibility. All right?'

William heaved a great sigh of relief.

'However, you are perfectly right about your sin of pride, William, and also of spreading falsehoods.'

William nodded. 'But the abbot suspects Gilbert of the murders and I know that it was not him.'

'I understand, but that is for the abbot to decide, not you. In this instance, since you have recognised your own sin and are obviously repentant of it, you will say your rosary twice, night and morning, until Milos recovers.'

'But he might not, sir.'

'But I am sure that he will. I may be wrong but I do not think so.'

Back at the sickroom, the infirmarium, the prior struggled sideways through the door, leaning towards the sickbed.

'Well, have they found anything?' the abbot asked quietly.

The prior nodded and became a little more vertical. 'We have come across the weapon, m'lord. A pole as thick as my forearm, with fresh blood on it.'

'Where was it found? Where was the boy found?'

'Near your chamber, actually, my lord. That short corridor that leads past the privy to the woodshed, the pole was just outside. Incidentally, your door was not locked. I realise there's nothing of intrinsic value there, but the records you have should not be so accessible.'

It was the nearest that the prior had come to censure and the abbot realised that the monk was near the limit of his fortitude. 'Thank you, Prior. I will make certain that it does not occur again.'

Rutilius left him and returned to the guestrooms. Along the way, the bustle of activity throughout the abbey could still be felt but it was abating. Within his rooms, the atmosphere was calm, and cool, he shivered momentarily. There was a dim glow among the half-burnt logs and grey ash. The abbot knelt down stiffly and poked at the embers of the fire, though he succeeded only in extinguishing the little that was left.

That was how William found him, kneeling among the coals that escaped from the grate, staring unhappily at the cooling ashes. William patted the older man on the shoulder and wordlessly urged him to shuffle back to a chair, while he blew a small glow to crackle into life.

'Are you hungry, Master? Thirsty?'

The abbot smiled and shook his head. 'Just miserable that all this should happen while the abbey is my responsibility, I suppose.'

'But it started before we came, Master. Brother Abbo was dead before we reached St. Jean de Fos.'

'That's so, boy. You're right. Let's go to bed and see if we can sleep.'

William told his rosary beads by firelight. And Anna-Marie did not come to his dreams.

The abbot was still snoring soundly, when William got up long before matins and washed his face. He made his way to the infirmary, saying his rosary along the way and shivering in the slight frost that silvered the grass on the garth. Brother August was not there, but a younger monk was sitting by the cot with a rush light illuminating Milos's face.

'How is he?' William asked.

'Peaceful,' said the other. 'He has moved a little in his sleep and his breathing is even, and when I felt his pulse a while ago, it was good. Not strong, but good.'

'You think he will live?'

'I think that he will. He may not have a memory of the attack but perhaps that is all to the good.'

William nodded and went on to the church for matins

before returning to the guest chamber in a pensive mood. The abbot was sitting hunched over another cold fire as William opened the door, and he hurried to make amends.

'Milos has had a good night. He is still asleep but the signs are good, they say.'

'Well, that's something we must thank our merciful Lord for.'

'Master?'

'Yes, William.'

'I have something to say that will make you very angry.' William hoped that by warning the abbot, the anger might be lessened.

The abbot leaned back in the chair and raised his eyebrows. 'Go on.'

'I said something to Milos that may have put you in danger.'

'Me? Not the youngster?'

'You, Master.'

'And what did you say?'

William told him about the rumour and explained his motive. He decided to keep the goading of Brother Sylvan to himself. 'I thought that if the murderer got to hear, he would do something foolish and betray himself.'

The abbot turned pale. His normally ruddy cheeks almost matched his undershirt. 'The saints preserve us, boy. You have put our lives in jeopardy and for no good reason.'

The abbot considered further and shook his head. 'Gilbert's away from the village, nobody knows he is here. No doubt he is skulking about the place, waiting, biding his time. Now I must spend my time behind locked doors, or find a pair of burly monks to protect me as I go about my duties.'

Again he fell silent, frowning, his eyes unfocussed. 'Merciful Father. This is a confusion. I can't think in a straight line. What about Milos? How is it that his life was almost taken?'

'I thought at first that he had been mistaken for me and that I should be lying there in the infirmary. But it didn't make sense when I talked to the rector about it.'

'The rector? What has he to do with it?'

'I committed a sin, Master, a sin of pride and I went to confess.' William, his eyes overburdened with tears, suddenly began to weep.

'No, you're right in that. It doesn't make sense if the rumour said it was I who knew all about it. Still, rumours change and grow as they travel. We don't know what was being said when it reached Gilbert's ears.'

'Gilbert? Master, Gilbert wouldn't do such a thing. Madame Brisenot said the other day that we should look closer to home.'

'Madame Brisenot? What does Madame Brisenot know about these things? She is good enough to convey to me the thoughts of the villagers but these cannot be confused with facts. No, something tells me that it is Gilbert and, furthermore, that poor Milos's injuries are a part of it all.'

He rose from the soft chair and crossed to the table by the window where the boxes of receipts and purchase notes were stacked. He looked through a number of the boxes without finding what he sought.

William wiped his face on his sleeve. 'Can I help, Master? What are you searching for?'

'That pin, the one that was found in Brother Abbo's clothes. I thought I put both parts in this box here, with the sealing wax and spare pens, but it might have been one of the others.'

They went through every one. In the box of sealing wax and spare pens, the abbot found the sharp end of the pin, the part that had actually killed Brother Abbo. It was twisted in a scrap of paper for protection, but the decorative part had vanished.

'Now that's a puzzle. I didn't think it was important until just now. I realised that it would be useful to show it to Gilbert, see his reaction. And now it's gone, that's really very inconvenient. Or perhaps,' the abbot pondered a moment, 'when you think about it, very convenient for someone. Do you think he was in here, disguised as a monk perhaps, hiding from the searchers?' He snapped his fingers. 'The prior took me to task for leaving the door unlocked.'

He crossed to the door, taking the key from his pocket. He tried it in the lock. 'It's broken! Look, the lock won't turn!' He twisted the heavy key this way and that, the locking bolt did not move. 'This place has been broken into.'

'It must have been broken yesterday morning, Master. Brother Sylvan was in here after we came back from visiting the kitchen. You lock the door when we go out. You gave me the key when I came ahead, I just didn't think when I saw the door was already open.'

'I'm tired of that one.' The abbot shook his head. 'After breakfast, boy, find him and bring him here. The sooner he gets off to the shrine, the better.'

'But that's rewarding him, Master, not punishing.'

'The lesser of two evils, boy. Now, I shall visit the young boy…' For a moment, the abbot was lost for the name, 'Monte? No, Mi…' and then it came to him,

'Milos. Then on to see the prior.'

He had forgotten the need for security, for the moment at least.

Arriving at the doorway, he asked Brother August, 'How is the child?'

In reply, August gestured towards Milos who was sitting up, eating from a bowl of porridge, 'As you see, m'lord. Hungry.'

'That's very pleasing, Brother. Does he remember anything?'

'Do you remember anything, Milos?'

'I'm sure the man wore a habit.'

'There, I felt sure he would be hiding behind such a disguise.'

The abbot continued to address the infirmarian, 'But nothing more? Nothing of more use?'

'You might ask the boy, my lord. He is awake and healthy.'

'Well, yes. I suppose I might.' He made an effort to look at Milos. 'Nothing other than the habit, boy? Nothing we might use to find out who it was? Did he have a limp, perhaps? How tall was he?'

'I didn't see him walk, my lord, so I can't aver as to a limp but he wasn't tall, I don't think. Not as tall as you.'

The abbot shook his head. 'Nothing reliable, then. Height can often be confusing, especially in the dark.' He went to pat the boy's head but noticed the bandages and aimed for the shoulder instead. 'I hope you'll soon be out of bed, young man. Splendid, well done.'

From the infirmary, he went to the chapterhouse and through to the conservatory. There was no sign of the prior. He tried the church, the parlour, the congregation's dayroom, he was not there. The abbot asked those he passed if any had seen the prior.

No one had.

Wondering where the man could have got to, he turned round to go back to the guestroom.

'Ah, Prior, I've been looking for you.'

'And here I am, my lord.'

'I came to say that we might as well get Brother Sylvan down to St. Jean.'

'As soon as you wish, m'lord.'

'As soon as we may, Prior. Let's hope that is an end to his aggravations. We can rest a little easier now.'

Fate had no intention of allowing the abbot peace of mind, however. At the guestroom door was a guard in a livery he recognised. The abbot peered at the man who kept his gaze fixed on the far wall, intent on ignoring him.

'Now, what is it, Comte?' he asked as he went in. 'Oh, it's you.'

'Yes,' the master-at-arms said. 'Me.' Without the Comte, he seemed less confident.

'And what do you want?'

'My lord, the Comte wants you, at the château.'

'Me. Whatever for? Am I suspected of murdering poor Abbo, now?'

Ramon, the master-at-arms, shrugged.

'When does he want me to go? Now? At this hour?'

'He does. Immediately.'

Rutilius turned to his acolyte. 'Have we had breakfast yet, boy?'

'Um, no, Master, certainly not.'

'Then you may wait outside, or anywhere else you please, sir. I have no intention of going anywhere before breakfasting. William, pray go and ask Brother

Giles to hurry, just a little.'

Brother Giles followed closely behind the returning William. 'My lord.'

'On the table, Brother Giles, wherever there is room.' The abbot turned his furious gaze on the master-at-arms. 'Out.'

The abbot did not feel the slightest bit hungry but he ate slowly and deliberately. William nibbled a piece of bread and drank some water.

A quarter-hour later, he left the guestroom. 'I have to see the prior before I leave. I shall see you at the main door. Is that clear?'

Ramon nodded slowly.

'Boy, bring Mariette to the steps.'

The abbot found the prior in the chapterhouse just as the morning meeting was breaking up. 'Prior,' he lowered his voice to little more than a whisper, 'I am summoned to see the Comte, why I don't know.'

'You, m'lord? Summoned? By the Comte de Fossard?'

'That's what I said.'

'Summoned though?'

When the abbot was safely settled into the saddle, William led the animal after the guard.

'Where is this place, Ramon, and how long will it take to get there?'

The master-at-arms turned in his saddle. 'It's about an hour, my lord. That's all.'

'And where exactly?'

'Not far from St. Jean, an hour's ride.'

They followed him at a brisk pace; he, on his destrier, making better time than the others.

'This is not the way to St. Jean,' said the abbot. 'I have been there and this is not the road.'

'The château lies nearer the river. We don't go through the village.'

The day was hot and the sky brassy. An hour had almost passed and no sign of a château was visible, the trackway they followed was narrow and erratic, a goat path, no more.

Perspiration ran down his neck beneath his undershirt and tickled, as it rolled across his stomach. The abbot scratched and thought about the prior's amazement when he had told him of the summons.

Josephus was quite right to be surprised, the situation was ludicrous. Who had the right to order whom?

He thought carefully about chains-of-command. *The Comte de Fossard was answerable to the King of France, Philip, who counted the Pope as his liege lord. Well,* Rutilius considered, *at least as far as the Pope was concerned.*

That seemed right, now. *He, Rutilius, was commanded by the Bishop of Avignon, who also bowed to Pope Martin, though there was probably a cardinal in there, too. Cardinals? Cardinals were beside the point; the point was, Fossard had no power over him at all. None.*

'Ramon, stop.'

The master-at-arms slowed and stopped, carefully remaining several paces away from the fuming abbot. 'My lord?'

'I refuse go another foot. Is this clear? If he needs me, the Comte may come to see me.'

'But, my lord, he is a busy man and…'

'Then, he need not see me and I have saved him a task.' Rutilius was pleased with the logic and preened himself just a little. 'William, the other way. Back!'

William turned the donkey round and set off.

'My lord Abbot, my master ordered me expressly…' Ramon looked surprisingly downcast.

'*Ordered* you?'

The master-at arms kicked his mount into motion. 'Just ordered me, m'lord.'

'This is a ruse, is it not, a ruse to lure me away from the abbey?'

'Now why would I do that, m'lord?'

And suddenly the abbot knew.

They came up from St. Jean, with Ramon many yards behind them. The abbot was noticeably wary, as they came into view of the abbey. He stopped and wiped the beads of moisture from his brow.

'Is something wrong, Master?'

'The Comte will not be expecting us back so soon.'

'Ah.' Enlightenment came to the acolyte.

And as the abbot had suspected, the Comte was within the abbey. When they came in sight of it, eight or ten horses had been hobbled and left to graze in front. A single man of the Comte's guard stood watch, leaning against a wall and obviously bored with his task. Ramon joined him, despondency evident in every movement, as he slid from his mount.

The abbot and the acolyte left the path and went around the end of the building to enter through the side entrance leading to the stables. Their only observer was a monk on his knees, with cuffs turned up to the elbows, as he tended the garden.

'Brother, will you take the donkey to the stables while I find out what is going on?'

Inside, there seemed to be guardsmen everywhere. Singly, in twos, threes, they stamped along the passageways, opening doors as they went, disappearing inside if the interior could not be seen at a glance.

'They're searching the place. It's just as I feared.'

'For Marcel and Gilbert?' asked William.

'Of course for Marcel and Gilbert. Yesterday, or more probably, the day before, they searched St. Jean. Yesterday, doubtless they went through St. Guilhem, now they are here. The prior put the two of them in the crypt; if they have the sense to stay out of sight, they may be overlooked.'

'Here he is, Master.' William tapped the abbot on the shoulder, and pointed to the prior who seemed strangely rigid.

'Ah, my lord. Thank God that you have returned.' The prior seemed to have gone far beyond apprehension and anxiety. He did not lean, sway, scratch, or itch. 'Turning the place upside down, m'lord.'

The abbot patted the other on the shoulder. The prior was shivering with suppressed anger.

'Where are they at the moment, Prior?'

'Everywhere, m'lord. They tramp about, they scratch the tiles with their boots, break down doors if they won't open to a touch, just everywhere.'

'Yes, Josephus, I do see that. What I mean is where is the Comte himself? Do you know?'

'In your quarters, m'lord.'

The abbot's face became an alarming puce in colour. 'Is he? My God, my God, give me patience with this... this ruffian.'

'There was nothing I could do, m'lord. Nothing.'

'Of course not, Prior. Do not trouble yourself about it, give it no more thought.'

The abbot turned about, and he appeared to swell as he walked, like an image painted on a pig's bladder blown up at a children's feast. He marched the length of the corridor, his features set as implacably as one of the pope's personal guardsmen.

Outside his own door, where a guard leaned against the wall cleaning his teeth with a quill pick, the abbot stopped and tugged his robe straight, made certain that the crucifix hung in plain sight, and then marched in, allowing the door to crash against the wall inside.

'God's wounds,' exclaimed the Comte. 'In the name of the Almighty, who dares come in here like this? Ah!' The Comte was standing with one foot on a stool, the investigatory notes spread out across the table. His fingers were stirring the contents of one of the small boxes of charcoal sticks and sealing wax.

'Ah. Just so, Comte, in the name of the Almighty. You enter this abbey with neither permission nor invitation, you deface the building, and you cause uproar. Now, I catch you going through my things like a petty criminal. It is *I* who come in here in the name of the Almighty. How dare you enter one of God's houses like common brigands?'

The prior hovered, with no idea what to do except to brandish like a weapon the little brass trowel he kept for his orchids. The abbot almost cried at sight of the plucky but ineffectual Josephus.

'You might remember, too,' he continued, now thoroughly into his stride, 'I am the Pope's direct representative, hmm? It's within my power to have you removed to the stocks.'

The Comte scratched his buttock. 'Why, we looked for you, Abbot. We looked and we could not find you. We asked your prior here. He seemed so distraught we could not understand a word he said. We simply had to assume that, as the good citizen you undoubtedly are, you would give us our right and proper permission.'

'You assume too much, Comte. Out with you and your ruffians now. I do not give you permission.'

The Comte cupped an ear with a hand. 'I fail to hear you properly, Abbot. Your words are unclear.'

'As God is my witness, Comte, the Bishop shall hear of this. I shall recommend excommunication if you do not leave this abbey.'

'Excommunication?' The abbot's trump card, which worked so well with most offenders, failed with the Comte. 'The Bishop? The Bishop will simply ignore you, Abbot. He knows from which side of the plate he eats. Excommunication! Whatever next.'

'God's retribution next.' More angry than he had ever been, the abbot slammed his fist down on to the table, rendering a great crack across its surface.

Simultaneously, there was a blinding flash of lightning from the gathering storm outside and, as everyone stood back in alarm, a cacophony of thunder rent the air so that no one could hear a word said.

For once, the Comte appeared disturbed.

'The Lord watches us,' the abbot cried out.

The Comte licked his lips and nodded. 'Perhaps then we will discuss the matter another…'

There was a knock at the door. 'Lord Girand.' The call came from the hallway outside. 'There's someone hidden in the crypt.'

A guardsman came in, his face wreathed in smiles until he saw the serious expressions on everyone else's.

'Yes, we know of that one. He's the poacher's friend. He should have been shackled by now and outside…'

'Someone else, my lord. Not him.'

The Comte regained his composure and turned a wolfish grin on the abbot. 'Someone else in the crypt, Abbot. Perhaps you'd better come with us, then you can escort us from your abbey.'

They stood outside the doorway to the crypt.

'Keys, Abbot.' The Comte held out his hand.

'Keys, Comte? You think I carry the keys to every door in the abbey around with me?'

'Prior. The keys.'

Prior Josephus looked at the abbot, who nodded very slightly. He felt in his pocket and brought out a bunch of keys.

The Comte handed them on to one of his guards and gestured towards the door. 'How did you find out there was another one here?' he asked the guard who had brought the news.

'The kitchen boy brought a tray of food, my lord.'

The Comte chewed his bottom lip. 'For the poacher?'

The other shook his head. 'He's chained to a post by the horses, my lord. The boy just slid the tray under the bottom of the door.'

'Hmm,' observed the Comte, as the door swung inwards. 'And there it is still, though the food is gone. Perhaps they have large mice here, or rats. Search the place, and more thoroughly than last time. Find me these rats.'

It was an awkward wait, standing around in two separate groups, with neither willing to speak to the other. Gilbert and Marcel were discovered and led out in less than a quarter-hour. Their expressions were grim, as they were led outside. They were lined up behind the novitiate Thomas, the poacher's ally in the kitchen; a length of rope was knotted around each of their necks, and tied to the saddle of one of the horses.

The Comte and his party mounted up and prepared to leave.

'I think we shall have the reliquary case in the vestibule, Prior. Next time this one comes calling, we'll see what a fragment of the true cross does to his arrogance. And the *clamour* too, for a carefully chosen curse on those who break the peace of our house.' The Comte seemed to have discovered a talent for stoking Rutilius's anger.

A slight pallor came over the Comte's face, though it was hard to see it behind the whiskers. He paused, then leaned down from the saddle and spoke softly to the abbot. 'I can confess my sins like that, Abbot.' The Comte snapped his fingers. 'And receive absolution. Just remember this, remember who really does have the power around here.'

As he straightened up, a second spear of lightning struck a birch tree across from the gates and, simultaneously, a blast of thunder added deafness to blindness. The predicament lasted long enough for a general panic to start. Several guards were thrown by their horses and one, who had been standing close to the tree, was quite clearly dead. The singed and twisted bodies of a score of starlings littered the path, and the remainder of the flock wheeled and whirled about the demoralised men with discordant cries, adding to the disorganisation. Horses, freed of their riders, were in turmoil, rearing and wild-eyed, attempting to gallop off in any direction.

Eventually, some semblance of order was restored and shaken guards caught all but three of the horses. With two riding double and another with the corpse tied across his horse, they formed up into a column once more. Girand, the Comte, looked even paler than before. He rode off at the head of the column without another word.

No one but William noticed that only two men – not three as before – were still roped to the last horse in the detail, as they rode off through the sudden downpour.

CHAPTER FIFTEEN

The weather for the day was yet to be settled. Sunlight shone without conviction from beneath the edge of a cloudbank; the wind tossed occasional flurries of rain at them. However, by the time they reached the descending road beyond St. Guilhem, the sun was asserting itself and the wind was dropping; the rain, never determined in its assault, retreated.

'I think it will be a fine day, Master.'

The abbot grunted. He was still concerned about his suspicions of Gilbert; increasingly he wondered if his reasoning had been flawed. He readily admitted that this was unlike him, yet it appeared that he had allowed personal feelings to influence his judgement. 'Objectivity, boy. As examiners, this is what we must strive for.'

It was not an answer that William had been expecting. He looked afresh at the sky and the sun in order to appraise the prospects once more. His was definitely an objective view. 'Yes, Master. I am certain that the weather will be good today.'

'The weather? Undoubtedly.'

William tugged gently on the donkey's bridle to guide the beast around a pothole, past a hollow filled with ooze, along the inner edge of the road where it skirted steeper slopes. An hour passed, and part of another; the red clay tiles that roofed the village of St. Jean could be discerned through the trees.

‘What is that?’ asked the abbot, rousing from his reverie.

The sound that had caught his master’s ear had been going on for some time but had risen in volume so gradually that the acolyte had remained unaware. Now he listened. ‘A discussion, Master?’

‘An argument, boy. An altercation of some force.’

They rounded a bend and, as the abbot said, so it was.

‘…And look at my holding; nothing left. What am I going to feed my hogs, eh?’

‘Rabbits, I keep telling you.’

The argument had been in progress for some time.

‘Bah. Maybe a rabbit as big as a goat; that looks like a goat; that eats like a goat. That rabbit there.’ The householder pointed at the animal in question, a sad-looking goat with its head drooping listlessly. ‘Look at it, ashamed of itself.’

‘It has been down at the shrine until last night. How could it have eaten any of the weeds off your land?’

‘Weeds?’ asked the incredulous householder.

‘Weeds. Stuff you feed to your hogs, stuff that my goat would have to be starving before it touched.’

‘Your goat is always starving. It would eat anything.’

Fists were clenched, the argument was about to become physical.

‘Gentlemen, gentlemen.’

Neither had noticed the abbot’s approach and both stopped abruptly at his words. They waited as he carefully descended from his donkey’s back and looked at the other beast.

‘Surely we can resolve this without resorting to violence.’

‘I don’t know, my lord,’ said the grower. ‘When there is

a voracious goat about and its owner won't answer for its depredations, a fist may be the only path to justice and satisfaction.'

'Is this the voracious goat? It doesn't seem very greedy to me.'

'Appearances are deceptive, my lord.'

'Genevre is very docile, my lord, very biddable.'

'Master,' William interjected at the first opportunity, 'the goat, Genevre, is choking.'

'She certainly does not look well.'

William crossed to the animal and touched the long neck where the lump of some obstruction was clear now he had drawn attention to it.

The goat's owner wrung his hands. 'She is always doing this, anything that takes her fancy. Let her die, at least she will make a few good meals, I am tired of taking her to the shrine.'

'No, no,' said William. 'She needs to be rid of this, then you must tie her up and make sure she doesn't stray.'

The acolyte held the goat's head to his chest and did something short and sharp and out of sight. The goat coughed, and again, and again. It vomited several undigested items on to the ground of which none were the green tops from the householder's turnips.

'The trouble with tying Genevre up is that she eats the rope.'

'A chain?'

'The cost of a chain would buy two goats.'

William did not hear the last remark. With the goat recovering, he had looked at what had caused the choking. The most recent object was a strikingly-coloured garment, of a kind with which only one of the men was familiar.

'So that's where it went. This morning, my wife accused me of hiding it,' said the goat owner, rubbing his chin speculatively.

'What is it?' the abbot asked, looking over William's shoulder.

'Why, it's um, my wife's,' the man made hand motions in front of his chest, 'she's quite big, it helps, you know, her…'

'Perhaps, I'd rather not know,' interrupted the abbot. 'The main point, though, is when did it go missing?'

'My wife spread it on the bushes behind the house with the rest of the washing.'

'But when?'

'Yesterday afternoon. It must have gone when she took everything in at dusk.'

'I ask, you see, because that second little bundle of cloth came from my, well, from my office. It looks as though it still contains a small item of jewellery, for which we have been looking.'

'That's an unusual thing to eat, even for Genevre.'

'Some pies had been wrapped in it. There would have been gravy on it.'

The goat's owner nodded. 'Genevre does have a savoury tooth.'

'William, be so good as to look inside the bundle, will you?'

William found a stick and, with a moué of distaste, he picked the damp and smelly bundle apart. Inside was the blue-winged butterfly.

'So, who has cut off the tops of my beets?' the gardener asked plaintively.

'Rabbits,' the goat owner said firmly. 'As I have been telling you since you accosted me and blamed poor Genevre.'

'Pah! If your goat had not already had a full load, it would have been my beets. There is no doubt in my mind.'

'Your mind is the size of a pig's. It comes from eating turnips that were meant for pigs.'

The gardener took a deep breath but the abbot intervened once more. 'Gentlemen, do not force me to lay a complaint before the Comte. He will take a very dismal view if the peace is broken in front of a religious.'

The threat of further bickering was stifled by another series of coughs.

'Here comes something more,' said William, as the goat regurgitated another morsel that had defied digestion. 'What is it, I wonder?'

'A tassel?' suggested the gardener, who was feeling overlooked.

They all crowded around the bedraggled object.

'Hmm. Is there nothing she will not eat?'

'Very little,' said her owner ruefully.

'William. There's a stream over there, clean the pin and the tassel, and wrap them in something.'

'Here. Use this.' The goat owner handed him the unnameable garment. 'I daren't give this back. If I did so, she'd only accuse me of taking it for some sort of joke.'

William washed everything and hung the bundle by one of the ribbons from the back of the saddle to dry.

The abbot began the process of climbing back on to the saddle. William helped but, without a mounting block, it was a difficult task. However, gardener and goat man came to their aid and, together, they installed the abbot side-saddle on the donkey. They set off towards the shrine.

'So, the goat could have swallowed that pin any time before yesterday afternoon. Late afternoon, probably.'

'Well, yes,' the abbot agreed. 'Before it ate that other thing, the thing belonging to the goat man's wife. That establishes the latest time.'

'Which can only be while the goat was at the shrine.'

'Probably. The important thing is that it shows the goat got the pin down here, at St. Jean de Fos. If I am right about Gilbert de Gignac, he might have stolen it from our room to get rid of the evidence.'

'But Gilbert was already hiding at the abbey from the Comte.'

'Well…' Rutilius replied doubtfully.

'And if it is not Gilbert, it must be someone else, perhaps it was Brother Sylvan.'

The abbot's forehead wrinkled. 'But why, boy? By God's great mercy, why?'

'I don't know. I don't think there's much to blame on Gilbert, though.'

The abbot sighed. 'Perhaps you're right, boy. This business is going around and around in my head.'

The main doors were open so that the sun illuminated the region just inside the shrine in a golden haze. By contrast, the deeper reaches of the cavern were impenetrably dark.

'Hello!' the abbot called out.

'Anyone there?' the acolyte shouted.

'He can't have just left the place open and gone off somewhere.' The abbot was disapproving.

'Perhaps he needed to piss, Master.'

'Don't remind me, boy. I am enjoying good health

thanks to that infusion of juniper recommended by the infirmarian. Let us not mention the subject again.'

'Of course, Master. I suppose we can wait a little while.' William tied the donkey's bridle to a door handle, and they went inside.

'I suppose we can.'

As their eyes adjusted to the gloom, they explored the shrine. It was deserted. The door to the storeroom was stuck.

'It must be locked,' the abbot said. 'Do you see a key hanging anywhere?'

'None, Master, is there a keyhole?'

'It must be jammed. I think we will have lunch while we wait.'

They returned to the sunshine and William took the viands from the saddlebag that Brother Giles had prepared for them. They dined on another of the pigeon pies and a loaf of bread, and drank weak beer from an earthenware jug, which had been wrapped in damp cloth.

Shortly after they finished, there was the sound of a cough from the road to the village. Expecting this to be Brother Sylvan, they got up to see better and found Marcel approaching slowly in the heat of the day.

'God be with you, my lord,' called Marcel, as he saw them.

'And with you,' returned the abbot. 'So the Comte released you? Thanks be to God.'

'Aye. He might have had His hand in it. I escaped yesterday when that thunderbolt struck. I came to the village and hid myself away.'

'So, Gilbert is still there?'

'I expect he is, though I cannot be sure, of course.'

'We have to do something about that. It is why we are

here. We need to see this Marie-Louise woman.'
'His sister-in-law.'
'The same. Do you know where she lives?'
Marcel seemed a little reluctant. 'I don't wish to show my face around the village, m'lord. The Comte's guard may be looking for me.'
'But we can vouch for you.'
'I heard no vouching when they took Gilbert and me away yesterday.'
'But we must establish your whereabouts. You have a witness, you told me, remember?'
'Aye. Just so.'
'God's blessings upon you all.'
Looking round, they discovered Brother Sylvan leading a huge grey and brown hunting dog with a sad expression and a large bandage around its left front paw. Understandably, the dog was limping.
'Cut his paw,' said Brother Sylvan as though he were already in an argument.
The dog growled and bared its teeth at the abbot.
Brother Sylvan tried to reassure the abbot who had taken up a defensive posture. 'He's really quite tame, my lord.'
William fondled the dog, and, happy at the friendly attention, it sat down, forgetting its bellicose attitude towards the abbot.
'He belongs to the Comte's daughter.'
William stood back and unwrapped the butterfly pin for something to do. Since the encounter he witnessed in the cloister, the subject of Anna-Marie was no longer a favourite.
'Oh, what's that?' Brother Sylvan was looking at the blue-enamelled wings of the pin that William held in one

hand. His expression seemed to be one of surprise.

'That is what murdered Brother Abbo,' the abbot told him.

Brother Sylvan appeared oddly fascinated by the object. He took the opened cloth from William and looked at the thing closely.

'God in heaven,' Marcel exclaimed. 'Begging your pardon, my lord.'

'You are surprised, Marcel?'

'I've seen it before. Gilbert bought it for his sister-in-law's birthday. In fact, he purchased it from my son. Where did you find it?'

'It was found in his clothing. The pin itself is broken off but this matched the part taken from Brother Abbo's wound.'

Marcel shivered. 'Gilbert bought it a month ago and I put it in the strongbox with the shrine's donations. Where did you say you found it?'

'I didn't, but it was inside the goat that is always coming here for help.'

'Benoit's? It was here yesterday, too. Benoit thought that it had lost its appetite since it wasn't gobbling everything in sight.'

'Benoit being the goat's owner?'

Marcel nodded. 'Poor Genevre. I have warned Benoit repeatedly that she would kill herself one of these days.' He took off his hat and held it in both hands, close to his chest. 'No doubt Genevre will make good eating.'

'Oh, it isn't dead yet. The boy made it sick somehow, and it seems to be fully recovered.'

Marcel let out a long sigh, 'That is good news. The animal is living on borrowed time though, my lord.' Marcel bent closer to the abbot and whispered, 'Perhaps you will make young William sacristan. He might be more use than the one we have.'

'Hmm, Marcel, you are a wicked man,' he whispered back with mock severity, then more loudly, 'Brother Sylvan, the pin, if you please.'

Brother Sylvan had already put the bundle away in his purse. Now, looking guilty, he retrieved it and opened it.

The abbot took the pin. 'Ah, Brother Sylvan.' He picked up the tassel. 'Not a tassel after all, is it?'

'How do mean, m'lord?'

'It's the end of a monk's cincture, isn't it? The knot?' The abbot looked pointedly down at the trailing end of Brother Sylvan's girdle, where the knot was missing. 'Yours, I believe.'

Brother Sylvan was a little mystified.

The abbot belaboured the point. 'The goat obviously chewed it off when you saw to the animal yesterday.'

'But I couldn't do anything for it,' Brother Sylvan responded, completely misunderstanding the abbot's reasoning.

'Well, time, I think, to see this friend of Gilbert's.'

'His sister-in-law, my lord?'

'Exactly so.' The abbot turned to Brother Sylvan and instructed him. 'We shall be away no more than an hour, Brother. I forbid you to leave the shrine unattended, is that clear?'

'Absolutely, my lord, absolutely.'

'Good.'

They walked the short distance into the village and Marcel indicated a narrow street to the right.

Here, the abbot halted. 'Boy,' he said, 'return to the shrine and make certain that Brother Sylvan does as I have directed. In fact,' some wisp of an idea had come to the abbot as they had walked, 'be discreet. Do not show yourself unnecessarily.' The abbot was coming to the same conclusion as the lay workers: Brother Sylvan was not to be trusted.

As William returned to the shrine, the others climbed the steep little street. Small patches of broken earth outside each of the houses were planted with flowers or vines, which crawled up the mud walls. On the steps sat women, younger ones with child at breast or sleeping, older ones, who spun wool, or embroidered linen stretched on wooden frames. Some watched their ascent. Others showed no curiosity at all. At several, small birds perched inside willow cages and sang above the doorways.

'Here,' said Marcel in a low voice.

A woman looked up from the child she was tending. A little more than a year old perhaps, just old enough to wobble from one side of the door to the other on chubby, uncertain feet. 'Marcel,' she said in surprise. 'Is Gilbert coming? I haven't seen him for a day or more, and who is this that you bring to my door?'

'Marie-Louise. I present my lord Abbot… My lord, I do not have your name.'

The abbot shook his head. 'It does not matter. Abbot Rutilius, Marie-Louise. I am happy to meet you; may God bless you and your child.'

'Thank you, lord.'

The abbot pitched his voice low. 'Marie-Louise, may we go inside so that what we have to say may be kept between ourselves?'

Marie-Louise was flustered. 'Of course, my lord. Is this something terrible?'

'Yes,' said Marcel, bleakly.

'Hardly at all,' said the abbot, simultaneously.

They went inside. The ceiling was low and the abbot had to duck beneath the rafters, a hazard he was unused to, and the small window on to the street admitted very little light. The tiny room contained a hearth near the back wall, a straw mattress on a ledge in a long alcove, and some straw pillows for sitting on. The hearth contained a small partly-consumed log and enough kindling to get it burning at the end of the day. A lamp, a tiny dish of oil with a floating wick, flickered in front of a cheap effigy of Mary, Mother of God.

The room was spotless. 'You will have to excuse the state of my house. I was not expecting someone of quality.'

'Marie-Louise, as far as I can see, your excuses are needless. Besides, I grew up in a fisherman's cottage no greater than this one, until my father was drowned, I remember my mother sweeping the place a dozen times a day,' the abbot reassured her. 'Now, some quite terrible events have occurred at the shrine and at the abbey.'

'The murders.' Marie-Louise nodded.

'You know? Of course you do, everyone in the village will know.'

Again, she nodded.

'Now, we have to make certain that no suspicion falls upon Gilbert.' Which was an odd way of putting it, he thought, considering that Gilbert had been his chief suspect, his only suspect, just an hour or two before.

'You are asking me to vouch for him?'

'Just so. Tell me when he was with you these past days.'

Marie-Louise wrinkled her forehead and put the baby

down at her feet. The child grasped her skirt and pulled himself upright. 'We went to my sister's, three days ago,' she said. 'We took my husband's cart and mule and he took me to my sister's. Her baby was due, and I had had word that she had begun her labour.'

'And when did you return?'

'Yesterday morning.'

'Exactly when did you return?'

Marie-Louise shrugged. The time of events was rarely exact. 'Before noon.'

'And he was with you all the time?'

Marie-Louise shook her head slowly. 'No, you remember the night we stopped at St. Trivier, it was raining? When we saw you at the door?'

'You? That was you and Gilbert?'

'Yes. He returned here the next morning, he left me there.'

'So, there was no question of his being here on the night of the murder?'

'Oh, no. We left as soon as they took the Virgin back to the church from our little shrine. The festival, you know.'

'Gilbert.' Rutilius frowned. 'I was so wrong. He always seems to be in such an ill humour.'

Marie-Louise giggled. 'I am sorry, my lord. He was anxious.'

'Anxious? Anxious about what?'

'He told me how he laughed at you and your boy that day. He thought you would recognise him.'

'Well. So that was Gilbert. Well, well.' He turned to go, narrowly missing a pitcher of water on the windowsill. 'That's good to hear.'

He stepped outside. Marcel was leaning against

the wall, next to the window.

'Marie-Louise?'

'My lord?'

'When did Gilbert come for you?'

'The day before yesterday.'

'The Lord be with you.'

'Marcel, where is this woman's husband?'

Marcel chewed his lip for a moment. 'Marie-Louise's husband left St. Jean almost a year ago; soon after little Gilbert was born. Marie-Louise's husband is Gilbert's brother. You would find it difficult to meet a more feckless, useless man.'

'Gilbert has no responsibility for the child, has he?'

Marcel looked at the abbot, who evidently meant exactly what Marcel thought he meant. 'Gilbert cares for the child as if it were his own,' he said carefully.

They walked back down the hill. A bird at the next doorway warbled sadly, dreaming of freedom beyond the cage.

'It doesn't give Gilbert any help, does it?' said Marcel.

'Indeed it does,' the abbot replied, and Marcel stopped in surprise. 'I saw them the night that Brother Abbo was slain, on their way to Gignac.'

'That is Gilbert's good fortune then.'

'Our Lord God protects those who love Him, Marcel. Remember this and be joyful.'

They resumed their walk. 'Now, however, we must look to your defence.'

'Mine?' Marcel asked. 'I am free.'

'Until such time as the Comte wishes to find you.'

Marcel shook his head. 'I have no one.'

'You mentioned a lady.'

'No. You must be mistaken.'

The abbot turned about and walked back to Marie-Louise's house again. He ducked his head below the lintel once more. 'Marie-Louise?'

'My lord?' She looked up in surprise from tending to her baby.

'Is there no one who can vouch for Marcel?'

Marie-Louise frowned. 'Madame Violle might be persuaded.'

Behind the abbot, Marcel broke into a fit of coughing that left him breathless and with streaming eyes. 'Marie-Louise,' he managed eventually, 'what has Madame Violle to do with you?'

'Why, nothing Marcel, nothing at all.'

The abbot, still blocking the doorway, looked at Marie-Louise then turned ponderously to study Marcel. He turned back to the woman. 'What is the problem?'

'None at all.' Marie-Louise's eyes were opened wide, limpid as a pool of water, innocent.

'Marcel?'

'She is a friend of mine.' Marcel cleared his throat. 'I see her from time to time.'

'On Tuesdays and Thursdays,' Marie-Louise offered.

'So…'

'Yes, yes,' said Marcel, far more testily than should have been the case for a man who was being given a defence against murder. 'Excuse me, m'lord.' He squeezed past the abbot. 'How many people know about Madame Violle?'

'Well, everyone,' Marie-Louise answered him, now looking less innocent than before.

'Everyone? What about, you know...?'

'Oh, no. Not him.'

'God be praised.'

'At least, I don't think so.'

'And Madame Violle would vouch for Marcel, even considering the circumstances?' the abbot asked.

'I'm sure, so long as she could testify in private. She may wish to speak to Marcel first to be sure there was a proper understanding…'

'Hmm. Well now, we should certainly see this lady. If the situation is as I understand it, Madame Violle's word, at such a cost, you understand me, might be a powerful argument. Thank you, Marie-Louise.'

'M'lord?' she said quietly.

'Marie-Louise?'

'I heard what Marcel said about Gilbert and my babe, which is absolutely true. I also heard the way he said it. Gilbert is ashamed of his brother, and he looks after us both as well as he is able.'

Marie-Louise's eyes were shining and brimming with tears.

'Gilbert is a true friend and no more.'

'Marie-Louise, I understand perfectly. You are a fortunate woman.'

Rutilius turned over Marie-Louise's last remarks. On reflection he saw that Marcel had made quite a number of comments concerning Gilbert's character that might be thought underhand and disparaging. He resolved to treat Marcel's information with reservation.

After they had walked in silence for some time, the abbot asked, 'Why Tuesdays and Thursdays, Marcel?'

It was a moment or two before Marcel understood the question, then, in a gloomy voice, he answered, 'There is a market on the following days in Gignac, in Montpellier and in Nimes. Victoir, Violle's husband is a leather worker; well, he was. Nowadays, he has other people who do that work, and he sells straps, and bridles and things, cups…'

'Comical in a way.'

'Comical, my lord?'

'I thought Gilbert to be a womaniser and we find him devoted to his sister-in-law and her child. You have a seemly reputation that is not born out by the facts.'

'Except that everybody knows. My reputation is in disarray.'

'Except for…'

'I hope so.'

They walked on in silence until they stood outside a fine house of two storeys. The door was set in an arch of stone, with a window next to it. The timber frames of the upper floor were painted a dull red, the window frames were covered with ox-horn.

'This is the one?'

Marcel nodded and knocked on the door. They waited for some minutes, and then came the sound of footsteps. A woman opened the door a little and looked out through the slot between frame and panel. She raised her eyebrows.

'I wish to see Madame. I have here my lord Abbot Rutilius?' He looked at the abbot and raised his own eyebrows in query.

'Just so. I have to speak with Madame Violle about important matters,' Rutilius said.

The woman pushed the door to without closing it and went away.

'Juliana,' said Marcel. 'Madame's maid.'

'Madame's maid?' More raised eyebrows, this time from the abbot. 'Her husband must be quite successful.'

Marcel did not reply. They waited until Juliana returned

and ushered them into a room, which opened off a small vestibule. 'Madame will not be a moment,' she said.

Nor was she. 'Marcel, good morning to you, and this…?'

'This is my lord, the Abbot Rutilius.'

'And what is this all about? Oh, and please be seated.' She gestured to a pair of chairs and the abbot eased his weight carefully on to the nearest. Marcel remained standing.

'Violle,' said Marcel, 'I find that I need to prove my whereabouts during the past week or so. Now, the abbot is aware of our, um, friendship and would like you to assure him that I am, that is, I was with you on the evenings of Tuesday and Thursday this week.'

'I can't do that, Marcel.'

Marcel's mouth dropped open. 'Violle!'

'Today is Thursday. How can I say what will happen before it happens?'

'Ah,' Marcel breathed a sigh of relief. 'Then, last Thursday.'

Madame Violle turned to Rutilius with an arch smile on her lips. 'Sir Abbot, Marcel speaks the truth. He keeps me company on those days every week.'

The abbot got to his feet. 'That is all I need to hear, Madame. You need say no more on the subject.'

But Madame wished to say more. 'Dear Marcel keeps me company, as he puts it so politely, on those days every week.'

'How loyal, Madame.' The abbot did not wish to hear anything more; he turned to go.

'Aside from, of course…'

'Aside from?'

'Aside from saints' days and feast days.'

'Of course, Madame. Good day.'

Outside, with the door shut, Rutilius asked what was wrong with saints' days and feast days.

'Victoir sells his merchandise here in St. Jean. Enough people come into the village to make it worth his while.' Marcel's tone was wary as though expecting further interrogation.

'Yes, I can see that that would be inconvenient.'

They set off to return to the shrine, but, hardly back into the village centre, Marcel suddenly stopped. They had just passed the tavern where they had dined before.

'A moment, m'lord, if you please.' Marcel went back and looked in through a window and then returned. 'Perhaps we might have something to eat, m'lord. In fact, allow me to buy something for us.'

'That's very kind of you Marcel, but I…'

'I insist, m'lord. You have bought a meal for me twice and allowed me to stay at the abbey so I must repay you in some small way.'

Rutilius nodded. 'I thank you, Marcel. I am happy to take a meal with you.'

They entered the tavern, which was busy with midday trade, pausing at the entrance to the main room.

'Ah, my lord, will you choose a seat while I have some words with a comrade of mine?'

Marcel left without waiting for an answer and crossed to stand by a man of middle stature, whom Rutilius found slightly familiar. His clothing was dark-brown fustian, his hands were grimy, his face was stubbled like an oat field after harvest; he wore leather boots and these, too, were encrusted with dried mud.

The conversation between the two men was quiet and intense. Marcel's companion seemed reluctant to agree to something; he bent his ear closer to Marcel's face and obviously asked him to repeat something. Marcel did so, tapping the other's chest with his forefinger. Rutilius recognised the word *me* uttered with some surprise, a pause for thought and then a slow nodding of acquiescence.

Quickly, the abbot sat himself at an unoccupied corner table, as Marcel looked round for him and then went to speak to the landlord, to give him an order for food before joining Rutilius.

'Sausage, m'lord. Today's dish is sausage.'

'Sausage is a favourite, Marcel. I'm sure I shall enjoy it.'

The abbot's enjoyment was small. The sausage was almost entirely oatmeal with just enough fat to bind it together. Since Marcel had bought it, there was little he could do to complain. He ate what he could, drank his ale and waited for Marcel to finish.

Rutilius thanked the lay worker and they returned to the shrine. Marcel was still tense, and the abbot put this down to the discussion with the leather merchant's wife and stayed off the subject. In effect, there was nothing to say and they remained mostly silent all the way back.

The shrine looked deserted, the sun shone down, baking the mud and bringing sweat to both men's brows.

'Hmm, well,' said the abbot.

'Brother Sylvan,' said William, materialising from the shadows.

The abbot jumped. 'Ah, you gave me quite a start, boy.'

William grinned. 'Brother Sylvan is still there. He shut the doors a little while ago and I've heard very little since.'

'I have a few questions for Brother Sylvan. He's mixed

up in something, I'm certain of it.'

'Just so, Master.'

They walked the last few paces and at a nod from the abbot, William pulled open the door. All was quiet, though it was the expectant sort of quietness that follows feverish activity suddenly halted. There was no one in the shrine.

'He's gone,' said the abbot.

'I don't think so,' said William with a laugh, striding forward and pulling open the door of the storeroom. 'That's what he called *exorcising*.'

William's grin widened; he laughed.

Marcel's mouth hung open.

Brother Sylvan's face was a mixture of surprise and distress.

Lady Anna-Marie appeared to be furious. Due to being discovered, or because of the interruption, was open to conjecture.

The abbot simply looked weary.

'Oh, you're going to be in trouble, Brother Sylvan,' the abbot sighed. 'I really don't like this, you know? I really, really dislike it.'

'Now we know why he murdered Brother Abbo, then,' said Marcel, suddenly at ease.

'We do?' asked Rutilius.

'Who? Me?' asked Brother Sylvan, startled.

'Brother Abbo caught them out. He killed the sacristan to keep him silent.'

'Brother Abbo never knew,' said Anna-Marie, now fully dressed and her manner truculent and defiant.

'Of course, you would say that, wouldn't you? He broke in and…'

'I thought *you* had killed him,' said Brother Sylvan to

the girl. 'That's why I took the pin. I was trying to hide it. I thought it was yours.'

Silence followed, punctuated only by the regular drip of water from the roof. Anna-Marie swung her cape around her shoulders and adjusted the hood over her hair.

'Hugo!' she shouted, her voice high, peremptory and *very* ill-tempered. Again, 'Hugo!' and all but Brother Sylvan looked at her with perplexed expressions.

There came the sound of a large animal tearing through brushwood and shrubs.

'A boar!' cried the abbot and, though far too late to be useful, desperately searched for shelter. Down the hill at the side of the shrine rushed a huge, grey-brown animal, with twigs and furze balls stuck in its coat, it had big yellow teeth in shovel-sized jaws. A dirty, frayed length of cloth was tied to its front leg and flapped in the air like a banner on a windy day. Now free of the bandage, Rutilius noticed the dog had lost its limp.

'Here, Hugo. Heel, boy!' The hound bounded across to the girl and stood next to her, panting. It licked a long red tongue along both sides of its muzzle and sat down, leaning against Anna-Marie's leg, a great amiable grin spread across its face. She left without another word, striding aggressively off towards the village.

Rutilius breathed a sigh of relief. Having seen so much of her recently made him feel uncomfortable in her presence; he was happy to see her go.

Brother Sylvan stood dejectedly in the shadow beyond the doors.

'Did you try to kill Milos?' William asked him, as the silence stretched on.

The abbot angled his head, seeing nothing untoward in a fifteen-year-old quizzing a monk ten years his senior.

'That was you, was it not so?' William persisted.

Brother Sylvan paused a moment and then nodded.

'Why? What had poor Milos done?'

Brother Sylvan suddenly grew quite animated. He looked directly at the abbot then back to William. 'That was your fault.'

'Mine?'

'Yours and the abbot's.'

'Mine?' The abbot was astounded. 'How do mean, my fault? Explain yourself.'

'You told me that William had evidence,' he said in an accusatory tone. 'You said it had to be discussed before you could decide on whether I was to be made sacristan.'

'I did?' the abbot frowned. 'I don't remember such a thing.'

Then, to William, 'And you told me he knew about meeting Anna-Marie in the abbey.'

William leaned forward and whispered to the abbot, 'We did, Master. You were teasing Brother Sylvan, to teach him that he was not as important as he thought. I just wanted to make him angry.'

'We did?' And the memory came back in a rush. 'I did, yes.' He looked across at Brother Sylvan again. 'But why Milos?'

'You mistook Milos for me,' said William. 'It was me you were trying to kill?'

Brother Sylvan nodded, matter-of-factly. 'In the dark.'

'My God, my God. How is deceit repaid, Lord?' He gave a great sad sigh. 'Well, what of Brother Anno then?' he asked tiredly. 'How had that kindly soul come to deserve such an end? Your attempts to confuse us and make us believe it was an accident did not deceive my assistant for a moment.'

'That was none of my doing.' Brother Sylvan was adamant.

'You expect us to believe that?'

Brother Sylvan shrugged. 'It matters little whether you believe me or not. The facts are as they are.' His scheme to become sacristan had come to naught; his erotic fantasies, likewise. Brother Sylvan had lost interest in his future.

'At least this makes things simpler in the short term,' the abbot told William. 'I can report to the Comte de Fossard that Marcel's whereabouts have been guaranteed by his, um, friend, and Gilbert cannot be involved; I can vouch for his movements on the feast of St Jean…'

'That is good news,' Marcel interrupted, with enthusiasm. 'Will you be going to the Comte's château now?'

'I must. Gilbert's life is threatened.'

'But how do you… how do we… prove Gilbert to be innocent?'

Rutilius made a moué. 'Well, we must trust in the Lord, of course, but simply put, I vouch for him. I saw him far away from here on the road Gignac when the killing was done.'

'Ah, your word is a valuable endorsement. I had better guide you as far as the road, m'lord.'

'Ah, um, yes, that would be a help, and William…'

'Master?'

'You will have to say here. We will lock Brother Sylvan in the storeroom. You will guard him. Hide the key about your person so that it cannot be lost.'

The situation had resolved itself, though it seemed that Marcel was the only person completely satisfied.

'Where shall I sleep?' asked William. 'The only place

is the storeroom, which you have already allocated to Brother Sylvan.'

'Would you really want to sleep in there now?' asked the abbot.

William thought about it and shook his head.

'I'm sure you can make yourself comfortable,' the abbot said, infusing his voice with a heartiness he did not feel.

'I'll get Marriette,' William offered.

'Thank you, boy. You do that, while we shall lock the brother in the storeroom.'

'That is inhuman. To lock me up like an animal in a dark little cupboard like that,' whined Brother Sylvan.

'You were more than content in there a while ago.'

Once more alone with Marcel, conversation dwindled to nothing. Apart from the regular clop of Mariette's hooves, the short journey was silent. They crossed the Devil's Bridge and Marcel pointed to the track which should take the Abbot to the Château Fossard.

CHAPTER SIXTEEN

William had become used to the comforts of the guestrooms at the abbey and now, having to sleep at the shrine brought back memories of the cheerless, draughty dormitory at St. Trivier.

At least there was no sharing the space with twenty old men with severe snoring problems, or worse, and Brother Sylvan seemed content with his lock-up. The acolyte was able to make himself comfortable with armfuls of straw from the animal pen outside, and a cloth that covered the lectern in the Lady Chapel.

It was the cloth cover that was responsible for his dreams; there was no doubt in his mind at all. The scent of lavender clung to it, *her* scent, Anna-Marie de Fossard, who had been praying here when they had first come. William had not dreamed of her, had hardly thought of her, since the day he had seen her in the cloister with Brother Sylvan, but tonight, as soon as he closed his eyes, she was there; she came closer as he slept, conjured by her fragrance.

The outer door opened with no more than the slightest creak of hinge and this was drowned by the evening breeze. Briefly, a cape-shrouded figure was visible against the sunset; black, unknown. The form entered, leaving the door open by a hand's breadth to allow a finger of light inside.

The person went straight to the storeroom and pulled at the door only to find it locked. There was a whispered expletive, and a hand felt along the top of the door frame followed by ledges where a key might have been placed. Nothing.

A lever? Something flat and metallic? Hard leather soles crossed the tiles going purposefully somewhere. The feet encountered William's makeshift bed. A little further exploration and the foot pushed against William's hand. The hand tightened.

'What's happened now? Hmm? Who's there?' The boy half woke.

A laugh, a tone of relief. 'Why, it's William, isn't it?'

And William grinned in the darkness and curled up again. 'Anna-Marie. Come on back here.'

'Well, an invitation like that, I can't resist, can I?' Anna-Marie sat down on the straw and stroked the boy's forehead. 'I came to pray, of course. You know that, don't you?'

'What were you coming to pray for?' William pulled on the ankle that he still held in his grip. 'Come on, come a bit closer.'

'Well, it wasn't for this.' She pulled his hand away from her ankle and kissed his cheek. 'Who do you think I am?'

'Anna-Marie, of course.'

'How clever of you, hardly any light in here and you know who I am. I didn't even realise you knew my name.'

'Almost real.'

'Oh, I'm real enough.' She put William's hand to her mouth. 'See, real.'

A drop of water fell from the shrine's rocky roof; it hit William's head, the cold shock startling him, drawing him from his dreams. He rubbed the wetness away and wondered. Things like that didn't happen in dreams, cold drops of water, girls with lips as soft as this.

'Have you come to find Brother Sylvan?' he asked suspiciously. 'Because if you did, you've come on a fool's errand.'

'Sylvan? What on earth makes you think I came for him? Hmm? He's so much older than me and he's ill-mannered and foul-mouthed, and rough too. Now you, you're much nearer my age. In faith, I doubt there's a year between us.'

Still very muddled between his dream world and the real one, William took Anna-Marie's words at face value. He was flattered, and, for the first time, was close to a girl who wasn't treating him like a twelve-year-old. It was just very wonderful.

Anna-Marie touched his sleep-tousled hair and smoothed it away from his forehead, and then ran her fingers down his cheek. 'I knew this was going to happen that night you came into the Lady Chapel. Do you know that? Did you feel then that we were meant to come together? Fate has it all fixed.'

'I remember that night. You looked very beautiful.'

'I looked up from my prayers and there you were, looking at me. I thought it was a new picture in the chapel, thought you were a painting on the wall.'

'So it isn't Brother Sylvan; he's not why you're here?'

'Him? I told you no. He's crazy, he deserves everything he gets.'

'Why did you come to see him at the abbey?'

Anna-Marie had been to the abbey numerous times, several of them in the past week, or so, and she wondered which one William knew about. 'At the abbey?'

'I saw you with him in the cloister.'

'Ah, the cloister, yes. Sylvan compelled me. He threatened me, made me…' Anna-Marie considered; William was, in fact, quite sweet. To what should she admit? 'He made me yield my body to him. It was because of Sylvan I've come to see you now.'

'How did he threaten you; I mean, with what?'

Anna-Marie was ready for the question. 'I've run away from home,' she told him, most of it the truth. 'Away from my father, who wants to marry me off to a fat old man. I'm staying with a friend in St. Jean and Sylvan, as he calls himself, is threatening to tell my father where I'm staying.'

'Hmm, well. He's not going to look for you here, tonight, is he?' William's arm went around Anna-Marie's waist and he squeezed a little. This was better than any of the dreams he'd had already.

Anna-Marie yielded to the pressure and she put her own arm around William's shoulder. She pulled at the tie at his throat, unthreading the lacing. 'And tell me this, why do you shiver when I touch your skin – like this?'

It was true, each time her finger touched against his skin, he shivered. William moved away a little.

'And why do you back away instead of coming towards me? Not very flattering, is it? Do my fingers sting like nettle leaves?'

Almost, he thought. *They almost do sting*. But he stopped moving away, he wriggled a little and leaned closer instead. Minutes passed. He found himself kissing her, pressing his mouth against her throat, sliding his lips slowly down into the cleft between her breasts. William's undershirt was loose now, it gave him ideas and he pulled at the ties at Anna-Marie's shoulders. Closer now to the soft fruit he had never tasted outside of dreams before.

'Hey, my fine friend, wait a little.' Anna-Marie pushed him gently away. 'Hold on there. There's a certain order in which we do things. First things first.'

She pushed him back to lie on the straw, and her perfume was heavy in his nostrils. She pulled his habit open and with a little help from William, pulled it off. 'We'll put it down here, out of the way.' She folded it and patted it flat, smoothed the wrinkles out. 'Hmm,' she said, and shook her head. 'Now your belt. Oh, you have a pouch too.' She undid the belt around his vest and patted the pouch. 'Over here too.'

William chuckled and reached for Anna-Marie's gown, which was already loose at her shoulders.

'Hey, you rascal, what're you doing?'

'Fair's fair. It's your turn now, sauce for the goose…' And a moment later, Anna-Marie's gown was around her waist, and William gazed, transfixed.

Anna-Marie's first intent was to discover where William had hidden the key to the locked store cupboard, where she was certain Sylvan had been confined. But, seeing the expression on William's face in the last of the evening's sunlight made her forget that. And when William's hand moved to touch her, she took it and guided the boy.

Both learned a lot over the following hour. The girl realised that Sylvan's rough-and-ready lovemaking was far from the only way. The boy learned that sex was a far more complex thing than he imagined, with far-reaching effects.

Anna-Marie abandoned thoughts of Sylvan. There was nothing she needed from him. And to be taught this truth by a virgin boy scarcely older than herself… Well, she kissed his ear as he slept.

It must have been well towards morning when both were awakened by an ear-splitting cry. 'I know someone's out there and if they don't let me out of here soon I shall be pissing under the door. And the stench of wax in here is making me sick.'

'Sylvan?' Anna-Marie said, rubbing her eyes.

'Brother Sylvan,' William admitted.

'In the store cupboard? You kept that quiet, you scoundrel.' She sat up and laughed. 'I thought I must have guessed wrong.'

'I don't care,' William shouted. 'Piss where you like.' He pulled Anna-Marie to him and whispered in her ear, 'I know you were looking for the key so don't "scoundrel" me.' He nibbled her ear. 'Not that I'm complaining, mind you, but I daren't let him out of there. The abbot's gone to see your father and he'll be telling him all about Brother Sylvan, so he's got to be in there when the Comte gets here.'

'You're right, my little rogue. My father's not a forgiving man and I'm afraid he's going to demonstrate that if he catches up with me.'

'How do you mean?'

'He's going to take a switch to my arse, believe you me. And we'd better get dressed. If the abbot went up to see my father last night, he could be here any time.'

Anna-Marie pulled on her gown. 'Can you do up my points?' William threaded the laces through the shoulder eyelets and tied a knot at each side.

'It's not that much of a sin, is it?'

'Sin? I told you about that fat old man he wants to marry me off to, didn't I?'

William nodded.

'I wasn't lying. And I wasn't lying when I said I was hiding from him in the village. You going to tell him?'

'What do you think I am? Anyway, why does it have to be some fat old man? Perhaps he'd let you marry me.'

'An acolyte? You think he'd do that?'

'I'm more than an acolyte, you know. My father was Duc de Castres.'

'Really?' Anna-Marie turned to him. 'Really?' She was interested, they were equals; possibilities spread out from this moment. 'Was..?'

'My father was sent to the galleys.'

'Oh, holy Jesu, why?'

'Cathars.'

'All the *old families* have a certain, um, allegiance to Toulouse but there are no Cathars left?' She ended the statement with a query.

'I know but father argued with someone; someone it would have been better not so to do. A cleric.'

'Ah. My poor boy,' she hugged him to her, and it almost made up for the calamity of his life. 'Poor William. It means that we could never… you know?'

William nodded.

'No land, no estate?'

William shook his head.

Anna-Marie finished dressing.

'Perhaps the Comte would give me a job,' William suggested. 'I could rise in his service.'

'I don't think so, William. Not marriage.'

'I suppose not, but we could dally.'

'Not after Sylvan, especially not after Sylvan. No.'

Grey daylight beamed through the still open door. 'Just for fun, where *is* the key?'

‘I gave it into the Lord’s keeping,’ he said. He pointed to the iron key, which was hanging on the left hand cross-piece of the altar crucifix.

Anna-Marie kissed him gently. ‘Goodbye, gentle suitor, my best and gentlest suitor.’

CHAPTER SEVENTEEN

The abbot felt lonely, and not just because Marcel had left. This would be the first time that William had not journeyed with him since that not-so-distant day they had left St. Trivier together.

He missed the boy, there was no doubt of it. Even when there was silence between them, it was a companionable silence for the most part, he reminded himself, remembering the day or two that William had so profoundly disagreed with him.

'And rightly so,' he said aloud. 'Rightly so.' The donkey flicked her ears; then, deciding that the words had nothing to do with her, concentrated on the uphill task of transporting the abbot's wobbling corpulence.

The abbot's stomach was already complaining about the meagreness of its last meal and, as he turned the donkey away from the main road, he was sorely tempted to return to the inn in St. Jean. The temptation was only momentary. *He would suffer*, he told himself, *it would do him good. Gilbert's freedom was what was important. A bowl of pottage would be good, though. A bowl of pottage and some really fresh bread, hot from the oven.*

No, this was Satan talking to him. There was no time to turn back not even for a draught of good red wine, or even one of middling quality… God's own wine was everywhere; streams abounded with good sparkling water in them.

Speaking of which, the road turned sharply and just

such a stream leaped down the side of the hill and along a bed of brown gravel, with pools placed *just so*, for dipping in a hand. And what was more; here were trees, set thickly to shield him from the sun.

He halted his donkey and wiped the sweat from his brow. He slid from the animal's back and pulled her across to the stream where she bent and slaked her thirst. When this was done, he knelt on one knee and scooped up handfuls of ice-cold water. 'One of Brother Giles's pies would be very welcome just now,' he said to himself. 'Very welcome.'

'God be with you, m'lord Abbot.'

The abbot stood up and turned around. 'And to you, sir. Now, I've seen you before, this day, at the tavern, um…' He concentrated, held up his hand, finger raised. 'Dondo, is it not?'

'An excellent memory, m'lord.' Dondo bowed. 'Dondo, at your service.'

Dondo wore his usual dark-brown clothes, which were well suited to the woodland. Patches of soil clung to the knees of his hose, and dirt rimmed each fingernail. 'Did I hear you mention a pie, m'lord?'

'You did, Dondo. It is a long time since I last ate a proper meal.' The patches on the knees of Dondo's hose reminded Rutilius of an earlier time when he had seen the man. *Where had it been?* he wondered. *Perhaps in the abbey kitchen.*

'Then you paused at just the right place, m'lord. Let me offer you a meal from God's own pantry.'

His thirst diminished, the abbot became aware of the smell of wood smoke in the air. He sniffed appreciatively at the breeze, for there seemed more than just wood smoke. Somewhat further from the road, at the side of a large still pool, a small fire burned redly within a ring of stones. He could see bread set close by to crisp. A thin twist of smoke rising straight up dissipated among the treetops.

'No. I think not, Dondo. I don't have the time to spare and, to tell the truth, I'm not sure it's desirable to be connected with a poacher.'

'To tell the truth, m'lord Abbot, you don't have much choice in the matter. I insist.' Dondo took him by the upper arm and pulled him towards the fire. 'In fact, I was about to request some meat from the good Lord.' He gestured towards the fire. 'Come, sit over here.'

So saying, Dondo took him back to the fire and took up his fishing pole. He put the end into the water and lifted the line up and down in a peculiar, though experienced fashion. The next moment, he lifted it clear of the water, as a long thick and wriggling black eel appeared to slide up the line against the pull of gravity. As the abbot watched with respect for the man's skills, the eel was banked and dropped into a creel made of rushes.

'Is m'lord hungry?'

'Certainly, he is,' he replied. *Well*, he thought, *it is not as though I have a choice. I wonder what purpose he has.* 'Very hungry, though I am still pressed for time.'

'Five minutes, no more, separate you from a meal fit for a king, or an abbot, for that matter. And the donkey can forage for herself.'

Rutilius had not eaten eel since he was a child and, even then, the eels his father brought home would not have come from a freshwater brook such as this one. Here was a new gastronomic sensation to be enjoyed.

Dondo had already caught several eels before the abbot had arrived. Now, he skinned them in exactly the same manner as removing tight hose from a leg. He wrapped the meat in leaves and placed it on the flat stones surrounding the fire.

'Do you have reservations concerning meat taken from the streams and heaths, my lord?' Dondo moved the bread back a little, in case it dried too much.

'No,' Rutilius replied at once. 'None at all.'

'Now, that's strange. I was told quite recently that you had imprisoned Thomas who works in the abbey kitchen.'

'Well, that's true enough, but not for poaching.' Rutilius used the word without inflection, as though it held no significance.

'Oh? Then can you explain to me why?'

'Thomas is a friend of yours?'

Dondo shrugged.

'Thomas was imprisoned because he defrauded the abbey. Because he brought the abbey into disrepute by using our innocence to hide his misdeeds.'

Dondo nodded gravely. 'If Thomas reveals who supplied the goods he moved through the kitchen, that one will also be as dead as Thomas.'

'That's very true, Dondo, very true. But those are the Comte's rules, not mine.'

Rutilius was not certain when it happened but while Dondo was talking, a pair of hand-sized mushrooms had been added to the hearth, and now they sizzled on the flat stones alongside the eels.

'I had no desire to pass Thomas to the Comte; he took the man along with Gilbert who is also blameless in this affair. I shall remonstrate with him when I see him later.'

'Hmm,' Dondo said, pressing the mushrooms with his knife so that black juice ran out of them. 'And will that be sufficient to save him from talking?'

'From talking?' The abbot thought about things for a few moments. 'I doubt it.' Rutilius was perfectly aware of the matters left unsaid. He went on, 'You might know that Brother Anno had information for me about the kitchen, but he was killed before he could tell me what was on his mind.'

Dondo's gaze became intense at hearing the name. 'Anno? Now, he would be the tall black one, I think, Huh? Never knew his name.'

'Had I known earlier about Thomas and, er, about Thomas's partner, I might have cleared up the business before the Comte became inquisitive.'

The poacher said little as he worked, as the eels steamed and cooked, as he stripped sycamore twigs of their bark. At what he judged the right moment, he skewered the meat on the twigs interlacing them with thick slices of mushroom, and passed two of them to the abbot with a chunk of warm bread.

'Try this, m'lord. You've already tried God's fresh water, but there's plenty more where that came from to wash down your meal.'

The abbot took a sample from one of the skewers and his mouth overflowed with juices, and they dribbled down his chin. His eyes opened wide as he munched and finally, swallowed. 'How have I never met such an admirable dish as this before?' he asked.

'Why that's a simple question to answer. You have never ventured into Dondo's kitchen before, m'lord.'

'That's a truth if ever there was one.'

The abbot finished his meal and tossed the twigs into the fire. One of the mushrooms still lay on the hearth stones, smoking.

A little while passed while Dondo finished his meal and wiped his greasy fingers on his hose.

'That was delicious, my friend, but I must be going now,' the abbot told him. 'My journey is quite urgent.'

Rutilius leaned to one side and then paused, a puzzled expression on his face. 'My legs won't work. They have grown quite numb.'

'Often it's the legs first, my lord. Often.'

'The legs? What are you telling me?'

'It's the mushrooms. Call it God's way of summoning you home, m'lord.'

'You've poisoned me.'

'I have to admit that you're right.'

Rutilius was silent for quite a long time; his face took on an expression of strenuous thought. 'You murdered Brother Anno, didn't you? For God's sake, why?'

'For Dondo's sake, actually and just a little for Marcel's. You really are a nuisance.'

The poacher got to his feet and looked around. 'Now, where's your donkey got to?' He went to find Mariette.

Rutilius did not bother to try to work out the details, he had no intention of meeting his Maker if he could avoid it, and there were things to try while he still had the use of his hands and arms which, actually, were strange and swollen and did not work very well. Resolutely, he thrust a finger down his throat and made himself sick.

Dispassionately, he looked at the pool of vomit and decided that there was still more to come. He repeated his actions and succeeded in bringing up some recognisable bits of the fungi. Perhaps because he had been hungry, he had not chewed as he should have done, the fragments of food were quite large. The abbot then allowed himself to fall over, hiding the results of his labours and pretending to be unconscious as Dondo returned.

The poacher dragged him away from the fire and, with great difficulty, heaved the abbot's deadweight on to Marriette's back. 'Now to rid us of this bothersome monk.'

The remark went straight over the abbot's head since he was really unconscious now and perched like a sack across the donkey's saddle.

He regained consciousness from time to time, just for a few moments. He was aware of the rhythm of the donkey and of his general discomfort, but they were like fragments of a bad dream. Eventually, the periods of lucidity grew longer, objects passed before his unfocussed eyes, things touched him. Finally, he regained consciousness fully.

The sight that met his eyes took some understanding. There was the donkey's shaggy coat at the bottom of his vision and he could smell the rank odour of the animal, and then the smell of sickness on his clothes. Beyond that was water, sometimes foaming, sometimes still, floating by in his upside-down world, as if it was in the sky.

Some clue turned his viewpoint around. The long skeins of weed, the occasional fish, the splash of waves were beneath him. He was belly-down across the donkey, his wrists and ankles tied, and lashed beneath the animal's girth, his head was much lower than his feet and there seemed to be some danger of his sliding off.

For the time being, the abbot stayed as he was. He was still numb in various places, the result of the poisonous mushrooms, and this saved him from the aches and pains, which would start if he drew attention to himself.

Dondo was leading the donkey along a narrow track at the side of the river. Behind him, his legs brushed against bushes and outcrops. Below his head, the river ran close to the donkey's hooves, high, flooding over the tufts of grass and reed that usually marked the edge of the bank.

Finally, they moved a few feet from the river and came to a stop. His arms and legs were freed and he was pulled off the donkey. The abbot collapsed immediately and his captor bent over and peered into his face.

'Still with us, m'lord?' Dondo asked.

The abbot remained silent.

'Who's the lord now, my lord? And who the servant, hey?'

Again, he received no answer.

'More surprises to come, I promise you. Come on, up you get.' Dondo took his arm and pulled him up. The abbot collapsed again, his legs as much use as a pair of hose filled with straw. The poacher kicked at the abbot's unfeeling legs. 'Well, I suppose I did expect to carry you; though I'd thought you'd be a corpse by now.'

Dondo dragged Rutilius across the grass into shadow. 'Caves, see?'

'The caves?' the abbot asked, and regretted speaking immediately.

'You must have the constitution of an ox, m'lord. Not that it will do you any good at all. Yes. Those caves, heard the legends, perhaps? People who don't know their way around shouldn't come here.'

He left Rutilius in order to tie the donkey to a bush and then came back. 'Donkey will be useful later. Now, these caves.' It seemed that Dondo could not stop talking 'There's a river in the caves, rises very quickly when the Gellone is full, like now. That storm yesterday filled it right up. Come on.'

Dondo took hold of the abbot's feet and dragged him along on his back, with his robe being drawn up towards his shoulders. 'Very dangerous, of course, and stupid.' The poacher stopped and panted. 'Slip and fall into the river in here and you're dead when it spits you out. Now don't run away, while I light a candle.'

The sound of flint being struck and, a few moments later, a candle stub in Dondo's hand grew bright enough to illumine the entrance to the caverns.

Wide curtains of translucent stone hung from the ceiling, cones of similar rock rose from the floor and some of these joined with those suspended from above. In the candle's uncertain light, the abbot saw colours running through the smooth stone, pinks and greens streaking the creamy surface. They glittered wetly in the uncertain light. From further in, there came the sound of rushing water.

They moved on, slowly now, for Dondo could only spare one hand. The abbot was squeezed through a narrow opening into another chamber, and suddenly the sound of gushing, spouting water was all around them. A haze of spume hid the far side of the long cavern; underfoot, the floor was a tilted sheet of wet clay into which they sank, as Dondo pulled the abbot towards the water.

The abbot came to a decision. He could wait no longer for his limbs to recover. The poacher slipped in the mud and lost his grip, and Rutilius kicked as hard as he could. The candle went up in the air and down again, trailing flaring drops of wax. The candle went out, the trail of droplets hit the ground and disappeared one by one.

...Darkness and the sound of water.

Rutilius rolled as far and as fast as he could.

'Damn you for a fool,' wheezed Dondo. 'You can run but not far, you fat old man, I shall find you.'

Even over the flowing water, the abbot could hear the squelch as Dondo pulled his booted feet from the clinging clay and began to stalk him in the darkness. As the sucking sound came nearer, the abbot rolled further, hoping that he was not too near the water. Dondo squelched past barely an arm's length away but the poacher had lost his sense of direction. He kept on going.

'Where are you, hey? I'm going to find you and then I'll push…'

Almost inaudible above the general sound of water flowing, a different sort of splash told of Dondo stepping into the water.

'Bones!'

Perhaps, if he had stopped at that moment, all would have been well for Dondo but he didn't. Panicked, he stepped back and trod on a smooth rock. There was another splash, as he lost his balance. More splashings, as he floundered about, trying to regain the bank, in the absolute darkness.

'Oh God, help me.' The abbot heard the water being churned about as Dondo lost all semblance of self-possession.

But God was not there to help, only the abbot. And his mind was in a quandary.

As Dondo shouted and screamed, the abbot knew there was only the one thing. He rolled downhill as fast as he could and plunged into the water. It was icy. It took his breath away, which explained why Dondo had not cried out immediately. 'Where are you?' he shouted. 'Call out so I can hear where you are.'

The flow swept them quickly through the length of the chamber, battering them against rocky boulders as it turned and swirled through the cavern. Faintly came the voice of Dondo and then quite suddenly, it grew louder and louder until it was right beside the abbot.

They had both been caught in an eddy. Searching hands found each other and clung in the darkness, as the eddy revealed itself as a sinkhole, sucking then down below the surface. Under the water, all sense of up and down was lost. They spun, were dashed sideways, forward and back, lungs bursting.

CHAPTER EIGHTEEN

For a few brief moments, the pounding was over. Long enough to find the surface and suck in great breaths of air. The abbot reached out and found a smooth ceiling just inches above his head, which whisked past fast enough to graze his knuckles. Then it was gone again, no gap, no air, just the smooth rock above. There was more of the same, six or seven or more, and then a long smooth stretch shallow enough to feel his feet on the river bed.

He struggled across the swift current and reached a shore. His legs were performing sluggishly and he crawled, panting and wheezing, on to cold wet sand. He lay there with his feet still in the water, all but unconscious. Somewhere, he could hear Dondo calling and then even that stopped, as sheer exhaustion took him away from the dark underground world.

The abbot woke to Dondo shaking his shoulder. 'Where are we?'

The abbot considered the question. For long moments, it made no sense at all. All he knew was that he was wet and cold, shivering as he'd never shivered before in his life, and every bit of him hurt most terribly. He thought about the question again. 'In the caves, of course.'

'You don't think this is Purgatory?'

'Purgatory? If we're dead, young man, this is the ante-room to Hell, which is where you're going to go without any doubt.' The abbot's feet were now drier, and the water had retreated away into the darkness. He struggled to a sitting position, and pulled his damp robe around him.

Apart from his chattering teeth, Dondo was silent for quite some time. The abbot could hear him breathing but nothing more until, 'Will you hear my confession?'

'I'm an abbot. You need a priest to give absolution.'

'You're the next best thing to a priest. You could hear me. Just in case.'

'In case of what?'

'In case we don't get out of here, and we die.'

The abbot remembered how he guessed that Dondo murdered Anno. 'Why did you kill Anno?'

The poacher remained silent.

'I thought you wanted to confess.'

'Ask me something else.'

'It's not me who should be asking, it should be you telling me. What about Brother Abbo, then?'

'Abbo? What has Abbo to do with me?'

'They were twins, the killings must be connected.'

'No,' said Dondo, after a time. 'There is no connection. I killed Anno, if that was his name. In fact I killed him so he wouldn't tell you about the business in the kitchen, and it was a stupid thing to do.'

'Well, yes. Very stupid. Why do *you* think it was stupid?"

'It was stupid because if Anno had told you straight away, my name may not have become known.'

'Hmm. That's so. But if you had not waylaid me today, it still may not have been known.'

Another silence ensued before Dondo spoke again. 'Marcel told me you knew all about me and were going to tell Girand.'

'Tell the Comte? Marcel said this?' The abbot grunted.

'Marcel is a liar.'

'Marcel is a devil.'

'Hm.' Rutilius considered Marcel in a new light. 'Marcel killed Brother Abbo, didn't he?'

'He did. Abbo caught him thieving from the alms box.'

And both fell into silent thought. The underground river, too, was silent; the level of water outside in the river was steadily falling and, at some critical point, it had failed to feed into the caves.

Now the cavern felt like the interior of a great cathedral without even a votive candle left twinkling in the darkness. The abbot could feel the vastness of the place, so wide that the presence of walls could not be sensed; there was not even that palpable feeling of the weight of stone that can be felt in most caverns.

Vast.

Sitting on his haunches, his arms wrapped around his drawn-up knees in the darkness and despite the presence of Dondo, the abbot felt absolutely alone. Each minute seemed like an hour, and there was no way to know how far night had advanced in the world outside. Perhaps it was already morning, how was he to know?

If only his young acolyte were here, someone he knew, someone he could talk to on an equal footing. He missed the boy badly; if only he would come walking along the invisible bank with a lantern in his hand.

No such miracle happened and in the absolute darkness, anything seemed possible. Dondo's fancy took hold of the abbot's imagination; they *could* be in Purgatory here, awaiting judgement. To one side, unseen, was the narrow path to Heaven; the other way, equally invisible but wide and easy to blunder along, was the tunnel down which the souls of the wicked would tumble to the fiery caverns of Hell.

When Dondo spoke, the words were muffled, as though he held his face in his hands. 'Will God show you the way out of here?'

But Rutilius was wrapped in his own thoughts, equally unsure of his future. *Had he led a life sufficiently free of sin? Had he truly repented when errors had been pointed out to him? He remembered his anger towards the boy. He had assumed an obligation to William. Anger was a feeling of which he must strive to rid himself.*

The abbot knew he was just feeling sorry for himself and that he should snap out of it, but he was so cold it sapped the will. He heaved himself to his feet and began, half-heartedly, to perform some exercises. It was oddly fortunate that it was dark, had he been out in the open, arm swinging and trotting on the spot would have made him feel absurd. But it worked, and after a little while, he began more vigorous movements.

With the shivering slowing and a tiny glow of warmth within his body, he began to walk along the underground river, feeling with a toe before committing his weight to the outstretched foot. He neither knew nor cared whether Dondo followed him or not. After a long time, he could hear water moving, a swirl, an occasional gurgle and he guessed that somewhere ahead, the much reduced current was emptying from the chamber.

Rutilius thought back over the events of the few days they had been here and nodded to himself. 'We arrived on the Wednesday at the abbey,' he muttered to himself, 'but we came to the shrine on the day before. Tuesday.'

He stopped for a moment. 'And it was a festival day, St. Jean's. Why, Marcel even told me so, he had brought the statue back the following morning and found Brother

Abbo, so he said. He cannot claim he was with Madame Violle. Urging Dondo to commit a second murder on my own person reinforces his guilt.'

Behind him, he heard Dondo's furtive steps. 'We're never going to get out of here, my lord. Nobody gets out of these caves.'

The abbot felt a thrill of fear run through him. 'Be quiet, for sweet Jesus' sake, be quiet.'

'We're going to drown.'

'I remember you, boy,' Girand said around a mouthful of hard bread. 'You want some breakfast, eh?'

Standing outside the shrine in the early morning fresh air, the sun hardly above the hills, the Comte's unfavourable reek was masked. 'Thank you, sir. I'd appreciate that.'

'Help yourself, then. Bread, some ham here in this basket. Ramon has had what he wanted. I have to say you're a happy little bugger for so early in the morning; not like the other day.'

William grinned and said to himself: *I have my reasons, Monsieur le Comte.*

The Comte and five or six guards had come clattering up to the shrine soon after the sun had broken through the early morning mist. William had been awake. He had been awake for most of the night and, judging by the noise from inside the store cupboard, so had Brother Sylvan.

'So tell me, young man, what's going on here, hmm?'

William stopped eating. 'Hasn't the Abbot told you?' he asked.

'I haven't seen anything of the Abbot since he frightened me to death outside the abbey.'

'He was going to see you yesterday afternoon. Marcel took him through the village to show him the way.'

'I'd not trust Marcel to show me the way to Hell, to be direct with you.'

William frowned, suddenly worried and anxious.

'Tell me something, boy: the Abbot, your master, is he?'

William nodded.

'Plucky little scullion, isn't he?' The Comte seemed to have gained a certain grudging respect for the abbot. 'Put the fear of God into me when that lightning struck, I tell you.'

The acolyte started to eat again.

'Now, you thought he was with me at the château. That right?'

'Yes, sir.' William swallowed his mouthful. 'He left the shrine yesterday afternoon; it was his purpose to come and see you.'

'And he didn't arrive. Do you know what he was coming for?'

'He had found proof that neither Gilbert nor Marcel could have murdered Brother Abbo.'

'Had he? That's very enterprising of him. What sort of proof, do you know that?'

'He had found people who would swear that they were both elsewhere when it happened. And...'

'Oh, very convenient. Your abbot's got a lot to learn about this sort of thing. They'll be hoodwinking the little man until he's ready to admit to the murder himself.'

'And Brother Sylvan had admitted to injuring one of the young boys at the abbey, trying to kill him because he thought it was me.'

'You live a dangerous life around the abbot, don't you?

What had this Sylvan been up to?'

'You might ask him yourself, m'lord. He's in there.' William nodded to the storeroom, which was now very quiet.

'Ramon.' Girand jerked his head towards the door.

The master-at-arms crossed to the storeroom and removed the branches that propped it shut. Brother Sylvan came out of the gloom and blinked in the sunlight.

'Phew!' Ramon flapped a hand in front of his face. 'What's that smell? Camphor?'

'God's wounds, I can smell it from here.' Girand screwed up his face. 'And it wasn't to keep moths out of the vestments, was it, Sylvan?'

Brother Sylvan remained silent, shoulders hunched, his hands hidden within opposite sleeves.

'Come on, you little fornicator, do you think I don't know what camphor's for? My daughter thought that too but she found out she was wrong. Why do you think I came here this time of the day, eh?'

The young monk said nothing. He shrugged, looked at the ground, stood.

'And damn me if I don't know you already.' He put out his hand and grasped William's shoulder, pulled him forward. 'How long's this Sylvan character been a monk at the abbey?'

'I, I can't say, m'lord.' William pulled his habit straight. 'I've only been here a week.'

'The prior will know; he knows everything. But it's been less than a year since I got rid of *this* Brother for helping himself to my larder. He was my dog handler, trained them to fetch what the hawks brought down except there was always fewer than I thought there should have been. Should have hung him.'

Brother Sylvan ignored the Comte's tirade and attempted to look pious by staring at his crucifix and whispering prayers.

'I'm finished.' Girand told his master-at-arms and pushed the basket away. 'Have them throw the rest away.' He stood up and looked down the incline toward the village of St. Jean de Fos. 'Ramon, kill him.'

Ramon and William looked round to Brother Sylvan, who was no longer there. He was running like the wind, habit bundled up around his hips. William considered himself rather fleet of foot but the young monk's speed was impressive.

Ramon strung his bow, nocked an arrow, aimed. There was a brief tearing sound as the arrow parted the air and a moment later, the young monk fell, tumbling over and over in the dust. He did not get up.

'Bring the body back and show it to my daughter.'

***

'Just get away from me, will you?' The abbot was disgusted with both Dondo and himself.

At himself in becoming fixated on the wrong man, for not seeking out Brother Anno and finding what he wanted to say; and for taking Marcel at face value.

At Dondo for choosing to kill an innocent monk to save his own skin.

Rutilius strode off into the darkness, following the sound of the river. He was deathly tired but he walked on anyhow, walked until exhaustion made him stumble; at least now he was too worn out to even think. That was good, he might sleep now.

He sensed, rather than saw, a pile of rocks heaving up from the sand and he clambered among them, and up until there was no more damp slime or weeds on the boulders. He sat down and pulled his robe tightly about his body. He hunched his shoulders and his hands tucked into the sleeves.

Rutilius fell asleep.

Time passed.

Dondo followed in the abbot's footsteps. He too was weary, sick at how things had finished, knowing that if ever he found a way out of these endless caverns he would be hunted down and hanged.

He stepped into the water, cold and icy up to his ankles. Dondo backed up and whined to himself, a thin keening of despair and misery. There was no hope for him in the bright world outside. Perhaps he should drown himself? He waded back into the underground river until the current swept him off his feet; Dondo floated in the icy water and the feeling drained from his body, breathing grew shallow…

Dondo suddenly clawed at the water; drawing himself to the side; climbing the bank with clumsy, unresponsive fingers.

A rufous light shone behind tall statues of grotesquely misshapen forms. To the left ran the river, thick and viscous, the colour of blood.

Ahead, the cavern narrowed to a single high archway. Great blocks of stone formed a perfect arch sealed in place by a huge keystone.

Beyond were the fumes of Hell, roiling smoke lit by the fires of torment. The silent cavern had brought him to the gateway of Hades.

Between the supporting pillars sat the Angel himself,

Lucifer, Prince of Darkness.

Dondo began to weep. He fell to his knees, buried his face in the gritty sand.

Through the archway, the sun rose higher, the mist turned from red to yellow, blue sky was just visible. The brightness woke the abbot and, hearing Dondo's mumbled incoherent lament, he turned around. 'Dondo?' he said.

'No,' screamed the poacher, pressing his hands against his ears, as Satan stepped down towards him.

CHAPTER NINETEEN

'Ramon, we'll take the road up through the village.' The Comte swung himself up into the saddle and pulled his horse around. 'And tell the men to look out for the Abbot. Spread them out once we're over the river.'

William rode behind Ramon. If it had not been for his missing master, he would have felt rather more excited to be among the guard detail.

Forewarned by the clatter of hooves, the villagers stepped to the side of the road and watched them go by. A few minutes later they crossed the Devil's Bridge and slowed as they began to climb the rutted path.

'Didn't you come down here?' William asked.

Ramon shook his head. 'It's kinder to the horses over the heath, and quicker too. Now, where did your master get to, I wonder?'

'Are there any houses, even ruined ones, where he may have rested overnight?'

'There's a few. Once we're through the woodland. We can ask when we get there.'

They continued on for another ten minutes. The undergrowth thinned out, as they got higher and the streams ran faster between the deep dark pools.

Ramon gave orders for the men to spread themselves out and look for any sign of the abbot.

'There's been a fire here,' one of the men called. 'Cold, but no older than yesterday. And fishing tackle, too.'

'Not a fisherman, your master, was he?'

'His father was, but no, I don't think the Abbot would have been fishing.'

'There's donkey shit here, too.'

'Come on,' the Comte told them. 'Just keep your eyes open.'

They continued without finding anything more, and William's hopes became a little desperate.

'I can hear something,' Ramon said and reined in his horse. 'Listen.'

All brought their horses to a halt. 'It's a donkey,' said the guard who had found the droppings.

'Got donkeys on the mind, you have,' Girand grumbled. 'Well, let's find the thing then.'

It was not difficult. The donkey must have heard them when it first brayed and now it let out a strident cry every time a twig broke under a horse's hoof. The animal was tied on a short tether, its head too near the knot to reach the ground.

'Recognise it?' asked Ramon, as one of his men released the animal, which stopped it making a noise, and it began cropping the grass.

'Yes. It's Marriette.' William was downcast now. 'I wonder what's become of him?'

'Well, we're not far from the caves. Maybe he went in there to shelter, and he's still asleep.'

'Let's hope he didn't try wandering around, then, m'lord Comte.' Ramon turned round to look at William. 'Dismount will you, then I can get down. Anyone got a flint and tinder?'

William followed Ramon, and two others followed them up a scarcely discernible track in the grass to a fissure in the rocks above them.

'Something's been dragged through here,' observed

one of the men-at-arms. 'Broken bracken all through here.' He gathered some dead bracken together and twisted some grass stems round it. 'See if we can get this alight.' The makeshift brand burnt quickly, but it was enough to see the footsteps left in the mud. 'Boots and sandals.'

Ramon went back outside to talk to the Comte. 'Could be in there. There's two sets of prints. Reckon it's worth following them?'

'We'd better,' the Comte decided. 'That fat little monk has got far more influence with the Lord than I'd care to ignore.' He pointed out a small copse. 'There's some pine trees over there, make up some decent brands and we'll do the job properly.'

It took them an hour. They followed the footprints to where they vanished at the high water mark. They found a crucifix with a broken chain, and a quite unpleasant-looking knife.

'Your master's?' Girand asked William.

The boy nodded. 'The cross is.'

'Well, I hadn't expected an abbot to use a knife this long. There's nothing else though. Looks as though he and whoever else was with him went into the water.'

'He's dead then? Drowned?'

'Probably, but not necessarily, no. There are stories of people getting spewed out at the other end, especially hermits and so on, holy people.'

'My master was always very holy.'

'I'm sure. Ramon,' he called, 'get the men mounted again and break them up into…I think there are three places the water comes out of these caves, aren't there?'

'That's right, m'lord.'

'Three parties, then. We'll take a look at the opening downriver.'

Another hour went by. The Comte took one party to the lowest of the three outlets, Ramon to the next one, and two of the men checked the nearest, and then caught up with Ramon, when there was no sign.

'I think it's him.' William said from behind the horseman, who was riding double with the boy. 'It's got to be. Oh hurry, please.'

'Let's just get there, young man. There's no point in breaking a leg in these deadfalls, is there?'

William didn't answer. What he had seen was not, in fact, the abbot; it was a bush over which the abbot's bedraggled habit had been thrown, presumably to dry in the sun. Beyond, was the abbot in his undershirt and drawers, lying on his back, asleep and snoring almost as loudly as Marriette brayed. He rested on a heap of dead branches and soggy rushes; behind him yawned a majestic archway of broken rocks leading into what looked like the blackest nether regions imaginable.

'Dondo?' he said, when he'd been woken up and had explained the course of events. He shook his head. 'I don't know where he is exactly. He killed Brother Anno, you know, and he tried to kill me, but he's gone for now.'

Ramon met them in the village at the inn where the landlord had given the abbot lessons in the economics of his trade. The Comte dropped a few coins in front of the man and called for mead of medicinal strength.

'Oh, we'll never catch the fellow now,' he told Rutilius. 'He'll be out of the parish as fast his legs will carry him.'

'I'm not so sure,' the abbot replied. 'He was under

some delusion that I was the Devil come to take him down to Hades. He turned around and went back inside.'

CHAPTER TWENTY

Madame Brisenot sat close to the abbot and clung possessively to his arm; she fed him slices of oyster from her own plate. The abbot did not seem to mind at all. Lucas Ferand, the rector, who sat next to them, and Jean Claude, the innkeeper, pretended not to notice.

'All that killing,' Madame Brisenot said thoughtfully, and ate a slice of oyster herself, 'and all in the space of a fortnight.'

Rutilius nodded. 'And largely because of Marcel's attempt to subsidize his old age. I checked the shrine accountings for the past half-year. Every time Marcel made a payment, the alms shrank in size.'

'It makes me very sad,' said Lucas. 'He hid a corrupt disposition beneath that cheerful appearance.'

'Corrupt and treacherous too,' added the abbot. 'Dondo murdered Brother Anno, but his attempt to drown me was entirely due to Marcel's deceit.'

'And do not forget the little monk he tried to kill, and fortunately, failed.'

'Passion, Adrienne. It causes a great deal of mischief.'

'You're right, of course, dear Rutilius. And think on this, Sylvan has paid dearly but the Comte's daughter will get away with it.'

'There will be a heavy penance, though,' Lucas said. '*I* shall see to that.'

'It alters nothing, Lucas. She deserves the same

punishment as Sylvan. If you or I tried to kill someone, we'd be dangling from a gibbet in the square within a day.'

'That's the way things are, Madame…'

'Adrienne.'

'Adrienne,' the rector amended. 'God has placed us below the Comte and his family and above these villagers,' he nodded towards the group of men who were celebrating at the other end of the room. 'We must be satisfied with our lot; anything else is blasphemy.'

Madame Brisenot was not happy. Her mouth was compressed into a line; there was undoubtedly a sharp retort behind her lips.

'And remember, Madame,' said the abbot before she could begin, 'Brother Sylvan must also bear the blame for seducing the girl. Once that sort of thing happens reason vanishes.'

'Seduced, Rutilius?' Madame shook her head. 'No, no, you are too idealistic. Anna-Marie de Fossard's reputation is well known. These events are no surprise at all.'

Lucas changed the subject. 'What surprised me,' he said, 'is the reputation that Gilbert has, or had. A reputation he didn't deserve at all.'

'But Gilbert liked to be known as a lady's man.' Madame chuckled. 'His reputation was a complete fabrication; he had built it all himself.'

'But did you know that before all this?' the abbot asked. 'He was quite despondent when he realised that he was no longer the disreputable Gilbert de Gignac.'

Madame pursed her lips. 'Well no, Rutilius, no, I didn't. I have to confess to being surprised. Only a little though, because nothing that a man does where women are concerned can surprise me very much. And as for Marcel, I never trusted him.'

The abbot nodded. 'Of course, Madame Vi…'

'Hush, Rutilius, my dear, the fellow over there, the one with the carved wooden cup, that is Victoir, husband to the lady in question.'

'Ah.' Both the abbot and the rector looked surreptitiously at the man in question.

'Of course, Marcel's secret was very well known,' observed the rector.

'Except for…'

'Just so, except for…' she nodded towards the man known as Victoir.

The abbot had left William to load their possessions on to Mariette's back. The expenses he had claimed included the price of a donkey to replace the stolen animal. Since he had already established a working relationship with the patient little donkey, Marriette's owner had been persuaded to sell her.

William rode the donkey and brought her to the tavern in St. Guilhem. Round the back, he found a water trough and tied her up to a post in the shade. He entered the tavern through the back door and came to a stop when confronted by the celebrating party of villagers.

'Aha, a good day, young monk.' Jean Claude had seen the boy come in. 'It's Victoir's birthday. He thinks he's forty so we're giving him a free drink or two.'

William nodded and skirted the small crowd.

'Now you're such an old man,' someone called, 'who's going to see to your wife?' This remark brought a roar of laughter.

'I'm sure I can handle that myself. I have always

managed it in the past,' Victoir shouted back and was rewarded by an even greater roar of laughter. He took a huge draught from the landlord's special drinking cup, a cup that seemed far bigger on the inside than on the outside. 'Should I need help with such a thing?' he asked and several of his neighbours collapsed with merriment.

William had not heard Marcel's secret and therefore did not appreciate the comedy. He found his master and the other two and joined them. He looked back at the party. 'This Victoir seems a popular fellow.'

'With some more than others, William,' said Lucas, who took the jug and poured a cup of beer for the boy. 'I suppose it will be some months before we see you and the abbot again?'

'I think it may be longer than that, Master Lucas.'

'Indeed, he is right,' agreed the abbot. 'The bishops do not care for an examiner to be too often at the same place.'

'William, my beautiful boy, come and sit here.' Madame pulled a stool over from an empty table and patted the seat. William, just a little wary, took the cup Lucas had filled and went to sit next to Madame Brisenot.

'I can see the reasoning, of course,' said the rector, leaning back and steepling his fingers. 'It is easy to imagine an irascible old abbot such as yourself and Abbot Roget salting away a fortune with no one being aware of it.'

The abbot's eyebrows climbed up his forehead, pink turned to red, red to mauve. 'Rector, I, I assure you, nothing…'

'Be easy, Rutilius.' Madame Brisenot was concerned

for the abbot's health. 'Easy. Lucas is joking, look at him.'

The abbot looked and noted the twinkle in Lucas's eyes turning to alarm. 'My dear fellow, a joke as Madame says. Surely you didn't think…'

'No, of course not, my friend. I should have known better, really.'

'Oh, Rutilius, you gave me a shock there. I'm going to miss you, you know and you, my beautiful young man.' And Madame Brisenot wiped the corner of her eye, careful of the cosmetics she had applied that morning. She leaned closer to William. 'You've changed since that time you first came in here, you know. You were a boy then, now you're a man. And remember what I said about girls, hmm?'

William nodded, embarrassed; he pretended a sudden interest in the celebrating villagers though his inner eye was focussed on Anna-Marie.

The abbot turned to see what the boy was looking at and his attention was caught. These people, he realised, these villagers, were what made the world work. Without their skills, oats would be neither planted nor harvested, fish would never be caught, sheep never sheared; an end to bread and beer, meat and fish, clothes and hangings.

The Holy Father, his cardinals, the bishops; the world as the abbot knew it depended on these people.

'Sorry,' he said, realising that he had been asked a question. 'What did you say?'

'More beer, Rutilius?' It was Lucas, looking as always, as though he had just stepped from a tailor's workroom in Montpellier. He held up the jug.

'Thank you, I will. One more and then we must be going.' His attention was drawn back to the villagers as

Victoir, obviously the victim of the complimentary beer, staggered backwards on to the toes of one of his neighbours.

The man got up and cursed Victoir for being a clumsy idiot, using the Lord's name in a profane manner. He was tall and very thin, his clothing was stiff with dirt, his voice was the sound of a rusted hinge.

The abbot felt angry at such language and behaviour but, more than that, he felt betrayed. This man was so far from the noble vision he had just glimpsed that his sparkling image of the *common man* simply vanished as a dream does on waking. He sighed and shook his head.

'I'm surprised God does not smite that one with a thunderbolt,' Madame Brisenot said.

'Too thin,' said William quietly, looking at the same fellow. 'He has only to turn sideways and the Lord will miss him entirely.'

Madame Brisenot giggled. Lucas snorted.

The abbot's mouth opened but he said nothing, he could think only of the near-blasphemy that William had uttered. Then he too laughed. Without the intent, there could be no blasphemy. William's remark was innocent and the good Lord had made laughter as surely as he had made solemnity.

The abbot laughed again. Tears overflowed and ran down his cheeks. Certainly William would not have thought of saying such a thing a fortnight since.

'Oh dear, oh dear. Oh my goodness.' What really shocked the abbot, now that he thought about it, helpless as he was with laughter, was that those same two weeks ago, he could not have appreciated the humour however hard he tried.

'Master, where are we going next?' asked William,

when the abbot had recovered.

'I don't know. Let us find out, shall we?'

Rutilius pulled a small packet from his bag and brandished it. 'Now.' He prised away the sealing wax with his thumbnail. 'This arrived yesterday, just before Abbot Roget returned to the abbey.' He unfolded the paper, smoothed it. 'The Bishop…'

Locked in her own room in the Comte de Froissard's rambling chateau, Anna-Marie lay on her stomach across the bed. As she had foreseen, her father had applied the hazel switch with gusto and sitting down was an option too painful to contemplate.

Not that it hadn't been worth it, from a certain point of view. She had transformed William from a boy to a man. It was not beyond imagining that, the Lord willing, their paths should cross again.

Printed in the United Kingdom
by Lightning Source UK Ltd.
127424UK00001B/1-42/P